Head Above Water

Buchi Emecheta

Head Above Water

Ogwugwu Afo
London & Nigeria

Hardback

ISBN 0 95081 77 32

First published in 1986 by
Fontana Paperbacks, 8 Grafton Street, London SW1 3LA

Copyright © Buchi Emecheta 1986

Made and printed in Great Britain by
Blackrose Press, London EC1
Typeset by Boldface Typesetters, London EC1

Contents

For Chiedu's Memory

I am still trying to work out why you suddenly died.
A part of a mother dies with her child. You were no longer
a child, you were then a young woman, and we did make plans and
did have a lot of laughter, and the two of us went through some
bad times together, yet you suddenly left, when I was in a position
to say "thank you daughter" for helping me raise your younger
brothers and sisters. We talk about you every day. You were sometimes
not very easy to understand, but you were my childhood friend who
I had when I was a child myself.
Since that afternoon in May 1984, when I was told of your death,
I am just beginning to realize that you are not here
any more. But it is a fact that will take me a very long time to
accept. Here is *Head Above Water*, the title we both agreed on
four years ago.

Daughter, I still thank God every day for lending you to us for
twenty-three years.

Acknowledgements

Several chapters in this book appeared in journals like *Kunapippi*, *Granta* and *West Africa* in versions which have since been revised and expanded in varying degrees. I thank the editors and publishers of these journals.

Other chapters were read out as lectures to many universities in many countries; again, I thank those listeners for their patience.

I am grateful to my daughter Christy Onwordi for first editing the whole work, and the editorial staff at Collins for the finishing touches and to the libel lawyer.

I thought I would be able to include my trips to America and the Scandinavian countries but had to stop as the work was becoming rather longer than I wanted it. It will have to be updated from time to time.

1

Introduction

For someone who has previously published more than ten books, writing an autobiography should be a fairly easy task. One has simply to look back into oneself, lift the lid off the great past and allow its timelessness to overflow into the present through the channel of one's pen on paper. But writing my autobiography is not going to be easy. This is because most of my early novels, articles, poems and short stories are, like my children, too close to my heart. They are too real. They are too me.

Nonetheless, I am going to make the attempt, though not in the manner of many autobiographies, on a day-to-day basis. If I had to write of all my forty or so years in full, the way I experienced them and the way some of them had been related to me by well-meaning big and little mothers, it would run into several volumes. I will therefore write episodically, touching lightly here and there on those incidents on which I have dwelt in depth in my other books: *Second-Class Citizen*, *In the Ditch*, *The Bride Price*, *The Slave Girl*, *The Joys of Motherhood* and *Double Yoke*.

The other works, including *The Rape of Shavi* and *Destination Biafra*, are imaginary works based on ideas and ideals. In *Destination Biafra* is my dream woman, Debbie Ogedemgbe. In *The Rape of Shavi* is my hope for us all — that not only will the nuclear war be a non-starter, but that the white European woman from the North will regard the black woman from the South as her sister and that both of us together will hold hands and try to salvage what is left of our world from the mess the sons we have brought into it have made.

In this book, *Head Above Water*, I hope to forge forward to those incidents that I have not previously touched upon, concentrating more on the little happenings that I think helped to mould and shape me into a fairly prolific writer. I cannot claim to be one of the best in my chosen profession but I have managed for the past ten years to keep my head above water on it, and hopefully after this I will live to write much, much more. For many of my readers, who are forever asking how an African woman could come to Britain and make a modest living writing books in a language that is not her first nor her second or third but her fourth, *Head Above Water* will throw some light.

I also have to stop looking back into the past of too long ago. Thinking about what might have been is lovely, but after forty years I don't want to be another Lot's wife. I did look back a good deal in my early novels, dwelling mainly on the first twenty years of my life, but *Head Above Water* is me in the almost Now: the last twenty years during which time I made England's North London my home.

If, however, some of the incidents described in the first part of this book are familiar to you, my reader, please don't be offended because some of them have to be touched upon again in order to highlight the present.

2

The Miracle

Writing can be therapeutic and autobiographical writing even more so, as it affords one a kaleidoscopic view of one's life. For instance, it was only when I started writing these autobiographical episodes that one question that had been nagging me for a very long time seemed to be answered. Why, oh why, do I always trust men, look up to them more than to people of my own sex, even though I was brought up by women? I suddenly realized that all this was due to the relationship I had with my mother.

My mother, Alice Ogbanje Ojebeta Emecheta, that laughing, loud-voiced, six-foot-tall, black glossy slave girl, who as a child suckled the breasts of her dead mother; my mother who lost her parents when the nerve gas was exploded in Europe, a gas that killed thousands of innocent Africans who knew nothing about the Western First World War; my laughing mother, who forgave a brother that sold her to a relative in Onitsha so that he could use the money to buy *ichafo siliki* – silk head ties for his coming-of-age dance. My mother, who probably loved me in her own way, but never expressed it; my mother, that slave girl who had the courage to free herself and return to her people in Ibusa, and still stooped and allowed the culture of her people to re-enslave her, and then permitted Christianity to tighten the knot of enslavement.

She never understood the short, silent, mystery daughter she had. Words said that she died not blessing me. That hurt, it did hurt and for twenty years I carried the hurt. But on going back to Ibusa in 1980, and seeing the people she lived with and the place she was buried, then the image of that tall, lanky, black woman nicknamed "Blakie the black" seemed to loom over me. Then I felt the warmth of her presence, then I knew right there inside me that my mother did not die cursing me.

Signs showed me that that was said to make me feel guilty, especially now they know that the marriage that caused the rift between mother and daughter did not work out for me. And of course nothing would satisfy our tradition better than to stir up the mud of an ambiguous past. But I have had time to think and that, thanks be to God, has made me stronger both emotionally and spiritually than that girl in *The Bride Price* whose immaturity allowed her to be destroyed by such heavy guilt.

This realization washed over me like an evening balm as I stood there, by the place she was buried. Relatives watching wanted and expected me to break down and cry, thereby devaluing my inner sorrow. Maybe if I had not stayed in cold England for eighteen years – England, a country where people cry in their hearts and not with their eyes – I would have done so. Eighteen years is a long time, and like the people I live with, I cried in my heart.

And as I walked slowly away, wishing Mother had been buried in a more private resting place and not inside our compound, where I could not speak to her privately, it seemed to me in the ears of my mind that I could hear that loud laugh and her voice saying as she used to tell me so many times when I was a little girl, "You think too much for a woman. This . . . tisha . . . it's nothing, all forgotten."

I looked back once, and I knew I was right. My mother, although she was very ill before she died, could not have cursed me. Unlike me, her mysterious daughter, she did not possess such inner depth. For, after all, did she not die alone, asleep on her bed in her room?

As if all that was not enough, my mother-in-law, Christy Onwordi, said to me later that evening when we were talking about my mother, "Your mother went home. The week she died, I saw Nkili Angelina Obiorah (my mother's friend, age-mate and lookalike), I saw her in white singing and she was profoundly happy. She joined a group of happy, white-gowned people. I knew then that your mother was not going to survive that illness."

Looking back in my mind's eye and remembering the night she died, which I described in *Second-Class Citizen*, I forgave myself and my mother because, you see, I am a woman now in my prime who has suffered and seen so much. If I do not understand the untalked-of agonies of that laughing and doubly culturally-enslaved woman who gave me life, who else is there on this earth who will take the trouble to?

I miss my singing, laughing mother very much and my village, Umue-zeokolo Odanta, did not seem the same to me any more without her and my other mothers to hug me when I arrived at Otinkpu.

As for my survival for the past twenty years in England, from when I was a little over twenty, dragging four cold and dripping babies with me and pregnant with a fifth one – that is a miracle. And if for any reason you do not believe in miracles, please start believing, because my keeping my head above water in this indifferent society, which is probably succeeding in making me indifferent and private too, is a miracle.

3

What They Told Me

Most of the events that happened before I was born had to be told to me by
my mothers. The history of the British Empire and her greatness I learned
from my English teachers at school in Lagos. But when it came to events
that happened nearer home, concerning my ancestors and me in particular, I
had to rely on the different versions told to me by my mothers. They never
ceased to fascinate me, especially as each member of my family had a slightly
different version. It was from this oral source that I learned from many
angles the story of my birth.

My father, right from the time I could first remember, had always called
me Nnem – "my mother". And my mother had always referred to my
moodiness and the mysterious habit I had of refusing food in order to
attract attention as coming "not from my side of the family but from that
mysterious woman who gave her father birth". I grew up under the
shadow of this. But it was my big mother, my father's elder sister, Nwakwaluzo Ogbueyin – this woman whom I see constantly when I look at my
image in the mriror; this soft, very fat woman who seemed to have all the
patience in the world; this mysterious woman who had the art of punctuat-
ing her stories with long silences and deep breathing – it was she who had
the patience to tell it all to me in one go.

It happened the third day after our arrival in Ibusa. We had finished eating
our evening meal and I could hear my cousin Ogugua shouting:

"Umu nnunu, umu nnu nta
Tunzanza tulu nza
Unu no nebo eme gide
Tunzanza tulu nza . . ."

I always loved this moonlight call: "Little birds, little birds, come out in front of Ededemushe's compound and dance with little bells in front and cowrie shells at your back . . . "

By the time she reached the end of her call-song, many of us were puffing at the feet of Nwakwaluzo Ogbueyin. We gasped our final response of *"Tinzanza tulu nza"* as we collapsed onto one another in a big heap, and wrestled ourselves playfully free on the white brilliant sand at Otinkpu.

My big mother, whom we called Nneayin Ogbueyin (Our Mother the Elephant Killer), laughed in her slow rich voice and cautioned, "Little children, my little children, you have just eaten your evening meal, you don't want to regurgitate it do you?"

"No, we don't!"

"Then sit down and sing your *inu* song once more."

We obediently sang *"Umu nnunu umu nnu nta"* once more and the *inu* song of "Agadi Nwayin" (The Old Woman who Lost her Sons) and by the time we did the last chorus of "Zomilizo" the echoes of our young voices went from one sand clearing and one part of Ibusa to another. At that moment it seemed to me as if every compound had emptied its young ones onto the moonlit sand to celebrate the joy of living and the joy of the new moon.

As our voices died, an indescribable peacefulness spread over us. We looked up to this magnificent woman with silver hair that fitted her like a cap, at her black, glistening and full face, and tried to peer into those brown eyes – eyes which we knew were becoming weaker and weaker as she progressed towards her grave. We studied her stick, lying between her legs like a rod of life as she sat there on her stool, and we looked up at her with expectancy to tell us what else to do.

"Do you want to sing once more?" We could hear the rich rumble of amusement in her belly.

"No, mother, we want stories!"

"I can't hear you."

"We want stories, we want stories, stories, tell us the story of Agadi Nwayin, please tell us our own Ogbueyin!"

She had succeeded in rousing our curiosity and expectancy and she knew it. She closed her eyes and slowly drifted into one of her story-telling trances. And when she opened her mouth to speak, the voice that came out was distant and mesmerizing.

"Whose father walked seven lands and swam seven seas to fight and kill a bad man called Hitilah?"

"It's me," I whispered hoarsely, afraid of disturbing the quiet grip her voice was having on us.

"Who is our come-back mother Agbogo?"

"It's me." This time I could not restrain myself any longer. I stood up proudly and this movement of mine startled all my little relatives sitting there on the sand at Otinkpu into reality. "It's her, it's her," their voices chorused. "It's me, it's me," I screamed intermittently.

"Who has a mother that can write and read like white people?"

By this time, I was dancing around singing "*O nmu. O mu.*" (It's me, it's me.)

Our excitement reached a deafening pitch, which amused her not a little. It was obvious that that night's *inu* story was going to be about me. And years later I could see why I was particularly singled out for this treat – the treat of being the heroine of our big mother's *inu* story.

Her real name, Nwakwaluzo, means "this child cleared the path". She was apparently expected to clear the path for some male children. She was only a girl child, so a man child was expected after her. It was almost like a command: she must have a male baby brother. I used to wonder sometimes what would have happened if, having given her such a name, her mother had had another baby girl instead of my father. Nonetheless, my father did come after her, although much, much later, and was given the name Nwabudike – "this child is a warrior". Although my big mother was a woman, through her strength and achievement she acquired the title Ogbueyin – "the killer of elephants". Words had it that she had led some elephant hunts, because she used to deal with the sale of their tusks. But by the time we were born she was getting old and looked more like a grand-mother than a big aunt, and due to the ignorant activities of many like her, elephants had long disappeared from that part of West Africa. However, she kept the relics of her great days. She had huge anklets and bracelets made from the tusks of grown elephants. Most people were supposed to wear such huge and cumbersome ornaments only on special occasions. Not Big

Mother! She had hers chiselled in such a curious fashion that she bathed with them on, she slept with them on, and she walked with them, a feat that required not only a unique skill but a lot of energy too.

When my brother Adolphus and myself first saw this swaggering lady, we ran. We were terrified for we had never seen such a person in Lagos, where we were born. And when our big mother tried to embrace us, we let out such a scream that people did not stop talking about it for a long time.

As I stood afar, shaking from fear, I saw my big mother cry and my heart melted and I felt sorry for her. I saw her walk with bowed head into her hut. Curiosity got the better of me and I followed gingerly behind her and stood there by her little door as she took her pestle *odo* handle and cracked to pieces those expensive tusk ornaments. Presently, she came out with her arms open to us in welcome. Although my brother still ran away from her after this, I did not run too far. Encouraged by my hesitancy, she dipped her now naked hands into her *nbunukwu* – waist skirt – and brought out a dark shiny *eshi* fish that had been dried in the sun until it was dark and mouth-watering, and lured me to her with it. Then I ran to her and our relatives laughed. The knots of bystanders were horrified at the loss of her expensive tusk ornaments, but with my hand firmly clasped in hers she reminded them, with her face beaming, "When has it ever been a virtue to be rich in wealth and poor in people?" The relatives nodded. They understood her very well – why have heaven and earth when you have no one to share it with?

With my free hand in hers and the other clutching the *eshi* fish, I looked up to the face of Big Mother. Never before had I seen anyone so full of happiness. And as a further treat she was that evening going to tell us the story of my birth. It was going to be my story, the story which she was going to cross seven lands and swim seven seas to get, just for me, because I was important. Because I was a significant person in our community at Umuezeokolo Odanta in Ibusa.

In her low, anaesthetizing voice she began. "Why all said 'Ah, only a girl' to Alice Ogbanje Ojebeta and her husband Jeremy Nwabudike Emecheta when a little girl was born to them was understandable. What trouble did she not cause as she ran out of her mother's belly in seven months when other children stayed nine? And there was nothing like a premature baby unit at the Massey Street Dispensary in Lagos where she was born. Most normal mothers did not have to go to such places. But because this little girl came into the world before her time, her poor mother had to be taken to those white people's birth places. Her mother did not know what to do and neither did the people who helped her deliver the girl child. Many of them nodded knowingly, thinking that she would not live anyway. She was a little bigger than the biggest rat you've ever seen, all head. So those people from the hospital sent Alice Ogbanje home with her scrap of humanity. She could not take her to her husband because she felt shame. Because, you see, Nwabudike married his wife here, according to our custom, and then when they got to Lagos, he had to marry her again according to the laws of the white people. Ogbanje wore a long white dress with another white piece that looked like a spider's web on her head. This latter piece was long, and she had her friends to hold it for her so that she did not trip over it. They both looked funny, but who understands the ways of those strange white people? After they had been inside that house, a big one where they prayed to their god, everybody came and took photos, and all ate rice and meat and drank plenty of palm wine and then they all danced all night. It cost my brother Nwabudike a lot of money, I can tell you. All that nonsense.

"And then if a man had done all that for you, what type of child would you give him?"

"A bouncing baby boy howling with life on a banana leaf," we replied, hypnotized.

"Well, Ogbanje did not do that. She presented Nwabudike with this scrap of humanity. So when she left that dispensary, she was crying, and the sky was crying with her, because the girl child arrived in July, our wettest month. She took her to her brother's wife.

"'And what is this? I want to be sick,' said her sister-in-law, Obi's wife.

"'It's a child, a girl child,' pleaded Ogbanje.

"'She cannot live anyway,' said Obi's wife. She should know because she had six children of her own, all boys and no girl.

"So they tucked the little wet bundle of flesh away with many rags to keep her warm, and dropped water into her bird-like mouth. But the girl child did not die. Instead she started to raise hell. Hm, what a voice she had. And her heart beat gbim, gbim, gbim.

"It was then that my brother Nwabudike saw in the child's determination to live the fighting spirit of our mother, Agbogo. And he too was determined to make his daughter live. But the daughter started to turn yellow. And Alice Ogbanje, because of the white training she had had in

Onitsha, took her girl child and ran back to the hospital where she was born. She cried and said, 'Look, my baby is turning yellow even though I gave her drops of water as my experienced sister-in-law advised. I know she has not got much chance of living but my husband said that she is his come-back mother. And he will not forgive me if I let his come-back mother die.'

"And the nurses in Lagos, they took the law into their own hands. They hailed abuse onto Alice Ogbanje and they said to her, 'How would you feel if someone fed you only drops of water for three days, eh? How would you feel?' One big Yoruba nurse threatened to beat her up, but took pity when she saw that Alice Ogbanje was still bleeding from the birth and that she was inexperienced.

"And those nurses stuck her virgin nipples into the child's mouth and she sucked and she sucked, and guess what!"

"She lived," we all shouted.

And I got carried away and I added my ending to the story. "And after a year, I brought a man child to the world, and my father and mother named him Adolphus Chisingali Emecheta!"

We clapped and danced that night. And I knew that I was forgiven for being born premature with a big head and small body and for being a girl, because I must have recommended my parents highly to the children living beneath the earth for Olisa to send my mother my brother, who arrived with no fuss, who stayed the whole nine months in her belly, and who appeared roaring his way into the world. And they did not need to tuck him up with rags.

My father and his friends must have been so proud of this strong, big baby boy that they named him after the man they thought was the toughest on earth – Adolphus Hitler. Sometimes as a child I used to wonder why my brother was called after the man whose very name we were later taught to fear. But then who knows what goes on inside the minds of ambitious, proud Ibo fathers? As most Ibo boys born around that time were called Adolphus after the German leader, Adol is still a fairly common name among the Ibos of Nigeria.

Whereas my brother was given the military names of Adolphus Chisingali Emecheta, meaning "God has ordered my promotion", my mother decided to call me Florence in reminiscence of the story of the lady with the lamp which the missionaries had told her when she was in Onitsha. My father decided on Onyebuchi, meaning "Are you my god?" The pet name Nnenna, meaning "father's mother", was not recorded as he and he only could call me that, just as my brother was locally known as Hitilah.

How we heap titles and ambitions on our children! Even today in the mid-1980s I have never seen prouder parents than typical Ibo ones. We expect our children to conquer the world, we push them into conquering the world and when they fail to do so we find it difficult to forgive them. I know many Ibo men in Europe and America who will never go home because they have failed to live up to the names given to them by their parents and Umunna.

4

Lorlu Onye Burma

It was during another visit to Ibusa that I heard the story of Lorlu of Burma. My father had died by then and I was growing up with the knowledge that whenever there was a war, most good and patriotic men joined to fight for their people. And I thought then that that was why my praise name included "the daughter of the one who went and fought and killed a bad man called Hitler". But with my big mother's version of the story of this monster man called Lorlu of Burma, it was not always the case.

At my primary school, we were told that our fathers had to fight Hitler because he said that all Africans had tails and should be killed. I did not know anything about the Jews except those written about in the Bible; nobody mentioned to us their plight or the Holocaust. I thought our fathers simply fought to save us from this bad man, Hitler.

We had by then started to call my brother Adolphus "Hitler" when he was really bad, which was very often. The name Adolphus stuck, as he was baptized with it, and I sometimes think that name somehow affected his behaviour. He still believes in belligerence.

I had a little argument with my brother one evening which led to a fight. He was much stronger and was growing bigger and healthier than I. He seldom had the patience for argument, but preferred to resort to the quicker way of fighting it out. Boys of his age were encouraged to behave that way, whilst girls were expected to cry for help and to forgive. But on this night, due to the hopelessness of my position – my father had just died and I was beginning to realize that my education was going to stop so that the money could be used to educate my brother – I was in no mood to forgive or run away. Jealousy fuelled my anger, and I set to work on his back with my teeth. Even at school in Lagos I was the greatest biter amongst my friends. It usually worked, rendering my opponent helpless in no time, especially if I dug my teeth into the really painful parts of his body. My brother's back until this cay carries the bumps and criss-cross marks of my teeth. People separated us, and while I puffed with anger he cried and threatened to do this and that to me.

Then my big mother came, stood there watching us, and cried, "How come children of the same mother and father become '*Abyssinia na Italia*'?"

I must say that I had heard my mother say this several times before, but had never bothered to ask what "*Abyssinia na Italia*" meant. I had to wait for over ten years to ask my husband. He read modern history, and you should have heard him laugh at my ignorance. "Even the old village women knew more about modern history than you," he mocked. The Abyssinians and the Italians were enemies during the First World War. I marvelled at this, at the power of the word of mouth. This was a fact known to women who had never read a newspaper, nor had ever heard anything like radio and television, yet they knew that these two countries were at war. And it buttressed the fact that if Africa had ever been a dark continent at all, it must have been in the Dark Ages and among people who lived in unapproachable and isolated places.

I did not ask my big mother the meaning of "*Abyssinia na Italia*" that night, but instead she called my brother and myself and all our friends together, and went into one of her trances and brought us the story of Lorlu of Burma. The lesson of the story was that if my brother kept fighting his wife the way he fought me, Lorlu would take him away and he and his friend called Burma would eat him up.

Lorlu was good at kidnapping husbands, especially bad ones, so my brother should watch it. I was now confused. Men in those days were conscripted into the army against their will and the wishes of their family, but until that night I had thought that people like my father volunteered gladly. Further probings would yield no answers, not even from Big Mother.

I know now that on this one, she did not understand. She did not understand why a man should go to work, and his wife cook for him, waiting for him to come and eat his evening meal, and then learn about three months later that he had been taken away to fight somebody he did not know called Hitler. And her version of the story was the only way she could explain.

There was this man monster called Lorlu and his friend Burma. They liked to kidnap husbands. But Big Mother did not like to press this lesson too much because after all my father, who was a violent person although a good Christian, was her brother. So we knew or suspected that my father had to be taken to fight Hitler by a monster man called Lorlu and his equally horrible friend Burma, because my father, being a stammerer, could not afford to talk. Like my brother, he had no patience for words. And that was the story I grew up with.

Years later when I came to England a friend lent me a book called *Edwina* – the life of Lady Mountbatten of Burma. For a long time I did not connect the late Lord Mountbatten with our monster man Lorlu. Nonetheless it eventually clicked. In Africa he was known as Lord Louis, and I think Mountbatten was simply too long a name to pronounce let alone remember. So to our mothers he was Lorlu, and you could imagine how astonished I was when I learnt that Burma was a place, not a bigger monster.

I was very disappointed, though, when I pursued my search to Sandhurst and knew that yes, there was a Royal West African Infantry and Riflemen who went to Burma. I think at best my father must have carried guns for an English officer. My father never saw Hitler, to say nothing of killing him single-handed. You can imagine how I felt. So I mentally dropped the description ''the daughter of the one who was so strong as to kill a bad man called Hitler single-handed''.

And from the big surprise that Lorlu the monster was none other than the much loved Lord Mountbatten who died tragically a few years ago, I am still recovering. I know that if my big mother had been alive and if I had told her how he died, she would have said, ''And what do you expect? All those curses we heaped on him and his friend Burma, they were bound to come true.''

In any case they are gone now, Big Mother, my father, all the poor black men forced to leave their wives and children in their prime of life, never to come back, and nobody explaining anything to anybody – they are gone now. Maybe they are all there laughing at the inaccuracies of history. But I get this feeling that Big Mother's laughter, her rumbling belly laughter, would be the greatest of all.

As for Hitler, my father never killed him. Burma is far from Germany, we do not know how he died and it has nothing to do with my family. I wonder where the man met his end. That is another story shrouded in mystery and I'm sure that most mothers would tell their sons and daughters their own version of it.

5

The Methodist Girls' High School

"I with avowed intent,
To be a Pilgrim..."

The lively young voices of the girls at the Methodist High rang out. Their vibrant silvery echoes burst out of their confines in the school's Assembly Hall, only to reverberate among the trees standing in front of the school compound, and to reach the grey hideous walls that separated the front of the school from the loco-yard opposite. Those grey walls and the elegant trees all seemed to take up the rhythm of the military Methodist tune in their determination to be like the khaki-uniformed girls within, pilgrims, pilgrims of Christ.

Hearing those voices from outside the school, the plaintive nostalgic tinge they gave the otherwise orthodox church hymn stood out. The girls did sing in tune – their Welsh music mistress, Miss Davies, saw to that – yet, and yet one could tell that those voices were voices from nowhere but Africa. Until a few generations back the voices of their grandparents were used in musical village calls, in singing ballads and telling stories in songs, in forest calls and in enhancing the vibrating rhythms of cone-shaped talking drums. Now these girls, the modern girls of twentieth-century Africa, still possess such voices, still with the same strength, still with the same vigour, but now with that added hope and pride, the pride that they were going to be the new women of the new Africa. They had been told that their position was unique in history, that they were going to rub shoulders with the types of Miss Davies from Wales, Miss Osborne from Scotland, Miss Verney and Miss Humble from England, Miss Walker from Australia, and many, many other white missionaries who had left their different countries to come to Lagos in Nigeria to teach the girls to value their own importance. There were a few black mistresses, one here in the needlework department, another there in the domestic department, but then, in the late 1950s, their influence was still minimal.

I was late again this morning in leaving my dormitory. I was far from being popular – too shy and too sensitive to be able to forget myself for a while. Because of this, although I craved and bled inwardly for company, when in it I was wont to make a fool of myself by doing or saying something wrong. And that wrong thing I would worry about, cry about, bite my nails to the point of almost eating up my fingers about. So, to be on the safe side, I always liked to stay behind deliberately when the others had gone, so that I could read a line of Wordsworth, or a verse of Byron or Tennyson, then make the short journey from the boarding house, through the trees that were still wet from the night dew, with only myself for company, taking my time and walking "as if next year would do" as our form mistress, Mrs Okuyemi, used to say.

I could deliberate, chew over and repeat the works of Rupert Brooke, Keats and Shakespeare, yet I was the daughter of scantily educated parents who came right out of their innocent and yet sophisticated bush culture, ignorant of the so-called civilized world. Yet in communal caring, and mutual sharing, and language gestures and music-making, they are unsurpassable in their sheer sophistication. But they had to leave all this, my parents, in search of this New Thing that was coming from places afar. They left their village homes, the habitat of their ancestors so many generations back, and came to the city, and there they had me, and they said that I was clever, and they said that because I won something called a scholarship – which my mother used to call "sikolakip" – I was to be brought up the new way. That was why instead of being in the village and claying the mud floor of my ancestors, I had to stand there in front of this school compound feeling guilty at having illegally enjoyed Rupert Brooke, and hearing the voices of my already assembled friends singing.

I sometimes gave the village life a good thought, especially as my people made sure I never lost touch with it. I had to go through all the rituals, yet

I knew even then that, like my parents, I was trapped in this New Thing. But of course to me and all my friends at the Methodist Girls' High School, it wasn't a New Thing any more. It was becoming a way of life. I was even then feeling like Byron's Prisoner of Chillon, when he cried,

> *My very chains and I grew friends,*
> *So much a long communication tends*
> *To make us what we are – even I*
> *Regained my freedom with a sigh.*

However much I admired the village life, I knew that for sheer survival I had to make a go of the education the school was offering me – free, when almost all the girls in the school were paying. I kept more and more to myself, because I did not pay for my education, a fact which made me feel awful, even though I was not given the scholarship out of charity but won it for myself. My parents could not have paid the high fees. My father had by then been long dead and my mother, although a Christian woman, had gone back to being a native in our village town, Ibusa, for the sake of survival. So although I felt guilty for being on a scholarship, I was grateful in a way for it – without the good start which it gave me, I wonder if I would have been able to write in English as I do.

Still, that morning I was late, and I knew that I was in trouble, so I ran in, stopping by the door, my eyes lowered and my fat navy blue Methodist hymn book clasped to my flat chest (I was a late developer, too skinny). But by one of those unhappy strokes Providence sometimes deals out to us, I walked into my form mistress, Mrs Okuyemi. She was black, she was young, she was beautiful, only she never allowed herself to be beautiful. The only day I knew she could smile was when I left school and ran to her house to tell her that I had done well in the West African School Certificate Examination. She even entertained me – she gave my best friend Kehinde Lawal and myself a bowl of mixed fruit salad. She treated us like people, so much so that my friend, whom I regarded as more sensible than I, said, "That lady really tried very much to help us, if only we had listened." Well, it was too late: we had left school by then, and I was married even before our school results came out. Anyway, all that was still in the future.

This morning, Mrs Okuyemi was sitting by the side of our row, as she should, being our form mistress. She did not immediately make way for me, but kept me waiting long enough for all the subject teachers to see me standing there. I knew what they were all thinking: "That Ibo girl has done it again." I stared at the cemented floor; I would not look at anybody's face. Then the other girls all pretended to be offended at my lateness. One would have thought that but for the disturbance I was causing they would have gone straight up the imaginary Jacob's Ladder in their desire to be the pilgrims whom Bunyan had idealized in *The Pilgrim's Progress*, on which that particular hymn was based. I knew they were all being hypocritical; I could see Kofo Olufowokan's perfect teeth flashing behind her hymn book. Then I collided with Bisi, and her chair clattered on the floor. Miss Davies stopped the piano; the Head, Miss Walker, lowered her glasses; and Miss Humble, a giant of a woman, always in sneakers, stood on tiptoe. She was the Physical Education mistress and also head of English and Literary Studies. I tumbled to the end of the row to make for the empty seat. Why didn't they allow the empty seat to be near the door? I wondered. But then, the latecomer would find life easier that way. Still, it was better to be late for an assembly than not to come at all: our dear Mrs Okuyemi would know, and would then have a "word" with the sinner. I would rather disturb the whole school than go for Mrs Okuyemi's "word"! It was Hamlet who boasted that he was going to speak daggers, but our Mrs Okuyemi's "word" was sharper than daggers.

The morning service went on after Miss Davies had put her glasses back on, straightened her already stiff shoulders, and swept her head back. We soon knelt in prayers and finished the morning assembly by singing the school hymn:

> *Lord grant us like the watching five*
> *To wait thy coming and to strive*
> *Each one her lamp to trim . . .*

I felt the hymn was having a go at me. I was the virgin who did not trim her lamp and was too late and unprepared for the wedding feast. Some people say this story of the ten virgins in the Bible was symbolic but some of us believed it was real. I remember that during one of my school holidays I was explaining the meaning of our school hymn to a distant cousin in Ibusa. She was at school too, but not in a "big school" like mine. At the mention of the virgin she gasped. "You mean Jesus Christ refused women, even though they were virgins, simply because they did not trim their stupid lamps?"

"Not just their lamps, Josephine they were not ready for the wedding," I began.

"I wish I was there. I can trim and fill twenty million lamps, if that is all it will take to make me a good woman. Not like this rotten place. You have to be a virgin, a virgin all the time."

I looked at her, too scared to say a word. We were coming to that age when we were not allowed to say everything that came into our heads. But I suspected that my cousin Jo would be in a big trouble on her wedding night. She did not say it; she did not need to. And as if to make me sorrier for her she said, "One can kill a fowl and pour its blood on the white cloth you use on your first night with your husband."

I shook my head. I did not know, but went on, "My mother said that any other blood would go pale before morning. But the real thing would always be red."

After an uncomfortable silence, Jo said, "I can trim lamps. I think Christianity is better. Think of all the beatings and humiliations one would have to go through otherwise. Trimming lamps is easier."

Jo and I belong to the same age group, yet she was saying this.

I was asking about her the other day, twenty years after this conversation; and I was told that she was a nun. Jo, with that beautiful narrow face of the Ethiopian maid, went into a nunnery because she probably thought God would accept girls who by mistake, curiosity or sheer ignorance had become adventurous. The fact that it needed two people to experience such an adventure and it was the girl who had to be penalized made me wonder, sometimes. Like my cousin Jo, I was taking the school song literally.

One thing that still surprises me about the discipline of my early schooldays was our maturity in human relations. No girl reproached you afterwards for disturbing the assembly, not to your face anyway. The thought of it would die with you, and the girls realized, even then, that that was enough punishment. It could happen to them as well. Or maybe the few people who took the trouble to tell me that I was doing something wrong noticed that I was not confident enough to take any kind of criticism well. I've now mastered a beautiful art in which I laugh at myself first, so that when criticisms come they lose their sharpness and pain. At school, I had not mastered the art of masking my emotion, so out of pity my classmates chose not to say a word. And, partly because of this, I was ignorant of so many things which the other girls knew and could get away with.

My greatest escape was in literature. I still remember clearly the first story I read in English by myself. It was the story of Hansel and Gretel, who walked hand in hand, and died hand in hand in their bed of flowers in the woods. I read this book several times at my primary school, so that I knew some of the words by heart. I used to imagine myself lost like that in the bush, so that the relatives with whom I was living at the time would be kinder to me and stop beating me for the slightest thing I did, so that my mother would come and stay with my brother and I, like she used to before our father died, so that my mother would love me so much that she would leave her native husband, who only had to inherit her and not marry her properly the way my Pa did. The second story was that of Snow White. I used to cry my eyes out for those seven dwarves. And during the school holidays, we used to go home to Ibusa. There, I virtually drank in all my big mother's stories.

Later, towards the end of my schooldays, my work started to suffer because the teachers were always intruding into my thoughts. I would dream and build a story in which I was the heroine, in which I always had enough to eat and in which I always had a nice bed and not the bug-ridden planks we slept on at Mrs Dedeke's boarding house. They used to be such beautiful stories. Thank goodness, I never spoke of most of them. Knowing what I know now of psychology, I would probably have been certified.

One of the reasons for my keeping all my imaginative thoughts to myself came about the day I was late for morning assembly. After prayers, our next lesson was English Literature. I guessed that Miss Humble did not like me that much. There was nothing to like about me anyway. I was forever looking serious, with formidable glasses, and not particularly tidy or exceptionally clever. My class work was steadily going down and this was making life more difficult. The situation was circular: I was afraid of leaving school – it was not a beautiful life, but it was at least safe and reliable. As a result of this fear, I began to dream of another world, but the funniest thing about this world was that I was always the mother of many children. And the more I wallowed in my dreams, to the extent of bringing them into the classroom, the more my work suffered and the greater my fear, because if one was on a scholarship and failed an exam, the scholarship would be taken away. I made a good grade in the end, but to achieve this I drove myself almost to the brink, knowing that the alternative was disgrace.

The tall and broad Miss Humble never liked me. I wanted her to like me the way she did my friend Kehinde Lawal. I used to really try in her Literature lesson, and her subject was my best anyway. I used to dream most in Mrs Osho's Maths lesson, especially when she came to the blackboard with her horrible-looking board compass. Girls who were clever in Maths said she was good, but I was not good at her subject. Much much later, how I wished she was with me when I had to take Social Statistics, when I was reading for my degree in Sociology. Anyway, Miss Humble did not like me and if she never favoured me, she had more excuse after my shameful behaviour in the assembly that morning. She went on reading Coleridge's "Christabel" and was going "Tu whit! Tu whoo .. And hark, again! the crowing cock, how drowsily it crew ..."

My mouth was agape in wonder. I was no longer looking at my young English teacher, with an MA in English from Oxford, but I was back in the village land of my ancestors. . . . I was listening to the voice of my big mother with her head covered in white woolly curls, with saliva trickling down the corners of her mouth, with her face sweaty and shining in its sweat, with me sitting by her feet with the Ukwa tree giving an illusory shade from the bright moon, and with the children, the too young ones who could not sit still for stories, playing Ogbe. . . . I was there in Ibusa in Umuezeokolo, Odanta, where all my people came from. I was there in that place, and did not hear the young Englishwoman, born in the Lake District and trained in Oxford, calling me, calling me. Suddenly somebody nudged me. Then Miss Humble's voice came through. Sharp and angry.

"Florence, Florence Emecheta, what are you going to do when you leave here?"

"A writer, Miss Humble."

Long silence.

"Pride goeth before a fall!" Miss Humble said in a hoarse, low voice and her protruding teeth looked as if they were going to fall out. Then she stretched herself, standing on her toes as if she was determined to reach the ceiling, and pointed at me stiffly, whilst the white hanky she tied around her watch with a masculine band twitched.

"Enh?" I was now fully awake. "I said I would like to be a writer." I began again just in case she did not hear me at first.

"Go out, out and straight to the chapel. Go there and pray for God's forgiveness."

"Enh?" I tried again.

"Take a bad mark!" It was almost a bark.

Then I knew that this was serious. I quickly made for the door, ready to run for it. Bad marks were added up and shown in one's school report. Some girls even said that they put them in one's school leaving testimonial. Nonetheless, I wanted to find out what exactly I had done to deserve this untoward punishment. I hesitated just for a split second, my eyes not leaving her face as she stood there in her ramrod erectness, her hand stretched straight like a poker, then I saw her mouth making the shape of another "bad mark". It was then that I ran, past the large glass window of our classroom that faced the verandah in the front part of the school. I did not stop until I was sure that Miss Humble could see me no more. Then I started to walk slowly up the stairs towards the chapel on the first floor of our large E-shaped school.

My mind was at first blank, with only Miss Humble's voice ringing in my ears. The voice of authority. The voice one had been taught to associate with correctness. The voice one had never questioned. The voice that simply had to be obeyed. Then as I neared the door of the chapel my own voice, the voice of my Chi, little and at first insecure, started to filter in. "What are you going to tell God, enh? What, Florence, are you going to tell Him, when you go inside there to ask His forgiveness? Are you going to say, 'Please, dear God, don't make me a writer'? And then at the same time say, 'But, dear God, I so wish to be a writer, a story-teller, like our mother Ogbueyin and her friends at home in Ibusa.' Unlike them I would not have to sit by the moonlight, because I was born in an age of electricity, and would not have to tell my stories with my back leaning against the Ukwa tree, because now I have learned to use new tools for the same art. Now I know a new language, the language of Miss Humble and the rest of them. So where is the sin in that?"

My Chi's voice suddenly grew louder, so loud that it covered that of Miss Humble. I reached the chapel door, and with my head up, walked past it. God had more important things to do than to start punishing me for speaking my dreams aloud. Not only did I not go into the chapel to pray, I did not call the "bad mark" either. I thought and worried about not calling the bad mark for many a night and I came to the conclusion that Miss Humble probably felt that her language was too good for the likes of me to want to use as a means of expression. But that was the only language I was being taught to write. If I spoke my Ibo language or any other Nigerian one in the school compound, I would be given a bad mark or asked to pay a find. And why did she take the trouble to leave her island home and come and teach us her language in the first place? I did not know the answer to this question, and thinking about it made my head ache.

On one point, however, she got me, and that was in ordering me out of the class. That kind of action was to us like that meted out to a leper, like being excommunicated for simply being a leper.

I laughed very much when I remembered this scene when I was in London in 1975, teaching English to English children, and had to order a very difficult and destructive sixteen-year-old Cockney out of the class. I was still a new teacher. Instead of being ashamed and sorry, the boy was happy and became noisier and started to make faces at the rest of the class through the window. He did not stop at this, but started to bang things at the wall, which brought along the school Head. I saw him talk to the boy, and with his face purple with anger he then asked me in front of the class what I thought I was doing, ordering a boy out like that. I tried to explain, but the Head refused to understand. He made it perfectly clear that in schools like his, the children ruled and the teachers had to obey. If you sent a child out of the class, you gave him the freedom to go and vandalize the school, the streets, and commit all kinds of crimes. How did those early teachers, then, manage to instil such values into us? I soon began to understand. England is a welfare state; one does not need too much education to survive. Nigeria was then, as now, a capitalist society where one has to work very hard in order to survive. In Nigeria there is no dole money, no unemployment benefit, and education is highly rewarded. The gap between the rich and the not so rich is very wide indeed.

I did not call in my bad mark the following Friday as one was expected to, because I felt that I had done nothing wrong. For the rest of my school career, however, I made sure never to anger a teacher so much that I was sent out of class. When I left school, my Head, Miss Walker, said in my testimonial that I was mild, pleasant and placid, and that she was sure I would do well in anything I set my heart on. Well, she was wrong about the latter: I set my heart on making a successful marriage, because they had taught us at the Methodist Girls' High School that prayers and devotion could move mountains. It did not work out for me that way. As for the former attributes, being mild and placid, I would have been something else, the opposite in fact, if I had been more sure of how people would take my outbursts.

6

The Holiest of Holies

Like the story of my birth, I cannot remember for sure when I first heard the name "United Kingdom". My father gave that name weight in my mind. Whenever my father pronounced the words "United Kingdom", it sounded so heavy, so reverential. It was so deep, so mysterious, that my father always voiced it in hushed tones wearing an expression as respectful as if it were God's Holiest of Holies.

Going to the United Kingdom must surely be like paying God a visit. It was around this time that my people living in Lagos were preparing for the arrival of our town's first lawyer, who was returning from the United Kingdom. The preparation went on for months. My mother and her friends were so proud of this, our new lawyer, because to us it meant the arrival of our own Messiah. A Messiah who had been to the "Kingdom of Heaven" and back to fight for the right of us Ibuza people. My mother was a seamstress, so not only was she kept extra busy, but I had a frock made for me from the remnants of the material ordered by the women on the arrival of this big lawyer. I always called this dress "my United Kingdom lawyer dress" and I wore it for a very long time, because my mother made it very big for me to grow into, and I grew very, very slowly in those days.

I did not go with the women to welcome the big lawyer. But the stories and songs of what it was like in the United Kingdom went on for months. My father and his friends would toast the river Oboshi, thanking her for not allowing our very first lawyer to go astray or bring a white woman home as a wife. My father was so happy during this time, and since I had come to realize that my being a girl child had been a slight disappointment to my parents, I made a secret vow to myself.

I made the vow between the two cracked walls at the back of our yard in Akinwunmi Street in Yaba, Lagos, that when I grew up I must visit the United Kingdom, to keep my father happy forever. That was going to be my payment to my family for daring to come into this world as a girl. It was a dream my Chi and myself kept to ourselves and it lived with me like a presence. Unfortunately my father died a few months after this. I was so young and yet so close to him. I loved my father so much that I still think I am going through life looking for him.

My mother did one great thing for me: she won agreement to let me stay in school for a while because she knew how much I wanted to, because she too had a little education, and because she knew that some basic education would qualify me to be the wife of one of the new Nigerian élite. But I had other plans. Without my father to look after me I had to look after myself. Secretly I sat for a scholarship examination to the Methodist Girls' High School and I won it. So I went to the missionary school, because if I had stayed at home I would have been forced to marry when I was only twelve. My mother did not understand me and did not see the reason for my wanting to stay long at school. How we both suffered in those days. Poverty and ignorance can be really bad even for a mother and daughter who apparently loved each other but did not know how to reach each other.

Because of this, I seldom went home during the school holidays. I would stay in the dormitory with the cooks and stewards and read all the books I could lay my hands on. Going home would have meant explaining to Mother that I wanted to go to the United Kingdom one day and that I would like to come back to Ibusa to tell stories like my big mother Nwakwaluzo used to. The longer I stayed at the Methodist Girls' High School, reading and dreaming among those huge trees that shaded us from the loco-yard opposite, the more Ibusa assumed the image of paradise.

I stayed at school until I was sixteen; then I could no longer avoid family pressures. I refused all the men kept for me and married the man I called Francis in my other books, but whose real name is Sylvester Onwordi – a dreamy, handsome local boy who, though older than myself, thought he too would make it big in the United Kingdom. But I soon found out that under his handsome and strong physique was a dangerously weak mind. It did not take me long to realize my mistake, and see that on this score my mother was right. But at our missionary school we were told that prayers could move anything, could turn a weak man into a hard-working one, and I believed in miracles. This miracle, however, did not happen. Sylvester did not change, and not only did he not change but he wanted to drag us all down with him. I was smaller, younger and a woman and I still thank the Lord and my Chi that they did not allow this to happen.

I got a nice job at the American Embassy in Lagos. It was a classy job and I was earning almost six times my husband's salary. Consequently it was easy for me to save and bring us all to England.

That was the time when English immigration was becoming difficult. A woman could not go there on her own with two babies, even if she could afford it, but she could go to join her student husband, so many "marriages" took place at that time in Lagos, marriages of wives going to join husbands.

My in-laws urged me to stay in Nigeria, because I was already earning more than those who had been to the UK and back. What they did not know was that I had promised my father that I would go to the UK. I would like to know that he is now in the land of the dead saying, "I am proud you went there as a woman, and a strong and loving woman who tried very much to be a good mother and a good wife."

I was almost eighteen in 1962, the mother of two babies, Chiedu and Ik, both still in their nappies, when my dream finally came true. I remember watching my brother on the shore, in a brown African robe which he had specially made to send me off in (and which was still too big for him), crying and wiping his eyes with the velvet hat that went with the robe. It was that sight that made me cry. Our mother had died only months before I left, so we only had each other and of course my young babies. But there was nothing I could do but pray very hard to God to look after him because he was the only male Emecheta left. God heard my prayers, because seeing him eighteen years afterwards, the proud father of five boys and two girls and owner of a palatial house to match, I just felt very proud of him and his wife Ngozi with her big laughing face. But meanwhile I had to follow my dreams.

I came to England in a plush first-class suite with a nurse for the children. I booked the best I could afford because I thought everybody lived like that in England. I thought people in England lived like they did in Jane Austen's novels and that the typical Englishman was like Mr Darcy, and the women like Mrs Bennet and her daughters. So when, thirteen days later, the nurse came bubbling into my room and asked excitedly, "Have you seen it? Have you seen Liverpool? We've arrived in England", I could be forgiven for dashing out on deck in a cotton housecoat. It was a grey, wet March morning.

England gave me a cold welcome. As I said in *Second-Class Citizen*, "If I had been Jesus, I would have passed England by and not dropped a single blessing." It felt like walking into the inside of a grave. I could see nothing but masses of grey, filth, and more grey, yet something was telling me that it was too late now. So I said quietly, "Pa, England is not the Kingdom of God you thought it was." It was too late now, I had sold all I had to go this far, so I said again to my Chi, "I must make it here or perish." And I was not going to allow myself to perish because if I did, who was going to look after the babies I'd brought this far?

With my mind thus made up, I went back into my suite, because the cold was beginning to touch my African bones.

Twenty-three years later, I am still shivering from that shock!

7

Culture Shock

In England, my marriage did not last long. We arrived at the time when it was classy to advertise for tenants and print in bold red letters, "SORRY NO COLOUREDS". My husband could only get a small room from one Mr Olufunwa, a man he met through another friend. It was a box-like room with just enough space for a bed and a chair.

When I was about to come to England, I sent £30 to my husband to buy me a coat and to meet me with it in Liverpool. But he decided to spend the money to buy himself a suit, and used the rest to pay a deposit on a rather beautiful studio couch. The couch was to serve as bed for Chiedu and Ik for two years. As for my coat, he borrowed Mrs Akinyemi's imitation fur coat for me to wear on arrival. For days, I thought it was mine. You could sense my humiliation a week later, when she demanded her coat back. An imitation fur coat cost only ten pounds in those days yet I had to wear a borrowed one even though I had sent enough money to buy one three times over. I eventually bought a coat for seven pounds, months later, when I started work.

Things were tough. I think Jake was conceived the very night I arrived in Britain, but I was successful in hiding it from a doctor who examined me before I was taken on as a member of staff at the North Finchley Library.

I started work there in June. Our neighbours and landlord could not take it at all. All the Nigerian women in the house worked at a shirt factory in Camden Town and they had taken the trouble to reserve a position for me there, but I refused because I knew I could get something better. I had already decided on a profession, and had started taking correspondence courses at home in Nigeria on British librarianship. I intended to continue it here. Working in a shirt factory would for me have been a damaging emotional blow. People were surprised that I was called for interviews at all, but what they did not know was that even in those early days I arrived with ten "O" levels and four "A"s – and all our papers were marked here in England. Most of my female neighbours had not gone beyond the equivalent of eleven-plus. Maybe if we had had time to communicate with one another, things would not have been so bad. But we were all busy being loyal to our husbands.

That was not the end of our problems. Our landlord and landlady were older than my husband and myself. They had been married for a while and for some uncertain reason were still childless. The wife kept seeing a specialist so that she could conceive, but it looked very difficult at the time. And here was I having the audacity to bring my babies into the house, refusing to give them away to be fostered, and being pregnant again. They complained that Ik cried a lot, that Chiedu wet our couch so that it stank, and that Ik was tearing the wallpaper. I must say we never caught Ik who was then only nine months old doing the latter. In short, they wanted us out.

Only people who lived in London at the time would know the power landlords used to have over their tenants. They could throw any tenant out at any time, and few people would think of taking a black family in. Our landlord was aware of this but nevertheless evicted us. Fate kept bringing our two families together however much we tried to go our different ways. My children have been taught never to seek revenge, and we are all friends now. But then, in 1962, it could have been the end of the world for my family, and Mr Olufunwa was the only one who had the power to alleviate our sufferings. Sadly he did not.

My husband always quoted this early shock we had at human nature as the strongest contributory factor to the break-up of our family. Maybe so, but I know that meeting the people we did at that time made him lower his standards considerably, and like his new friends he began to settle for second best. I could have followed him, but for the sake of the kids we were bringing into the world I was prepared to hang on to the edge of the cliff with my teeth, or to keep swimming with my head just above water.

I watched helplessly as the little confidence he had in himself slipped away as we faced rejection after rejection. No respectable landlord wanted a black family. We realized that however well educated we were, our colour which we had hitherto regarded as natural was repulsive to others and posed a great problem. Our hosts in our new country simply refused to see beyond the surface of our skin.

As we wandered from street to street, looking for a place to rest our heads, we heard about one Nigerian landlord. He was a Benin man. Like us, he was an outcast. People told all kinds of unsavoury and untrue stories about this man: how he could kill, how he could do this and that. As beggars can never be choosers, he took us in. Needless to say, he did not kill us. In fact the only trouble we had was when my husband started to befriend his wife. But the man himself always made me laugh and he loved children.

By the time we left his house to live at the Olas', in 1964, I knew I was eventually going to leave my husband. Knowing this did not make me want to go immediately. I kept hoping things would improve and that I would not have to make the break.

The day I brought Christy home from hospital, I caught Sylvester sleeping with a white woman friend. I telephoned him for hours from hospital to ask him to come and collect us, but he ignored my calls, so I packed my new baby and arrived on a sunny May day. The sunshine disappeared as I went upstairs and saw why my husband could not come for us.

I thought I would die of sorrow.

Then I looked at Chiedu, who was then four, at Ik, three, Jake still crawling at seventeen months and at Christy who was only twelve days old – and I knew that I could not afford to die of sorrow. My kids would suffer.

My mind went back to my childhood days and to the beatings I had from people like Vincent Obi, and to the innumerable lies told against one, simply because one's parents were not there. I shook my head. I must, please God, be around until my kids needed me no more.

I staggered up, washed them all and put nice clothes on them. I went down and told Mrs Ola that I was going to leave Sylvester. The woman, a good friend at the time, told me to forget it. She was frightened to come too close to me as she did not wish to be accused of giving me ideas. However, she was able to recount all that she had gone through for her marriage. Her experiences were such that they almost made me forget my woes, but I knew she was luckier than I for at least her husband was working, studying and passing his exams. We were still there when he got his Masters degree in Law.

Her claim that most women put up with such husbands did not move me much. If a husband was going to be unfaithful, he should have the decency to do it outside and not on his wife's bed and especially not on the day that she was bringing home their new baby.

After that incident I wanted us to move, because the woman in question lived in the same house. She was ashamed of herself, but somehow I felt more shame. And anyway, with Christy we needed bigger accommodation. We lived on the fourth floor with very narrow stairs, so there was no room for Jake to learn to walk.

I had by now learnt the tricks of finding accommodation. I did not go looking for a flat as a poor black. I was beginning to learn to make stupid and superficial jokes, sometimes at my own expense. I got a flat in Malden Road within a week. The house belonged to a Pole with an English wife. We made the agreement and paid the deposit before the wife saw me. In the event, I don't think she liked us very much.

I was delighted to get this flat because it was near to Chiedu's school in Queen's Crescent. Also, the library I had worked at in Chalk Farm before having Christy was within walking distance, so I could visit my colleagues.

After the incident that day I brought Christy home from hospital, I told Sylvester that he had to get a job as I was no longer prepared to go on working with four young children while he sat at home, an eternal student who could afford to hop in and out of bed with the women in the house. Mr and Mrs Ola supported me and he eventually got a job as a clerical officer at the newly built GPO tower. The job had a good future, since the post was in the Accounts Department, and he was reading to be an accountant. Consequently, we were all delighted.

I never learnt. With this new job of his, I told myself that I was going to make our marriage work: once he went out to work, his confidence would soar and he would learn to enjoy the new power he had over his family – the power to be the breadwinner, a feat which Sylvester had never achieved in all his life. And I was going to make it worth his while. I was going to practise all those things I learnt at the Methodist Girls' High School. I was naïve then – all I wanted was to be a full-time housewife and mother. I would have been perfectly happy living in Sylvester's reflected glory. I was going to be an ideal housewife with all our meals ready on time. I was going to teach our children to read and write before they went to school, and take them to music and ballet classes, where they would acquire confidence. I was going to take them to elocution classes and they would be taught beautiful table manners. Housework, I told myself, could be very creative if there was a breadwinner.

But Sylvester refused to go to work! He had been used to staying at home for too long, and regarded each day that he went to work as purgatorial. He insisted that he came to England to study, not to work for me to stay at home simply to wash nappies, knit jumpers, and indulge in my lazy dreams.

To show him that I did not just stay at home to wash nappies and knit, I wrote my first book, *The Bride Price*. I was so excited about this that I took the manuscript to my friends at Chalk Farm Library. And the Canadian librarian with whom I worked and argued and discussed black literature for hours during our lunch period, told me it was good. I knew then that it must be good, because he was a sincere critic whose taste in reading was catholic. He said the book was my brainchild. Somehow, that phrase "brainchild" kept ringing in my head.

With great exuberance, I showed my "brainchild" to my husband. He at first did not want to read the manuscript because, he said, "You don't know much, so how can you write a story?" Nonetheless, I pleaded with him to read it. He did so secretly and his reaction was to burn it. He was still burning the last pages when I came into the room from Queen's Crescent where I had been shopping.

I knew then that my dream of being an ideal wife and mother was buried. Society never prepared us for lone parenthood. As children we are encouraged to play the ideal mother or father, but as adults the fear of failing to achieve this ideal becomes very stressful. For me the fear made me clutch at straws for a very long time, even though I had by then learnt that one happy parent is better for the children than two warring ones. Nonetheless, the burning of my *Bride Price* decided me.

A Caribbean friend of mine, Mrs Hamilton, agreed to look after Christy and the others for me during the day and I got a job at the British Museum. I refused to cook for Sylvester and I refused him sex because I wanted to leave him very badly. He gave up his nice job as soon as he saw that I was settled in mine. He promised to go back to his studies, but those were his dreams and I told him I was no longer part of them. Nonetheless, he would corner me, demanding sex, when he knew that I was about to go to work. I had to give in because of the children. I remember Jake drinking the contents of a bottle of Domestos from sheer despair. I remember Chiedu dashing out and calling a man in uniform to come and save her mummy. The man was from the railways, but at five she thought any man in uniform was a policeman. I remember Mr Olufunwa, Mr Olufunwa who had thrown us out but who now had his own son, Ronald, coming in and telling Sylvester off, so much so that the two men started to quarrel on my account.

I was leaving, that I knew, and this time I was telling no one.

I soon got a flat from another Yoruba landlord by telling him that I was a Yoruba woman. I did not feel a qualm about this since human discriminations were just becoming too much for me. First I was discriminated against because I was black, and at that time West Indian landlords would not take Africans and Nigerian landlords would not take Ibos. And as for hoping to get a place as a one-parent family, one would just have to forget it. I told my landlord that not only was I a Yoruba, but that my husband had just gone home to take up a big position in Nigeria. Before he could open his mouth to ask any more questions, I paid him several months in advance by cheque. He was a slow Yoruba man from the hinterland who had probably not seen a woman write a cheque before in his whole life. But he was shocked at my married name. He said, "Why is it that a nice lady like you should marry a Yanmiri?" I smiled and said nothing. I knew that the fat cheque I gave him had done its work.

The problem now was how to leave Sylvester without a fight. Now that he had given up his job, he stayed at home all the time. Our move must be sudden.

He was shocked when he woke one Saturday morning and saw that three of the children were already in the street. Jake was too slow, and as usual he was making a lot of noise and kept asking me where we were going. In the midst of the argument his father woke. In desperation, Sylvester seized Jake's arm and said, "You don't like him that much because he looks like me."

I stood there for a while looking at Jake and wondering what I was going to do. Pulling him would confuse the poor three-year-old child the more. I decided to take the others away and get the police to help me with Jake. But

Jake suddenly shouted and shook himself free of his father. "Leave me alone, you're bad, you beat me all the time. I'm going with my mummy. I'm going with my mummy!"

I looked at Sylvester's face, and for that split second I felt really sorry for him. Shocked, he quickly let go of Jake's hand and I waited for my son as he struggled into his dufflecoat. He was still in his urine-soaked pyjamas but it did not matter. I carried him down the stairs into our new life.

Sylvester found out where we lived and came to demand what he called his "sexual rights" as a husband. I was virtually raped for Alice to be conceived, though, looking at her now, I'm glad it happened. My doctor, who told me that I was pregnant, reported the case to the police.

The case came up only weeks before Alice was born. There, in Clerkenwell Magistrates' Court, Sylvester denied his children and recommended that I should have them all adopted because, being a student, he did not wish to be saddled with five kids. He said that we never married, so I had no claim on him.

I was too shocked to be coherent. I just kept shouting anything. We were married but he burnt my Nigerian passport, the children's birth certificates, and our marriage certificate, knowing full well that to get those documents back from Nigeria was impossible. The country of our birth, Nigeria, is not particularly noted for the unearthing of such records. All I had to show were wedding photographs. Somehow, I wanted to rid myself of this man and did not want this court to know that I was his legal wife. He made me so sick with anger that I almost convulsed.

In front of the court I waited for him, and I cursed him and cursed him and really cursed him! I said in our language, I said:

> From now on, Sylvester, you, the son of Onwordi,
> The day you come out to make fire,
> God will send rain, unless any of these five children
> Belonged not to you but to somebody else.

That curse still makes me feel guilty to this day. But then what did the world expect a woman to do to a man who had just disowned her and said that all the five children she had for him were not his, simply because he did not wish to pay for their maintenance?

Our people can be superstitious. They say that if a pregnant woman curses the father of her child, especially if the father is denying responsibility, he will never achieve anything again. Well, I did not know that. The father should not have denied in the first place. A woman could never deny, not when the child was inside her. So what was there for a woman to do, enh?

8

Pussy Cat Mansions

I left Clerkenwell that day wobbling on my feet. I was eight months pregnant. Before I knew it, I had walked from King's Cross to Camden Town. Then for no reason at all, I stopped in front of a butcher's shop just staring at the chickens hanging by their necks.

Suddenly Chidi called me from behind. I don't know how he recognized me. The last time I had seen him I was a fraction of my size in my khaki school uniform and school beret. That was almost seven years ago. Since then, I had given birth four times and was on the verge of it again.

I turned, and the smile vanished from his face. I could not talk. If I had opened my mouth, I would have cried. But he knew me well. We were good friends, able to communicate with our eyes rather than our voices.

He got the message and his only remark was, "So you married Sylvester!"

I said nothing and he hailed a taxi.

"Where to?" the cab man asked.

"Take her to her husband," Chidi said without mirth. It was like a sentence. Although I did break a few hearts in my time, I was not beautiful, but I had that cultivation which the new breed of men from Africa were beginning to look for in their women – the so-called Western education.

"Yeah, but where?" the cab man persisted.

Then I gave my address aloud. Maybe I wanted Chidi to memorize it, maybe not, but at that moment I hardly knew what I was doing. He did memorize that address; he told me so years later.

I did not see him again for a long time and I forgot the incident. My baby was due and I had to worry about that. I refused help from anyone and I decided that I was not going to involve others in my problems more than necessary. Everyone had his or her own cross to bear. I stripped from my mind any idle or wasteful thoughts and forced myself to elevate the job of childbirth to a grand and beautiful level. For once, I felt I had a little control over my life. I knew that this child, which if a boy I would call Jeremy after my father and if a girl, Alice after my mother, would be my last child. I loved children but as I was not yet twenty-two, I felt that five was enough for anyone to manage in a country like Britain.

I did not want help and could be really hurt when offered it, but then I came across a woman who was emotionally stronger than myself. She was Mrs Burns, the head of the welfare section at the British Museum. She persisted and saw beyond my proud humility. She got the Establishment to give me three months' paid leave, at a time when a privilege like that was unthought of, to say nothing of giving it to somebody who had not even worked there a year. She must have wheedled it out of this person and that, and at the end of the day she got even the pillars of the Establishment nodding in agreement like lizards.

A few days after I stopped work, I knew that my baby was ready to be born.

I got the others ready, sent the older ones to school and wheeled the younger ones slowly to the nursery. After that I phoned the social workers at Bidborough House in Camden Town to tell them that I would be going into hospital. Like typical officials, they were infuriated that the child was arriving earlier than scheduled. I smiled to myself. To think that the angry voice at the other end was that of a woman!

By three o'clock that afternoon, after I had tidied the flat, I took a Number 24 bus and admitted myself to University College Hospital in Huntley Street. The only thing I feared in childbirth was a Caesarian section. But I was assured that this birth would be normal.

I thanked God for this, because after the break with Sylvester four weeks previously I had worked myself up emotionally and spiritually not just to want this baby but to desire it with all my heart. I would do all the exercises, cooing to Alice or Jeremy. Sometimes I was convinced I was going to have an Alice, at other times a Jeremy. And by the time I was ready for the birth of my child, I was sorry for Sylvester not being around to share with me those beautiful, beautiful moments.

A young doctor who sensed that I lived alone sat by me and we talked for hours, while the contractions kept coming and going. By about nine-thirty, I suggested he should go and have his supper. He did. And as soon as he left, Alice made her quiet appearance.

My other babies used to cry as soon as their heads were out. This one was just grunting and making sounds like somebody enjoying being kissed. She was painless and hairless. I thankfully took her from the black junior nurse who was around at the time of the birth.

The nurse was so young. I have never seen anyone so excited on seeing a baby. Alice arrived so quickly that it was me telling her what to do. She kept saying, Let's go and call Dr this and Dr that. And I kept saying, Yes, after you've tied that knot and given me my baby.

"Jesus, my first baby, all by myself," she cried. "I'm so glad." She wiped her hands and demanded, 'Mrs Onwordi, would you like me to phone your husband now?"

"Which husband?" I asked.

I have never seen a young person so disappointed. Her face fell and grew a shade darker. She cried, and I cried a little but not too much, because my own was the cry of joy and the cry of freedom.

I asked for a piece of paper and before our room was ready I wrote the poem I called "Alice". I still read this amateur work of mine in public whenever I want my audience to wallow a little in self-pity.

We slept that night in peace, Alice and myself. But by eleven o'clock the following morning, I asked the social worker that came to visit me where my children were. She told me that Chiedu and Ik had been taken to Essex and that Christy and Jake were with another woman in Kentish Town.

"I want my children back this minute," I cried. I put on my dressing-gown, picked Alice up and made for the door.

"You can't do that. You have to discharge yourself first," said the ward sister.

"Then I have discharged myself!" Those kids should have stayed in one home. I had begged and pleaded for this in the past three months. I could imagine Christy, who would not go to sleep until I had rocked her, crying her eyes out. I did not allow myself to think of Ik, who would not open his mouth in front of any stranger. The only child who could understand what was happening was Chiedu and she could have explained it all to her brothers and sister if they had stayed together. Though she was not yet six, they all trusted her. She was like their little mother.

My feet shook in terror at the mere thought of what those social workers were doing. They said that Alice had arrived eight days earlier than expected, and they had not prepared for this emergency. It was no use explaining to them that after eight and a half months, babies could arrive at any time. It was not their fault, I kept saying. It was the fault of my Chi, who landed me with Sylvester, of all men. Never mind, I'd survive.

People looked at me as if I had gone mad. Perhaps I had. None of them could see what I was seeing, feel what I was feeling. I was particularly worried about Christy and Ik. Those two children were never extroverts; they bottled up their feelings inside, like me.

Somehow, of all people, it was the young black nurse who had helped me with Alice who understood, she begged the ambulance men to drive me home and promised to see to it that they sent me a home nurse. "If they refuse, I'll come myself." Without my saying a word, there was a kind of affinity between us. She was so young, yet she understood; but then we were both blacks and maybe, like me, she knew what the word "family" ought to mean.

At that time, I was living in Wellesley Road, Kentish Town, and some friends, Mr and Mrs Hamilton, who came from Jamaica, were very helpful. Mrs Hamilton used to take Chiedu to school for me, and when I left Sylvester she became a good friend. Her husband would invariably knock at my window around ten o'clock on his way from the pub and say, "Mrs Odowis, everytin' is going to be aaraat." He and his wife could neither read nor write, but his nightly call was like a prayer.

I used to laugh and say, without coming out of the house, "Good night, Mr Hamilton." He would grunt again, "It's going to be aaraat", and then go on his way.

It was so nice with all those people popping in and out of our flat at the time and even though I did not ask for help, everyone did what they could. It's sad to know that all those nice people have now been moved and the strong Afro-Caribbean community we were innocently building at the time dispersed.

One Sunday, when Alice was four weeks old, there was a knock on our door and Chidi came in with another friend, Mr Eze. From then on, we seemed to have been discovered by the Ibo community in that part of

London. Chidi would call with friends and we would all stay till late, talking politics. Through him I came to know the Ejimofos, the Chimas, the Ezes and so many others. When the civil war in Nigeria started soon after, I was among friends. But the war put a dividing line between me and many of my Yoruba neighbours, and consequently my Yoruba landlord wanted us out.

Unlike the Olufunwas before him, he was unlucky. By this time I had grown emotionally tough. I went to church regularly and prayed hard. Chidi and his friends gave me all the moral and emotional support I needed. At one time, it looked as if the civil war in Nigeria was being fought there in Wellesley Road. I learnt later that nice people like Mr Chucks Ejimofo used to fast and pray for us, especially when we all knew that my landlord was resorting to mysterious *juju* methods.

All these harassments helped me get a council flat. It was by no means an ideal one, but it was the only vacant place available when the court told the council that my son Jake started to run at the sight of any black man. The Camden Council told us that I'd be there for a month or so because the flats were by that time in need of re-doing. Moving to that flat at 'Pussy Cat Mansions' as I called it in *In the Ditch*, gave me another kind of freedom that I'd never enjoyed in England. Freedom from private landlords. We moved into Pussy Cat Mansions when Alice was ten months old.

Friends still came to visit us, and by now I had the courage to invite home colleagues from the British Museum. Somehow I started shying gradually away from my Ibo friends because I guessed they would not understand my being friends with Whoopey, Mrs Cox and the Princess – the women friends I made at the Mansions. They would not understand that when people reached the bottom of the ditch, they needed each other. It did not matter which colour or what educational background, one had to be friends with them for survival. My Ibo friends and relatives would not be able to see beyond their rough language and obvious poverty. But I could: I lived with them and had seen the warmth of their hearts.

After twelve months, during which time I had resigned from the British Museum in order to be able to give more time to my children, I knew that I was not going to allow them to grow up there. I had to pull myself out of the ditch for their sake.

I was not quite sure, but I always feared that despite everything, they might like it here in England – after all, was it not the only country they knew? – and to live and survive here as black people they would have to be a head higher than the average white boy or girl in a similar situation. So for their sake I could not afford to wallow in the mire of our powerlessness for long.

My faith helped me. I prayed and sometimes harangued God. I got angry with Him for being so slow and would invariably boycott going to church just to show Him how angry I was. I always went back, though, when whatever it was that precipitated the worries melted dew-like in the air. Hence my favourite hymn is still "O love that will not let me go", especially the line, "I see the rainbow through the rain".

I realized that shouting our anger at the Social Security men and rent collectors was not the answer. I had to leave Pussy Cat Mansions. I started letting people know that although I was black, I still had some education. I began to write about our plight in the local papers like the *Ham and High*. I refused to consider any inferior flats and consequently was given one of the best, in Rothay, Albany Street, near Regent's Park. I gave thanks to God that at least environmentally my family would not suffer. If they did not turn out quite right, I would always console myself that I did all I could. And that, I think, is what most parents crave – the opportunity to do their best for their children.

9

The Matchboxes

In June 1969, I moved from Pussy Cat Mansions into Rothay in Albany Street. Although these flats belonged to the council, it was still a giant move for us. The area was very good and the flats were new, with the promise of central heating.

The June day on which we moved was mercifully dry. I left the bigger children at the new flat with the Gas Board engineer whilst he fixed in our old cooker. Before I arrived with the removal van, however, my eldest son Ik who was then eight had explored the whole of Regent's Park and its environs. He told me in no uncertain terms, "These are really, really posh nosh flats, Mum." I could not help agreeing with him. I felt a lump in my chest as I watched his chubby cheek relaxed in a vain attempt to smile. He was shy as a boy, too shy even to let people know that he could smile, but I always knew when he was pleased. Two funny dimples would form at the top of his fat cheek and the bottom part of his mouth would look as if he had two boiled sweets, one in each cheek. Looking at him now with his narrow face, I wonder where those chubby cheeks have gone. Our children, how they change.

Children get very excited at the thought of moving. Mine were too happy even to sleep. They jumped, they sang, they climbed around the new flat and I noticed that nobody banged the wall to complain of our noise. No one could hear us. The walls of these "posh nosh" flats were as thick and solid as those of Jericho! If I had a cold or could not cope with my family, I could no longer raise my voice and call Whoopey as I used to in the Mansions. For the first time since I left my husband with my five dripping kids, fear seized me. But as usual when things were beyond me, I prayed and begged God to give me energy and good health to cope with it all. As if God wanted to make me aware of all the bounties I was taking for granted – good health and warm friends – I became ill from sheer fatigue. I thought I would never be strong again. I always hated moving house. However gradually I planned it and however much I enlisted the help of others, I always ended up palpitating like a tired dog.

But with five young and rather lively children, what time had one to indulge in tiredness? Like the fabled Pied Piper I once more stepped into the street, but unlike him I was not piping a song, I was looking for a school for my children.

I went first to a clean, modern-looking one, but the teachers and the Headmaster and most of the people who had anything to do with the school were still glorying in its newness and regarded taking in four black children with the possibility of adding a fifth in a few years as a mini-invasion.

"Could you allow one of the dear children to come and start here with us, whilst you look for places for the others in other schools?" asked a plump and comfortable-looking teacher, smiling sweetly and making me feel as if I were setting loose the whole black population to invade her school. I thanked her very much, but no; where one child went so would the others, too. I was not going to spend the little energy I had in taking one child to this school and that one to the other. Besides, I was not particularly keen on its forced concrete newness. It looked too modern for my lively children anyway.

Again I stepped out, and asked the local people about the other school, St Mary Magdalene. This one was an old building, which I thought must have been built in the time of Chaucer. It had a beautiful church attached to it and from the outside one did not know where the church ended and the school began. It looked like a huge medieval edifice, somewhat out of place, surrounded as it was by concrete buildings. Nonetheless, I went inside.

The tiny door that led to the main building reminded me of the small vestry doors of All Saints' Church at Yaba in Lagos. Though my head did not reach the top of the door, I felt I had to bend to go inside. That was the effect of the small door. There was a dark narrow hall, the walls of which were pasted with legends, Biblical passages and children's drawings. But one particular drawing captured my attention. It was a child's painting of a piano keyboard. There were the usual black and white keys, but underneath the painting were written the words, "To make harmonious music on the piano, you have to play black and white keys." I was intrigued and lifted my brow, not knowing what to expect.

The Headmaster, Mr Harper, was a bright little man with beautiful grey hair. He had the face of the English schoolboy whose nanny had made sure it was well scrubbed. He spoke like one too – those public school people who "speak well", as one of the teachers, Miss Greenwood, used to put it. I knew at once that Mr Harper liked to talk: he talked and I talked. I told him I liked his idea about the black and white keyboard and praised his originality. He liked that very much. Since then my daughter Christy has told me that it was not original at all, and that someone had said it before.

Well, that might be so, but that afternoon it made Mr Harper relax towards me and it gave him an insight into my capabilities, because the conversation progressed to the folly of human nature. "Look at you whites," I cried, "you have straight hair and you're not satisfied but go to your hairdressers to have it curled. You have pale skin yet you spend a fortune to darken it. And look at me, God gave me tight curly hair, and what do I do? I spend my hard-earned money straightening it, and our black skin, some of us spend a fortune on creams to lighten it. So if you were God what would you do, Mr Harper?" He agreed with me that he wouldn't know what to do with us humans.

My children told me later that he quoted this many times in assembly. That was not bad. One seldom meets an Englishman who is prepared to learn. We got on so well that he forgot to ask me if my children had a father or not. But before I left that building of St Mary Magdalene, my children's names were all written down and they would start school the following Monday.

I lost my friends at Pussy Cat Mansions and before I knew my way about the universities and polytechnics, my friends were the Head and teachers of St Mary Magdalene. The school became an extension of our home. As it was a small school with less than a hundred children, this was not particularly difficult. I am glad I had this relationship with my children's teachers because it helped them all later in life and they were very happy there.

10

The Sociology Degree

It was lovely to be given a nice maisonette in Regent's Park, but what was I going to do to maintain it and my fast-growing family? How was I going to earn a living? I could not go on living on the dole, as the amount of money given to one was only just enough to keep one off the streets with a begging bowl. Besides, I had done that for a year and could see myself sinking slowly but surely down and down. If one stays on the dole, one starts to disintegrate. And whereas my neighbours at Pussy Cat Mansions had been friendly, these new ones were definitely not. The best of them were indifferent.

I was told that my new neighbours had waited years for the new flats to be built and did not understand why I should be given a brand new one just like them. The family living close by was the worst in the whole neighbourhood, in fact people later identified us by saying, "You live next to them." They had several children, all very lively, who immediately took a dislike to us. That meant having rotten tomatoes left on our doorstep, while calls were made to council workers to come and see how dirty it was. They told the council I did not deserve the flat given to me. We went through the stage of stolen milk bottles until I cancelled all my milk and started fetching it myself. Then we reached the stage where my doors were sprayed and rude things written on them. If one dared complain to the parents, one would be told that they were only kids. The mother threatened once to pour all her rubbish on my door if I did not stop complaining. "After all, they are kids, I didn't do it," she howled.

To keep sane in such a place one simply had to lock oneself inside. And keeping inside meant thinking. "I can't go on living in places like this," I kept telling myself, and was determined that when next I moved it was going to be to a house of my own. Now, how was a single woman still in her mid-twenties with five children and completely unsupported to buy her own house in England? But I was determined to do this and because I was always alone, I talked to my Chi about it.

I seem to have lost sight of her. She used – well, I think she is a she – to push me into doing things. I remember my first day at school, how I got fed up with watching my mother chatting with her friends and plaiting and replaiting her hair and me just standing there looking at them and missing my brother who was already at school. I was not then at school because, being a girl, it was decided that I would not need much education, so my younger brother started school before I did. I remember how my Chi whispered to me, "Go on, take a scarf and go to school, go on!" And to this day I'm glad I listened to her voice, because I went to school that day. And after all the ballyhoo and the punishment the policemen meted out to my mother for being neglectful of her child, I was enrolled at the Lady Lak Institute. I even got more than I bargained for, because it was then a very good fee-paying school. That good foundation helped me so much when my father died and there was no more money for such luxuries as sending dreamy me to school when there was a boy in the family to educate.

However, during my first few years in England I seldom saw or spoke to my Chi. Occasionally when I walked in the parks in early spring, all alone, and I could see the birds hopping about full of happiness, I used to stand and smile at the joy and would hear my Chi say, "Now, aren't they beautiful?" And I would reply with a knowing nod, "Yes, they are beautiful." I would then pull myself together, looking this way and that to make sure nobody saw me. For I have read of women locked away simply for talking to themselves.

Sometimes talking to my Chi would not be sufficient and I'd want to let someone into my thoughts. One afternoon soon after we moved into Regent's Park, Carol, my social worker, came to see how I was settling into my new flat. She still begrudged our leaving her care, and was soon to be transferred somewhere else, but in the meantime she would call on us occasionally to tidy up her notes about us. She refused my cup of tea and to impress her I announced, "You know, Carol, one day I am going to buy a house of my very own and I shall leave this unfriendly place."

She turned round slowly and raised her brows as her hand ran indulgently through the many beads she wore. "Oh my goodness, what next? You wanted a new flat, and you got the best; now you are complaining about loneliness, and as for buying a house . . . " She laughed and continued, "We all have dreams, don't we?"

"I am going to buy a house – I don't know when, but when I move from this place it is going to be into a house which I will be buying."

Carol narrowed her eyes, maybe to study me closer or maybe because she was thinking, "Poor girl, she's probably taken leave of her senses." She looked away and made for the door. "And where are you going to get enough money to buy a house, may I ask?"

"I don't know yet, but I think I am going to be a writer. Yes, I will write."

"I don't know how many would-be writers I have come across," she said, adding, "Writing does not necessarily make you rich enough to buy a house." She left, having made the hollow in my stomach bigger than ever.

Sometimes it is very good to meet people like Carol, Miss Humble and Sylvester. Such people were particularly good for me and my Chi, because one way to set my mind on achieving something was for another person to tell me that I could not do it. I would then put all my thoughts into it, I would pray for it and go out for it, in search of the miracle. And when I saw the miracle flying about, I would grab it like Jacob grabbed Jehovah and forced Him to bless him and make him the father of Israel.

I could hear the tone of her voice saying that my making a living from such a profession as writing was a dream. "Anyway," I said, as I shrugged my shoulders at the bare white walls, "I'm still a long way to forty. I'm quite sure Big Mother in Ibusa did not start telling her stories before she was that age." My mind wandered back to the first story I wrote and my husband burned. "If I had that now, I would have shown this patronizing woman, my social worker, that I could write."

Nonetheless, I kept writing little pieces and sending them out to editors. I would think up my subject on Saturday and Sunday and type it out on my old typewriter. On Tuesday morning, after dropping the children at their school and nursery, I posted the manuscripts. Well, one could call them manuscripts, because the typing was the worst I have ever seen. As I could not and still cannot afford a professional typist, I type my ideas myself. A friend came to see me the other day, saw me typing and laughed until she cried. She said my fingers on the typing machine looked like a hen dancing on hot ashes. Sometimes the red ribbon would come instead of the black and many a time some letters would not show at all and I'd have to rewrite them in ink – oh, my manuscripts in those days looked odd! But I sent them to editors all the same. And religiously every Friday they would return them.

It soon became clear that I was not going to become a writer overnight. I knew Carol would soon leave us completely and we would be given a new social worker. After Carol, however, I was not going to allow the next one to pry into my life. That was one of the promises I made myself when I left Pussy Cat Mansions. She was not bad, just typical of her time. She did not quite know when help ended and humiliation began.

I told her I would need help for my evening classes. She knew vaguely that I wanted to study for a degree but I now realize that she probably did not know how one should start. She came for me and we went to this educational trust and family help office to see if they would pay for my books, as the dole money was not enough. As usual I was introduced as her "charge" or as "one of my cases". The office was near the Embankment and, because of traffic, we were late in returning. My children were sitting by the door making so much noise by the time I arrived; to make matters worse, one of the girls peed in the lift because she could not get into our flat, and my neighbours had a really big laugh. My daughter said she did not do it, but I knew she did. I knew then that I would not need Carol any more. She might be a social worker but she did not know how important it is for hungry children coming home from school to be welcomed by their mother.

Luckily Chidi came to see us that evening and I poured out all my woes to him. He listened, screwed up his narrow face, scratched his balding head, drank what he called "sergeant major tea" and said nothing for a while.

"You were stupid to leave your job at the British Museum; tell your friend to give you a job and then you can study in the evening."

"I'd like to study sociology, I'm fed up with librarianship."

"There . . . there . . . is a lot of money in librarianship, you know . . . " he stammered. Chidi stammered a lot and was very careful with money.

But I did not want to study for money alone. I wanted the type of discipline that would help me to be a good writer when I was forty, and the type of study that would allow me to be there at the door to welcome my kids when they returned from school.

Chidi liked to play the male, though he was lanky where Sylvester was stocky and his eyes roamed like mine. He liked women to do all the talking, whilst he remained silent. And then, when he was about to leave, he would say whatever he came to say at the beginning. One day he left me the Sociology prospectus for London University. "I think you are more than qualified for direct entry," he said as he closed the door on his way out.

Hours later, I was able to settle down to it and read it all through. He had brought it just in time. The autumn term was just beginning at the polytechnics. I was too late that year for the full day courses and I had no money anyway. So without saying anything to anybody, not even to Chidi, I marched towards the Polytechnic of Central London.

To my surprise, they said the grades of my "A" levels were good. And I did not even know it! All those years, I had thought I needed another "A" level – Latin – which I passed after four attempts. Now I was told that I didn't need it at all. Chidi was right. And soon I was ready for my first lecture.

A cuddly white man who looked like a walking teddy bear came and introduced himself as Mr Griffiths. He was to give us the first lecture in Social Theory. We sat there glued to the hard chairs as this man went on pouring out gibberish like "structuralism, functionalism, *Gemeinschaft*, *Gesellschaft*" until my head started to spin. I had bought a large writing pad and biro pen. Half the way through, however, I found I had covered several pages with drawings of palm trees by the lagoon in Lagos. I looked to my right and watched a blonde girl licking her contact lenses before putting them in again. I looked to my left and saw a black girl with a long chin reminding me of Chidi's. The blonde girl caught my eye and I smiled at her. I offered her a bar of KitKat, which she refused. She pointed at herself and mouthed her name, "Brenda", and I did the same and mouthed, "Buchi". She nodded and smiled again. I thought she knew all there was to know about the course. She must understand what "concomitant variation" was. I offered the chocolate to the black girl. She accepted and we smiled at each other. I stopped drawing palm trees but "Griefs", as we later learnt to call him, went on rabbiting about "social engineering".

The black girl, Faye, and I walked down to the bus stop. She was four years younger and walked on her toes like a model. She would pull in her backside and jut her chin forward, and when she tied her scarf she would tie it not under her chin but at the tip of it, thus making her face narrower still. Her nails were clean and varnished and she was very sophisticated. "Good Lord," I thought, "I'm glad I left Pussy Cat Mansions!"

"Do you know what the teacher was saying?" I panted. I was much shorter than Faye, who had such long legs that one stride of hers equalled two of mine.

She looked round as one would look at a small child, then lifted her mouth and laughed. Then I saw that she had a broken tooth by the side of her mouth and in a funny sort of way I felt happy, because at that time I had not lost the tooth I later lost in Calabar when chewing a bread roll that had stones in it. I still remember the nice feeling I had. "Well," I told myself, "you may walk on your toes like a young horse and carry your neck like a proud flamingo, but you have lost one tooth and I have all mine!"

"You mean lecturer? He is not a teacher."

"Oh yes," I gulped, "I don't understand 'em ... do yer?"

"Ah, you have a charming cockney accent. How very refreshing."

I clamped my mouth shut at this, and after a while Faye said, "Do you mean functionalism and dysfunctionalism?"

We both collapsed in laughter. Faye is still a very good friend, and so is Brenda. Later I met Meriel, Sue, Roberta, Freda and many, many more students. but I am glad I met the women from Pussy Cat Mansions first because they taught me how to laugh – a habit which my Western Anglican upbringing made me lose. It was all right to smile or giggle at nothing, but to really laugh in sheer enjoyment was bad manners. I still cling to this legacy from my Pussy Cat Mansion days.

11

The Grant

When I put in for a Sociology degree, I was made to understand that it would be a formidable task. I thought then that it was an unnecessary attempt to scare me off by the Head of Studies, Mr Ashton. But after a few months I realized that what he said was an understatement. Sociology was proving impossible for me to understand.

Studying with eighteen- and nineteen-year-olds, who seemed to have no cares in the world while I had a full house to look after, did nothing to alleviate my perilous position. For months after I registered and started the course, I still did not know what it was all about. We had to sit through lectures ranging from Philosophy and Criminology to Comparative Social Institutions, and somewhere in between were the most hated ones – Social Statistics and Applied Economics. Maybe I was clever as a child, but I never overrated myself. I knew where my power lay. It lies in the written word, but when it comes to anything remotely connected with figures, I have this indescribable mental block that used to freeze my brain and send me into a loud sleep even in the lecture room.

The word "Social" placed before Statistics deceived me. Social Statistics, they said, would entail a little figure work but to me it was real statistics strewn with chi-square and standard deviation. And in a desperate effort to glimpse at what I was letting myself in for, I would sneak into extra lessons.

I was in one of those lessons one day with Meriel sitting by me. Meriel was a mature student. Anyone over the age of twenty-one was regarded as mature. I sat next to her this evening, with my pen poised to take notes I knew I would never understand later. I started my loud sleep. Meriel, a nice and understanding lady, was amused and allowed me to use her shoulder for a head-rest throughout the lecture. When there was a break, she not too gently pushed me away and cried, "Look, Buchi, I may be nice but I am not your cushion. Why the h ... don't you become a day student – then you'll have more lectures and extra tutorials and seminars."

"Sorry, Meriel," I said, "I'm just tired and I still don't know what that man is trying to say."

"How can you understand when you can hardly keep your eyes open the minute he opens his mouth? He is not a bad lecturer, you are just too tired after a full day's housework. I would put in for a full-time day course rather than try to squeeze five lectures into one as a part-time evening student. Or are you just studying to get away from the children and meet a nice young man?"

Meriel wanted me to laugh at the last remark, but I did not find it funny.

"Of course I want a degree at the end of it. What do I want a young man for, I have a house full of kids. I want something for myself as well, not a man. Oh Meriel, how do you become a day student? It must be very expensive and I can't afford it."

Meriel started to laugh rather uncontrollably. She had a loud laugh and was well known along the college halls. When she laughed, her pretty face would go red with dimples at the top of her cheeks. The rims of her glasses would gleam and twinkle and she would give you a gentle pat on the shoulder as if to remind you of her amusement. I did not mind her laughing, because something told me that I was going to need very badly the information she was about to give me. And I was right. I was glad I did not sulk or move away: her laughter at my ignorance was the price I was going to pay for the information.

"I am going to be a full-time student after my Part One," she said. "I can't see myself getting a good degree this way. And I have no money either but I will get a grant from my local government."

"Local government? Who are they? Why should they give me a grant? I was not born in England." All these thoughts whirled through my head, and I did not know which question to put first. This was a place where one learnt to think a little before speaking, unlike at Pussy Cat Mansions where nobody took offence at any blunders. I peered at Meriel and offered to buy her tea, which she refused, and bought me an orange instead. She preferred to give rather than accept, and woe betide anyone who refused Meriel's help. Tea was bad for me, she said, and I agreed with her.

So in between rolls and orange drink I ventured again, "Meriel, who is my local government?"

"Oh for Christ's sake, Buchi. How do you expect me to know? I live in Coventry and you live somewhere in North London – how am I expected to know your borough?"

I smiled, but my brain was working fast. I was quite sure that most of my Nigerian friends did not know this, and that my husband had never heard of boroughs or grants. "It must be like a scholarship," I told myself. The only authority I had was Carol and if she had not told me about it, then she did not know. Should I ask Chidi? No, I felt somehow that he would not like it. After living with Sylvester, I was cautious about what to tell men. (Now I tell them what they want to hear.) He was earning good pay at the Ministry of Environment and doing all his study in the evenings. He wanted me to do the same. But I knew that with my children that method would take forever, so it was better not to let him know. I needed his company.

I was restless for the rest of the evening. The following day, I went to Faye and said, "Do you know that they give scholarships here for full-time courses – how do you compete for them?"

I saw her breaking into laughter but I was quicker. "If you laugh at me, Faye, I'll put an African curse on you."

"Your curse would do nothing to me, and my grandparents were Africans too, so you can't frighten me, gal. We don't call it a scholarship, it's a grant. And I think you should qualify. How long have you worked since you came here?"

"I only stopped work last year. I've always worked," I said.

"Oh, Buchi, and you did not know about grants? I wondered sometimes why you had to study this way with all your children."

So it was with high hopes that I marched to County Hall the following week and, like a dream, I was told that yes, I could get a grant when I changed my course from part-time evening to full-time day. What they did not say was how long it was going to take and what endless forms I would have to fill in. Many of the officials kept wondering why I had delayed my university education until I had five children. I cannot remember how many times I said, "But look, Madam, when we scream in labour pains in the wards, we do not scream away our brains. The brains are still there intact. We have babies with another part of our anatomy, not through our brains, and having education does not mean that one has to be child-free."

The authorities apparently did not believe me. I remember one saying that it was a sin to toy with culture, especially if it was all going to be at the taxpayers' expense. When people say things like this, I still feel the flutter of guilt in the pit of my stomach. Where was all that confidence Faye gave me – all those sub-sociological arguments that I was going to use in baffling the clerks? I mumbled an apology and left that office. But one thing was sure, I was going to get a London degree in Sociology and I was not going to do it on part-time basis. People either took it for granted that I was on a grant or that, being a Nigerian, I was being supported by my country. As soon as I was admitted, I went to the ABC bakers in Camden Town and got an evening job as a cleaner-cum-envelope addresser.

I would be at home in the mornings to send the kids to school and then get myself ready and go down to college. I did not have lectures every day, thank the Lord, but on my free days I would not stay at home. I went to college anyway and spent my time at the Senate House Library. That huge building, tucked in between the British Museum and the College of Tropical Medicine and Hygiene, was the saviour of so many borderline students like myself. The corridors in those days were filled with Nigerian students quoting law at each other or arguing about the war that was raging at home. My mind was too full to listen to such talks and my body too weak to want to waste any energy just standing there listening to Nigerian men. One simply had to nod, smile and dash past them. I worked steadily from ten in the morning to three in the afternoon, then I would shop on my way home and be indoors by the time my kids returned. I would be ready with a smile, cheap apples which I usually cut into pieces to make them look more than they were, and brown bread sandwiches.

I had discovered that the English were like any other race beneath that veneer of stiff importance, and if one was really determined to help oneself, one would usually find a helper. Those were the days when it was shameful to be unemployed, when people looked down on you if you deliberately shunned jobs or were felt to be workshy. The Social Security men would call on you on any day, and you had to have a reason for not being there. But since I became a full-time student and yet was not given a grant and was too scared to push my claim, not knowing who those people at ILEA were and how powerful they could be, I decided to face the devil I knew. I told a fairly young man from the Security that I was not using all the money given to me just for my kids but was saving some of it, after paying my rent, for paying my university fees.

"And how can you afford that?" the man cried, bewildered. "The money is not even enough for people to live on."

"Well, I have to afford it, because if I don't do anything now I will be on Social Security forever. But if I work hard now, I will be off the dole in three years. With a degree I can get the type of job that will fit in with my family."

The man, I don't remember his name now, was ahead of his time. He saw my point. "Yeah, that's right. If you get qualified, and you get a nice teaching job or something, then you can look after your kids during the holidays and be at home by the time they return. You can even take a part-time teaching job if that's what you want – "Then he stopped abruptly and considered. "But you're not allowed to do that. Being on the dole means you have to be at home. If we allow people to leave home and do what they like, they might start doing jobs and being paid for them."

"But they can't get away with that," I said. "They'll have to get their insurance if they are paid over four pounds a week."

"Ah, you are talking like a woman. Many men get away with it, especially those in building trade. They get paid cash for work done and still claim."

I did not want to argue, though I knew that it was illegal. But what I was doing was the only way to save my family and myself. I was not going to sit around and rot in those hospital-like flats that caged one in as if one was in solitary confinement, and allow myself to disintegrate. The neighbours were not even nice. They were aggressive as well as foul of language. If I stayed in and allowed all that to take me over, I would end up in a mental hospital and that would cost the taxpayer even more.

"But you know that I am not doing that, working for more than four pounds a week. I do clean at the ABC in the evening and I use that money for our food."

The man lifted his brows and said slowly, "Now I really respect you. You mean after the university lectures you go and clean in the evenings?"

I nodded.

"I'll try to be your officer. I can't promise. They might change and give this area to somebody else. I see the sense in what you're doing, in fact I wish I were qualified for direct entry to a university course myself. But we have to pretend we don't know what you're doing. And don't kill yourself with work."

"I won't," I cried after him as he left.

I sank down into prayer by my door. "Oh God, please forgive me, don't let this nice man get into trouble. And thank you for sending me some really nice people." Somehow when one saw people like that one did not mind uncouth neighbours who did not know better.

What I did not tell the Security man was my reason for choosing to work at the ABC bread factory. There were usually loaves and loaves of damaged bread left. They were not really damaged, they were either unsold or slightly overcooked and as for cakes, we had more than enough. There were so many "accidents" during decorations that the workers simply took them home. My gov'nor knew I had young kids and she was always on a diet, so I had more than enough for my family. We could even afford to shun white bread. We wanted brown, brown bread with fibre, I told my family. The pay was £2.75 and with the free bread and free dinner for the kids, I was really well off!

The year soon passed and I failed my Part One degree examinations with distinction. I should have given myself more time. The anger I felt was choking. With this anger, I poured all my bad words into a letter and sent it to the ILEA. I wanted a grant, and I had by now learnt from Social Theory that the grant was my right, since I had paid full tax for six years. The letter was not very nice. One of those letters one should write and never post, because one knows that no one would be happy to read it. But I posted mine. I accused them of persecuting me because I was black, because I had children, because I had no husband, because I was still young, and because they were all heartless, brutes and slave drivers and I hoped God would condemn them to an everlasting fire where all the African *jujus* would make sure they roasted forever.

I got a reply within four days. And at the beginning of the new term, I got a full grant, back paid. I marched to my nearest garage and bought a car for £300 and used it to learn to drive.

When one does these things, one does not sit and plan them. But in my case, writing about my life years afterwards, one would have thought that they were all planned. I like to read what critics and students make of my character from my books. They tell me things I did not know about myself. I think that I am a shy, jelly-livered woman with no shred of confidence. But when people read the patterns of my life, they usually do not agree. Can you imagine somebody packing five excited children into a car and driving it around London after only two hurried lessons round Albany Street? I still drive badly, with my foot on the clutch all the time, and seldom go beyond thirty miles an hour. I always crawl behind buses, sometimes waiting when they wait. Maybe that is why I have never had a single accident – I am never in a hurry and I forbid anyone to start a conversation when I am at the wheel. In fact these days I use more public transport than private, because of the fear I had implanted in my subconscious during those student days. When the distance becomes too great, I lock my car up and take a train or bus.

When I retook my Part One the following year and got through, I knew I was on my way to achieving something in England. But for those first precarious years, when I was pulling myself gradually out of the ditch into what is sociologically called the lower middle class, I had people like Meriel, Faye, Brenda, Sue Kay, Roberta and even the men from the DHSS to thank.

Incidentally, I did not get that man in any trouble, because one gets off the dole automatically on getting a grant. The grants covered my university fees, and the council reduces its rents for students. Hence as a student I was much, much better off. I could now take my family's clothes to the laundrette every week instead of washing them by hand; we could now afford pure fruit juice instead of the cheap over-sugared ones; and when I wanted peace and quiet in the house, I could afford to pack the kids in the car, put them down at the Odeon cinema and come home to do some sewing or study. The children, now adults, are still great moviegoers.

Sometimes on my free evenings I would go on my own. I used to love the cinema until they started the disaster movies. The last I saw of that series of horrors was *Soldier Blue*. I was eating peanuts when those Red Indians were being killed, and the peanuts in my mouth started to taste of blood. I have been off peanuts ever since. So shaken was I that I ran out of the Odeon in Camden Town, leaving my car behind as I was in no state to drive. I went home and had a good cry. It would not have been so bad if the makers of the film did not state at the end of it that all those horrors had really happened. I used to love the movies, but since that episode I am very careful about the things I allow myself to watch.

My children have graduated through *Jaws* to *The Omen* and other horror films. I prefer to stay with my musicals. Maybe that is very old-fashioned, but that is my way.

12

That First Novel

I was beginning to be aware of what was awaiting me outside the college. The question I kept asking myself was, what could I do as a sociologist? I had a vague idea that it would help me to write some day, but until that day arrived, what was I to do?

When my grant was confirmed, I packed up my ABC bakery job and within a year my lifestyle changed. My life was strictly determined by my family and my degree course. I suddenly became too busy. I had to make the best of every minute. No longer did I take a whole day shopping at Queen's Crescent market. I would go to my local Co-op where things were slightly more expensive, or phone Maliki, the Indian grocer at the Crescent, to deliver the African foodstuffs to my home.

Those Indians, what would one do without them in England? They supply us Africans with all the foodstuffs we need, they would deliver them to us and would sometimes make jokes with us. Maliki and his wife grew so rich that they left the business and sold it to a kinsman of theirs. But I am forever grateful to those hard-working Indians. I don't know how many times I relied on them for that last-minute hitch on Christmas mornings. In 1972, for example, I invited people to stay over on 24 December only to realize that I had bought all we needed except loo paper. The same happened in 1973 but this time it was salt. In both cases I relied on Maliki to save the day, and he did.

Knowing that in a few years I'd be out of college, and be grantless as well as jobless (albeit this time probably with a fairly good degree in Sociology), my mind went back to my pet dream which was to be able to write and maybe make a kind of living from it. This idea which had been nudging me since childhood seemed suddenly to look real. The more I went into sociological theories the more I could find their equivalent or what I termed their interpretation in real life. My life at Pussy Cat Mansions only a few months back could be regarded as "anomie" or classlessness. I found I could relate my lack of any hope for the future and near personal despair to the same concept. Then why didn't I write about that, and not the romantic happy-ever-after story that my first draft of *The Bride Price* had been? For a long time I debated alone whether that would not be revealing a great deal of me to the reader. "Who will be interested in reading the life of an unfortunate black woman who seemed to be making a mess of her life?" I asked myself many, many times. Then the answer came to me after reading Nell Dunn's *Poor Cow*, and books like *A Pair of Hands* and *A Pair of Feet* by Monica Dickens, books based on "social reality". I must add that the phrase "social reality" and sentences like "One must be pragmatic" seemed to be in vogue for many Social Science students in the 1970s. I decided to start writing again about *my* social reality. After all, I had nothing to lose – one could never tell, somebody might even find it interesting. I myself found such documentary novels not only interesting but very informative, too. So for the second time in my life I started consciously putting my thoughts onto paper. Again I went to our local Woolworths and bought three exercise books and two Bic pens and wrote on Saturday and Sunday mornings before starting the day's work.

I noticed a difference with this type of writing. I found it almost therapeutic. I put down all my woes. I must say that many a time I convinced myself that nobody was going to read them anyway, so I put down the whole truth, my own truths as I saw them.

Because the truths were too horrible and because I suspected that some cynics might not believe me, I decided to use the fictitious African name of Adah, meaning "daughter". Well, time proved that to be a vain hope. People could tell straightaway that Adah's life was over fifty per cent mine, but meanwhile I continued to wallow in my ignorance. I wrote the story of my life as if it were somebody else's.

Reading my first novel *In the Ditch* years later, I saw that using the fictitious name Adah instead of Buchi gave the book a kind of distance, and the distance gave the book the impression of being written by an observer. I was writing about myself as if I was outside me, looking at my friends and fellow sufferers as if I was not one of them. I am always embarrassed when people read that book to me now. Some scholars say that I was probably too harsh on myself, and that many writers start like that. Well, they are kind, very kind, especially at the American universities like the one in Middletown, New England where *In the Ditch* is still studied.

I decided to write for four hours every Saturday and Sunday. That way I brought together all the happenings of the week. The language was simple and to give it weight I sprinkled a lot of sociological phrases here and there. Then I would say it did not matter as nobody was going to read it anyway.

After writing for about five weeks my "diary" about "life in London for a single female raising five children", I thought I would start typing it. I cleaned my old typewriter and started. The result was terrible, I told myself. I could never be a typist.

I phoned a girl called Gloria. She was a friend I made when I worked at the British Museum. "Can you type manuscripts for me?" I asked.

"Yes, of course. But I thought you were reading for a degree. What is the manuscript for, is it your thesis?"

"Thesis, I don't even know what a thesis looks like. This is a story."

She took the first exercise book, read through a page and complained about my writing. "To type your work, I would have to be with you all the time because I can't read your writing."

"Do the best you can," I said, dreaming of seeing a well-typed piece which would convince newspaper and magazine editors of my commitment to writing. Gloria spent weeks on it and when I phoned her from the public phone boxes, she would ask me what I meant by this word or that. Eventually I begged her to return the exercise book. She returned it, neatly typed but with so many gaps in each line for words she could not understand, and a bill for eight pounds. By this time I found I had changed my mind about this sentence or that idea, and we argued about the money because I knew that my typewriter which was bought from the Crescent had cost only five pounds. I paid the money, but lost a friend.

I cleaned the typewriter again and as I did not have the patience to type according to Pitman's, I started picking the letters out one by one using only two fingers. I screamed with joy when after four hours of banging and rubbing off, I had a first full typed page (or should I say a page half typed and half filled in ink).

This was a laborious way to write. Being one of those people who do not make elaborate notes in advance, and who tend to write as they talk, I found the method of first writing in longhand and then typing inhibiting. I would sometimes cut a whole paragraph simply because I was too tired to type it out. At another time, I would drop a whole idea for the same reason. Then it dawned on me: a writer in the twentieth century must master her machine – the typewriter.

Big Mother in Ibusa did not use a typewriter since her stories were simply for us, the children in her compound. And that was one of the big misconceptions about Mother Africa: because she did not write down her stories and her experiences, people of the West are bold enough to say that she has no history. I must not fall into the same trap. I must not allow myself to.

So with my two fingers I plodded on. I worked on "Life in London", which I later called "The Ditch", from about six in the morning till eight or nine on Saturdays, depending on the mood of my family. Some days the kids slept late or just stayed in their rooms talking school politics. They were all by then at the same school, St Mary Magdalene, and the poor teachers were usually torn into shreds. At other times, they would be up by seven screaming for toast and marmalade. We had grown so sophisticated that we could afford to have a full continental breakfast. Since I was not given a lot of meat as a child, I did not give much to my family. A good thing, because meat was then too expensive. We had chicken on Sundays and maybe one or two pounds of steak for the six of us for the rest of the week. We never acquired the art of eating bacon and eggs for breakfast and in a curious sort of way, we still live like that. Poverty has a way of staying with one for life.

As soon as they woke, I would be in the kitchen, occupied for the next four hours until everyone was dressed and out to play. I found that even with the noise of children coming in and out and banging the doors, I could type. I am not saying that typing is a mindless job, but it does not need the type of concentration one needs when first writing the idea. So I worked out a plan. While my family slept I wrote the ideas, and when they were awake I typed them out. Hence the dedication in one of my early self-documentary novels, *Second-Class Citizen*, to "my five children, Chiedu, Ik, Jake, Christy and Alice without whose sweet background noises this book would not have been written".

Critics have since doubted the sincerity of this dedication, saying, "How could the noises of five young children be sweet?'' But they forget many things. They forget that when I was that age, I did not have a place I could call my home. I know I lived with relatives, but these were relatives with their own children. It was nice in Ibusa, but I only went there during school holidays. After a while even that luxury was denied me as my father had died and there was no money to pay the fares to Ibusa. So I had to stay in Lagos and help in the house. My children had a home, a proper breakfast, clean clothes on their backs, and by God's grace they did not have to worry whether they would be having any lunch – they knew they would. Thus I found the mischievous noises of my contented children sweet.

Then critics have asked, ''But how can you write with the children?'' Again, I have to write because of them. Their father had recommended adoption and since I did not agree to this he washed his hands of us. I saw him only a few times in over five years; whining to him for help was out. He would only repeat his famous sentence: ''I told you I would not be saddled with five kids.'' Pity he was one of those who believed that babies always remain babies. Still, one has to be grateful to him in a way, for without him I would not have had them. Also, as a professor friend I met in Chicago once said, ''I bet if your ol' man did not give you a kick in the ass, you probably would not have written.'' I think she was right. If my marriage had worked, I would probably have finished my library course, tucked myself away in a public library and dreamed of becoming a writer one day. Day dreaming was not new to me. I enjoyed it, even as an adult. When things became intolerable, I would recoil into myself and could spend hours just staring into space, dreaming away. My life would have been like that had I had a happy marriage. That is why I can now forgive everybody. That is why I am not bitter any more. The realization of all this came much later; when I was banging away on the old typewriter putting together *In the Ditch* I was not so philosophical.

Having one's first novel published is not as glamorous an affair as the media would have one believe. The would-be author would convince herself that ''This is it, this is what I want to do, I must write, I must tell a story or do nothing else. It is novel-writing for me, no matter how long it takes, no matter whether I'm published or not. Write I must and a novel it must be.''

Then follows that secret joyous state of actual writing. Some lucky would-be male authors are at this early stage surrounded by good friends and doting members of their families who actually believe in them, believe in what they are doing, hopeful that one of them would be a real author one day. Many are regarded as authors simply because they are writing a book. The clap-clap of the typewriter is greeted with reverential awe as believers await in hushed silence the gradual approach of their priest. This treatment has its compensations: one is hailed as an author by a doting mother, a would-be girlfriend or wife. Many would-be women writers are not so lucky – they are invariably viewed with suspicion. I know this because in 1981 – 2, when I taught my books at the University of Calabar, none of my seventy-eight students was female. The world, especially the African world, still regards serious writing as a masculine preserve.

The only bad effect on a still unpublished male author treated in this way is that of facing the crash when it comes. This arrives when he suddenly realizes that writing takes longer than he had previously calculated or when he faces a plot that becomes suddenly too unwieldy to manipulate, or worse still when those admiring relatives and friends become stingy with their praise. They want to see his book not only in print, but also an overnight best-seller currently being filmed in Hollywood, and soon they expect to see his yacht on the Riviera. Here, alas, the would-be writer finds himself alone. He has to be really determined to be able to continue on from here. Some hitherto hopeful authors perish at this stage and are never heard of again. They have had their glory, their praise, short-lived though they were. Invited to parties by hopeful hostesses, the writer is charmingly asked, "But what happened to that lovely book we were all going to buy and read?" He stammers an explanation, usually long, about this and that in an attempt to explain why the book has failed to materialize.

There is the other would-be author who has only himself to blame, only himself to disappoint, and only himself to attack when the crash comes. Many people still maintain that the sharing of personal pains makes them lighter. There are no doubt instances when this is true, but when it comes to any artistic creation, I doubt it very much. Maybe the old masters knew the answer, for how many times does one read of great painters never unveiling their work until they had satisfied themselves that everything they intended had been captured on the canvas before them. Those lucky artists! I should by now have learnt my lesson either from Miss Humble or from the experience I had of watching my first attempt, *The Bride Price*, burnt in the fire in front of my eyes while I stood there wringing my hands and coping with the agony of it all in my heart. But no, I never did. I was still not that secure, although after meeting the women at Pussy Cat Mansions, I have at least practised and learnt to laugh at myself first.

As a result of this conditioning, I now belong to that group of writers who have convinced themselves that they are going to write but are not courageous enough to tell others about it. The few who know are encouraged, wickedly maybe, to make light of it by the would-be authors themselves. In my own case, this attitude kept everybody happy for a very long time. With two fingers I went on picking my letters out on the typewriter. The old typewriter has long given up the ghost, after the onslaught it received when I was typing and retyping my fourth book, *The Slave Girl.*

The third stage of the would-be author's life is the most cruel and disheartening – this certainly could be the end of the road for many. The endless trips to the publishers coupled with the unceasing flow of letters to newspaper and magazine editors. In my own case, for instance – not a typical one by any means, as I sometimes think that I was one of the unluckiest would-be authors that ever lived – I spent almost every week of 1970 and 1971 trying to persuade publishers to read my work. I did not care whether I was paid for its publication or not – my only wish was that it should be published.

I soon got used to the sound of returned manuscripts thudding onto the lino-covered floor of my council flat – a sound which dug an immediate pit in my stomach. It took years for that pit to be filled. But during those long, lonely weeks, over ten years ago, the feeling was too horrible to describe. It was more of a mental thing. The physical reaction was not so bad. My stomach would start rumbling and then graduate into strong protestation, just as if one had eaten some poisoned stuff or drunk polluted water. I used to cure myself of this by simply leaving the returned manuscripts there, completely ignoring them. I did not need to read the accompanying letters because by now I knew almost off by heart how the nicely worded photocopied notes went. The publishers thanked me very much for letting them read my lovely manuscript which they enjoyed enormously, but it could not be published at that moment. I used to ask myself, "But when can it be published?" After a while, I accepted this as part of my life – this constant rejection. I went purposefully to work at the post office during Christmas 1970 and 1971. The money I got from working those endless nights I used partly for my children's Christmas presents, the rest simply to buy typing paper and postage stamps. It was a good thing I kept all this to myself, for if people had asked, "But look, woman, what are you doing sending all those typed pieces to publishers who never read them?" I would have told the enquirer that I knew people who for ten to fifteen years gambled on football pools, hoping that one day they would win the jackpot. The possibility of my getting my work published was that remote.

So, what kept me going? Maybe I was young and naïve, or perhaps there is something in what those who believe in horoscopes say – that people like me, born under Cancer, are crabby and tenacious – or maybe just being twenty-two I was stubborn in my own quiet, determined way, still very hopeful, and thought that nothing was impossible. Or simply a combination of all this. Anyway, I slogged on.

My failure in getting my writing appreciated hit me head on at this time. I kept telling myself that I would get an Honours degree, then what? Go back to the British Museum and start working again among the mummies? Not on your life! I was not going to do that. Go back to Nigeria? The Nigerian civil war was still very fresh and anybody remotely connected with the Ibos was not then welcome in the country of my birth. My brother Adolphus had told me in his last letter that being born in Lagos, coupled with the fact that we all speak the Yoruba language like natives, could make one forget that one was Ibo and almost think of oneself as a Nigerian. But the Nigerian politicians would never let you forget that you were Ibo, Yoruba, Hausa or Efik first, and Nigerian second. Indirectly he made me conscious of my Iboishness, a fact which I too was then playing down, hoping that being a Nigerian was enough. Well, thank God, all that is now a thing of the past. You could trust politicians always to bring the tribal facts out, because nationalism as it is known in the Western world is a novel thing for us. But we are catching up fast.

I had given my brother up for dead before I received his letter, as he had not written for the duration of the war. I did not know then that he was living somewhere in the bush and doing his best to protect his life. My in-laws and ordinary relatives? They had probably written me off as a bad debt, for doesn't everybody love a winner? Who in his senses wanted to put up with a relative who could not make up her mind what she wanted to do with herself and her five screaming kids? So all that was left for me was myself, my children and the English editors and publishers.

I plodded on, my language becoming more and more pragmatic and in parts offensive. I did not care about its form, I did not care that my subject was not intellectual, I just let it pour, all my anger, all my bitterness, all my disappointment, into those Woolworths exercise books, and then retyped later. My social realities, my truths, my life in London.

As I said earlier, I never learn from my mistakes. One evening in late 1971 Chidi came to see us. Instead of my thinking of some witty conversation to amuse him with, I almost drove him crazy reading my "Observations" or "Social Realities" or "Life in London" – I gave the piece so many titles at this time. I did not know whether he was listening, but I had by now got to the stage when I did not care.

I knew that after that day I would not see him for a very long time, as he always stayed discreetly away when I was in my "literary" mood. So what did I have to lose? I went rabbiting on about my "Observations" of London. He listened patiently as he sipped his tea. Then he said suddenly, "There is a funny Englishman who has taken over a paper called the *New Statesman*; he may be interested in reading your 'Observations'." He quickly left after this, not bothering to tell me whether my work was good or not. Where do those gorgeous women get their menfriends who encourage them to greater heights from? I suppose I should be grateful that he did not burn my essays. But thinking about it all these years later, and reading them all over again in my diary, I must have bored him.

I suspected that Chidi had made that suggestion by way of ridicule. Yet I was prepared to put even such a ridiculous suggestion to the test. I retyped the first three "Observations", sending one out every Tuesday. I chose Tuesday because that was the day most parents went to the post office to collect their Family Allowance, now called Family Benefit. It was only a few pounds but even this was useful in restocking the fast diminishing foodstuffs in the larder. I felt guilty in a way for using part of this money to post my writings, but my argument was, well, if ever I became a writer, the children would gain more. So I felt justified in spending those threepenny pieces in posting my "Observations" instead of using them to buy the kids a pound or so of potatoes.

The first week after the piece was sent nothing happened, not even a rejection did I receive. Now that was very odd, I thought to myself, because each typescript usually came back the following Friday. Undaunted, I sent another one: nothing. Still I sent a third, and it was then that I think the poor man on the receiving end decided to put a stop to it by sending me a note saying that he was amused and interested by my "Observation of the London Poor".

I screamed with joy until I almost lost my voice. I was going to be a success at long last. I showed the letter to all my friends at the college and tried to tell the children what it was that was happening. They were too young to understand the full implications of what that little note meant to me, but they were happy with me. Well, they could not help it, they had no choice, because I was all smiles and sang away at my work. Success, success, success!

Then I waited; the first week passed, nothing; the second week, nothing. The man whose name was Richard Crossman had told me that he would write in due course. But as time passed, I could hardly face those friends who only weeks before had started calling me a writer. They told me that the man who signed the letter was a big person and a former MP in the last Labour government . . . they told so many conflicting stories about this man's importance, I guess that was why I was nice enough to wait a whole six weeks for his "in due course" before taking the bull by the horns.

The children were particularly trying that morning, so after I had got them off to school, I came back to the flat. The day was damp and cold, the heating in our new flats had broken down and I tried to heat the place up with an old paraffin heater only to realize that I had run out of kerosene – which did not stop the heater from letting out the choking smell that paraffin heaters are well known for. To let out this impure air, I had to open the windows; and that brought in more cold air and drops of rain. I normally would have gone to the Senate Library on days like this when I had no lectures to attend, but the thought of meeting one or two of my friends put the idea right out of my head. For as soon as they saw me they would say, "You still have not heard from the *Statesman*? They do take their time, don't they?" I'm sure one or two were already wondering whether such a big man would actually have condescended so low as to have written the letter at all. So that Crossman man was making me look like a liar. Another gust of cold air blew in, chilling my bones, and this wind woke the Ibuza person in me. "Who the hell is this man that has kept me waiting all these weeks after sending such an encouraging note?" If I had had a telephone, I probably would have phoned him. But since I had none, and since I could not go to the college that day, I decided to find the office of the magazine myself.

People told me that he was a big man and could be nasty, yet my anger fuelled my determination. He had no right to keep me waiting for six nail-biting weeks. I later realized that luck was certainly with me that day, because normally that narrow office in Turnstile Lane was always busy, but the only person who stopped me or tried to stop me was a tea lady or an elderly woman who looked like one. I passed her, not too politely, and followed the sign pointing to the office of the editor. It was when I was half way down the narrow corridor that the woman asked me if I had an appointment. It was too late, I was determined to go in, and in I went. To say that the big man was not at all pleased to see me was an understatement, but a few weeks later his assistant Corinna Adams, a very nice lady, came to my flat and we went through the scattered sheets of paper that formed my "Observations of London", which by now had acquired another working title, "Life in the Ditch".

"Life in the Ditch" is a documentary novel of the daily happenings of my life when I was living in the place officially known as "Montagu Tibbles" off Prince of Wales Road in North London. By the time I moved in there, however, the block of flats was locally known as "Pussy Cat Mansions". By then it had become a place which by accident or design looked as if it was set apart for problem families. If one had no problems, Pussy Cat Mansions would provide problems for one in plenty. Despite all this, I made friends there, and it was there that I met my social worker Carol, very desperate women like Whoopey and her mother, and many others who are still my friends. The place was unique, stranger than fiction, and that was why "Life in the Ditch" was serialized. A few weeks after the lady editor visited me, it started to appear in the *New Statesman*.

The *New Statesman* then and to a certain extent now was *the* Socialist paper and well respected in English sociological discipline. One simply had to read it in those days – before *New Society*, *Time Out* and *City Limits*. Big names used to contribute articles to it. So when my articles started to appear, I was almost like one of those early English poets who said that he woke up one morning and suddenly found himself famous. Agents wrote to me, journalists wanted interviews, and there followed a series of talks over the radio at Bush House and Langham Place. It was at the height of all this that the *Statesman* phoned me to say that a literary agent by the name of Curtis Brown was interested in making me a writer, and not only that, a publishing house called Barrie and Jenkins would like me to compile my "Life in the Ditch" into a book! I thought the excitement of it all would kill me. Well, it didn't. There were months of going through this and that, for I never realized until then how long it takes to produce a book.

That year, 1972, was a good year for me. Somehow I managed to keep my enthusiasm for my forthcoming book under control. This was very difficult, and many a time I was tempted to pack up my studies, which were becoming more and more difficult, and face writing. Each time this tempting thought came to me, I'd go and look at the pile of rejection slips that I had acquired and that usually reminded me of how precarious living as a writer could be.

Before the serialization I was a nobody, and in fact had to plead to be allowed to repeat the Statistics paper I failed at my first attempt. As I said, adding up makes my head go in circles. This was before the abundance of calculators. That subject, Social Statistics, could have put me off Sociology for life. Now that I started feeling rather conspicuous, I suspected that my struggle at being a sociologist was being watched with curiosity by my friends and with amusement by my lecturers. But I worked hard, and for the first time started getting my Statistics right.

It was around this time, in early April of 1972, that I got my first real pay as a writer. It was a cheque for £80. My heart kept pounding, for I had never really been paid for anything I had written. I waited for the children to return from school, and we celebrated by going round the corner in Robert Street and ordering several packages of chips; I even allowed the children to buy sausages as well – a great luxury. We ate and laughed and planned what we were going to do with the money. But I had other ideas. I was not going to cash the cheque until I'd shown it to all my friends. Even the children's headmaster knew about it. He wrote a letter to congratulate me, and advised me not to spend it on a fur coat.

I showed it to Chidi and he snorted and warned me that if I did not keep quiet about it I would be asked to pay tax on it because I was now self-employed. (I did not have to pay tax on it as I was still a full-time student and was allowed to earn over £200 or so a year, but that statement soured my enthusiasm somehow.) He was always like that, too English for an African. Nonetheless, we talked so much about it that my second daughter Christy made a song of it, "We'll all grow rich with life in the ditch."

I eventually went to Oxford Street, bought dresses from Marks and Spencer for the girls and bought striped jumpers for the boys. But because I was still worried about my degree, I only bought a bottle of Avon handcream from my local Avon lady for myself. And all that made me feel rich.

The children wore the dresses to school and I remember their getting offended when Mrs Gardner said to them, "Is that your *New Statesman* dress?" I was not put off by this cynicism, because I wanted everybody to be happy with me. But with the £125 I got on signature my life changed slightly. I felt like Onassis, and could now afford proper lunches when I went to the Senate House Library. I could also afford to buy books which I knew would be of help to me in chi-square and standard deviation problems.

When May came, I sat my Part One Sociology exams with more confidence than I had done before. After the exam I had time to keep phoning my then publishers, Barrie and Jenkins – "When will *In the Ditch* be out? What will the cover look like? Is it good? What colour is it going to be?"

I don't think John Bunting, one of the chief editors at Barrie and Jenkins, had ever come across such an enthusiastic author, to say nothing of my lively family. He took this opportunity to get to know us very well, and whenever I went for a meal with him he used to allow me to take away all the leftovers from the huge helpings people used to serve in those days. I thought this was antisocial behaviour until I started visiting places like California, and big cities in Norway, where such services are provided as a matter of course.

How could I ever forget the day *In the Ditch* arrived from the printers at the publishers? One would have thought that with all the anticipation I had built up over those years, all my dreams richly textured and nurtured with hope and anticipation, all my dreams so ardently desired, a day like that might be an anti-climax. It was not.

The telephone rang and John Bunting said, "Buchi, they are here, the books."

"What books?" I asked stupidly, forgetting that I had just put my new gleaming kettle on the gas cooker to boil.

"Your books, you silly. They really look like books."

"My book *In the Ditch*? And you think they really look like books. What is the size? Are they too thin?"

I had always worried that they had cut away so much from the original manuscript that my first effort was going to come out looking apologetically small. And people were going to read it and say, "Well, she did not know that much", not realizing that many pages had been chopped out because some people thought that the original "Life in the Ditch" was too depressing and that I had to stop somewhere.

"Are you still there?" Mr Bunting asked.

"Yes, I am. I was only thinking."

"We are sending you your first few copies in the post, and you will get them tomorrow."

"Tomorrow? No, I am coming straightaway. I can't wait," I shouted back before he had time to make any protest.

I stood there looking out of the window into vacancy. Me, an author! Me, a writer... Then the smell of burning kettle hit my nostrils. I had burnt the new kettle I bought that very morning. I put the fire out, opened my kitchen window to let out the smoke, put on my best African skirt and a blouse I had made myself, and with a big smile on my face, went down to Barrie and Jenkins.

All the big bosses had gone for lunch when I arrived. The young assistant who gave me the first six copies of my very own book was around the same age as me, but unlike me she had not had five children. We talked banalities for a few minutes, but I was dying to get away and be by myself to examine the new book thoroughly.

I had come a long way, and only people who have set their hearts on achieving something and eventually getting it will realize how one feels at a time like this. I have always compared the feelings I have for my books on their first arrival to the ones I used to have after going through child labour and then being left for a few minutes with my brand new baby. I don't know whether other mothers do this: I always made a little speech to my new child, who was invariably asleep (except for Jake who screamed his head off!). Then I would strip the baby completely naked to make sure it was perfect. And when I was perfectly sure that all was well, I would then thank the Lord and smell my child. I don't know whether people have noticed that a new child has a natural smell which is unique and which always reminded me of the smell our farmers in Ibusa brought with them from the farm. It is like that of forest fire, mingled with rain and human sweat. A new child still has all that human heat from the womb about it. I would fill my nostrils with that smell, and allow it to flow down into my very being. Four-legged animals are luckier, for has not nature dictated to them that the mother licks her new born with her tongue? We have progressed from that stage, so we allow the friend who has helped us with the birth to wash the baby.

Each of my books was like a child to me. I felt every page, smelt the shiny cover but, unlike my babies, I even imagined it on a library shelf – a thought I had cherished since 1962, when I was a library assistant in North Finchley. Whenever I shelved books, especially those by authors who had written many, I would stand back and tell myself that one day, just one day, my books would be among them. Now it looked as if that dream would really come true.

Something else happened to me as I stroked those shiny books on my lap. I am one of those women to whom nature gave a great capacity to breed. I got pregnant very, very easily and would never have aborted a living embryo. I am not saying that this is the right decision, but this is me. I don't believe in abortion. This stand used to cause a great rift within me so I allowed my friendships with men to be platonic for a very long time. But *In the Ditch* changed that. Not immediately, but the very first step was taken that afternoon when I was nursing my new book.

I could hear the voice of my Chi saying, "As long as you keep writing and producing books, just as you used to make babies, you'll never be pregnant . . ." This may sound outlandish to readers but a contraceptive pill had never passed my mouth, I don't even know what they look like. It is very possible not to regard sex as the main reason for our existence. Women are capable of living for so many other reasons. That afternoon, those first copies of *In the Ditch* made me aware that probably one of my reasons for being here is to write. And because writing that comes from one's innermost soul is therapeutic, it could also probably be contraceptive. But maybe this is because I came from a culture in which women are so busy living other, richer lives that they find sex a bother. How much of ourselves do we really know?

13

Part One Sociology

In the Ditch brought me some modest publicity but, being my first book, I kept wondering how long it would be before it was forgotten and started to gather dust on the shelves of libraries and bookshops. I talked about *In the Ditch* for weeks, partly because of my pride in my modest achievement and partly because I was trying desperately to deaden the other fear: the fear that I could fail my examination again. This was all the stronger because I knew that another failure would mean the end of my career as a sociologist.

The fact that this fear did not come uppermost and cripple me mentally was because of the literary critics. In most cases they were kind. Many of them pointed out that *In the Ditch* was the first book they had read about the English working class written by a foreigner living among them. *The Times* said that it was an important little book. Despite all these kind reviews, it was the bad ones that stuck in my memory. *The Times Literary Supplement* didn't like what I wrote about my social worker, simply because Adah collected the dole. The critic resented the fact that a parent with five children should be collecting Supplementary Benefit and still have the audacity to complain about a social worker who repeatedly dehumanized her. Another paper said, "If Adah had been that educated, why did she allow herself to be in the ditch?"

The first impulse was to write to all my critics and explain to them that any woman, black or white, with many children would find herself in the ditch unless she came from rich parents or her husband supported her. But

Adah was not supported because it was impossible to make men pay for their children's maintenance in those days. Adah's husband first refused his children, then when he came to his senses he was advised by his friends no longer to refuse them because "You never know, one of them may become a brain surgeon or the Prime Minister of Nigeria or even that of Britain". So he told them at Clerkenwell court that he had changed his mind, that the kids were really his but he had no money to support them because he was a student. Six years later, when his children were growing into teenagers, their father was still a student. He never qualified.

And as for the fact that someone on Supplementary Benefit did not have the right to complain and even write a book about the Social Services, I had little to say other than that those on Supplementary Benefit are people, and many of them would like a job if they could find one, and women in particular would like work that fits into their child-rearing routine. Adah gave up her job when one morning she saw her second son, with his nose running as thick as candle, shivering in the school shed in the dead of winter. She had to leave the children earlier in the school open shed than most parents in order to run to her job at the British Museum. Some of these explanations were in *In the Ditch*, but at that time I did not know much about critics: that they read what they want to read into one's books. However, all this set afire the kind of frustrated anger one feels when one can't talk to one's critics face to face. I determined to write another book in which I would trace Adah's life from Nigeria and explain why she had to be where she was, in the ditch.

It was in the middle of all this self-doubt and uncertainty that John Bunting's secretary rang me in excitement. "*Nova* is going to serialize *In the Ditch*!" she cried.

I had seen *Nova* on newsstands and just glanced at it. It was a very glossy high-class magazine for the liberated woman. It was around this time that such glossies were springing up all over the Western world like mushrooms. Some, like *Cosmopolitan*, are still around.

Nova soon wrote me to say that they were sending a photographer to take my photographs. We had a lovely time with her, a girl called Sally Watts, and she had a nice time too, I think, because she photographed the children dancing and jumping, and with their mouths open, and with funny faces. When eventually the serialization started to appear, my kids felt they were celebrities too. I wanted this, because I liked them to share in the fun whilst young. I knew even then that when they got older, that part of my career would have to diminish.

It was the *Nova* article that brought Faye to my house a few weeks later. She wanted us to go window-shopping because she had just had a baby girl, Chioma, and of course nothing was too good for her. The only trouble was that we did not have much money.

We talked about the *Nova* article as we wandered through Heal's, Habitat and Maples, touching almost everything but in the end buying nothing. The prices were beyond our means, but somehow I was reluctant to go home. I knew why she had come, not just to talk about the article but to ask about my results. She had gone a year ahead of me because I had failed the year before. She knew the exact date the results were out. And as she was about to take her train south of the river, where she lived, she said with her chin jutting forward, "Well, I know you'll tell me in good time, when you're ready."

"Are they out?" I asked.

"Ah," she laughed, "you want to pretend you did not know."

I stood there stunned as the image of my first failure came to my mind. Faye had phoned to tell me she had passed, and asked me what my number was. Of course I did not know, but after a frantic search I found it on one of the question papers. By then it was too late in the evening, so I decided to go the following morning, the morning that the children were leaving for Norwich to stay with one Mrs Walls and her husband, a holiday arranged by the Church of England Society. I ran to the Senate House and stood in front of those terrible boards where numbers were printed. I looked up and down and down and up but did not find my number. I could not wait to cry, neither did I have time to be sorry for myself, but ran home to get the children ready for their Norwich holiday. I would have borne the hurt and the pain better if Ik had not seen me first.

He had on his holiday clothes with a yellow hat and was carrying a spade and bucket, waiting for me to get them to the station. He was full of excitement, but one look at my face and he dashed headlong to his brother and sisters and wailed, "Mum has failed, Mum has failed."

"Won't we go on holidays now because we have failed?" Christy, then six, asked tearfully.

"Of course you will," I answered with determination. "You are going to Norwich."

I packed them off quickly, but the image of two disappointed children whose mother's failure almost ruined their holiday haunted me for months. That was last year. Another year had passed, and I was now faced with going there again. I was determined not to let Faye come with me and I was not going to let the children know. I was going there all by myself to face my disgrace. When I had finished that paper, months before, there was a little confidence, for I thought then that I had done better than the year before. But now I was no longer sure.

I was determined not to go to Senate House that very day. I hate suspense normally, but if I suspect that what lies at the end of my waiting could be a really bad surprise I would rather wait forever and go on biting my nails.

The children did not know why I suddenly became snappy when they returned fom their pottery class at Cumberland play centre. I could not talk to anybody about it. Faye, the only close friend I had, had passed her exam, and I feared that she would only force me to go and see the results myself. If I failed, would I be her friend still? She would be a full sociologist, and I would be a tried and failed one. I remembered what Sylvester, my husband, used to say to me: "Look, a dog with a full belly does not play with a hungry one." He used to say this whenever he saw me talking to any unmarried female. It was his way of making me feel that a woman who is married even to a beast is luckier than one who is not. And how it used to work with me in those green and innocent days. Now I.was using the same premise to judge my new friend.

When Brenda heard of my previous year's failure she sent me a commiseration card and begged me to keep in touch. But somehow our paths did not seem to cross again, though I knew that she was coping with her work. However, Faye would never let me be. She was always phoning me and telling me all sorts of things about her baby Chioma. And anything I said, she would reply to with, "I must tell Dennis."

Dennis was her new husband. They married as soon as Faye passed her Part One examination. The marriage took place somewhere in Balham. I remember telling her that I did not know what Caribbeans wear at weddings and she had retorted, "Why not wear your African costume?" which I did. But that was the first time I had gone to the south of London. I could not find the church and it was raining. My costume clung to me and I was very cold and angry after hours of wandering in my high-heeled shoes and my most expensive silk. As if that was not enough, I got home to find that my baby Alice had chewed off the lovely golden tips that beautified the six egg cups I bought Faye as her wedding present. Weeks later, I gave them to her and she said, "I am pregnant and maybe I'll have a girl." And I said to her, "You will, since Alice chewed the tips of your presents." She did have a girl and she gave her an African name, Chioma, which she pronounces badly, "Shoma". In actual fact Chioma is a well known Ibo name for girls, meaning "lovely Chi", or "kind Chi", or "blessed Chi". After that incident, I stopped regarding her as a West Indian. Faye is still one of my oldest friends and Chioma is now a tiny, dark, pretty girl, with the same musical voice as Faye.

Well, I thought, maybe I would phone her and ask her what I should do. But on remembering that she would only say "I must ask Dennis", I put the phone down. "I am going to lose her anyway. She's married and I'm not. And as Sylvester had always said, I am now the hungry dog." The only trouble with Faye was that it did not bother her whether I was married or not. She was too busy with other things to realize that she was the full dog and I the hungry one.

The sun was shining the following day. I decided to go and find out for myself. I walked gingerly past Gower Street, then branched into Malet Street and began to walk round Senate House. I stood in the middle of the car park making a desperate attempt to fish out my number. Then a girl came up to me. "Do you know where the numbers are listed?" she asked in a small voice.

"Yes," I said courageously as I led her through the building to the compound at the back, where papers containing the numbers of candidates were pinned. Somehow this strange girl gave me courage. She was even more frightened than I was, she looked younger and she was Indian. With her, I felt like an old veteran even though I was not yet twenty-six. I fished out my number, and in no time at all I saw it there, clear. I had passed.

I had rehearsed in my dreams that when I saw my name or number among the list of the chosen, I would jump and scream and pretend just for a second that I was not a mother of five. And true to my dream, I placed my hands on my head ready to give a joyous bellow when I felt the breath of someone behind my head. It was the Indian girl. "You passed and I failed," she said quietly.

And my scream died in my throat. The agony I had felt the year before came flooding back. I told the girl that this was my second attempt. She asked me where I found the courage to repeat a killing course like that. "Because whatever you want to do in this world, if you set your heart on it, you will always get it." I don't know whether that helped her or not, but she nodded wisely and went away, her beautiful sari sweeping in front of Senate House.

Then the song we used to sing at Methodist Girls' High School when doing needlework came into my mind and I hummed it through Malet Street, along Gower Street, past Thames Studios and into my flat in Albany Street.

> *When my heard is full of glee,*
> *Help me to remember thee...*

I kept remembering the face of the Indian girl, so much so that I forgot to tell my children until the following day. And when I saw how happy they were, we decided to celebrate by going to the Zoo. The London Zoo was close to where I lived, but I had never had the time or money to visit it or take my family there.

14

The Zoo

I always guessed the importance of fruit for growing children and coming from Africa, I never lost touch with having a whole meal of fruit. In England, people eat salad. I reckon our own salad at home was when we had slices of pawpaws, mashed avocado and diced coconut, eaten in any order. So on our trip to the Zoo, I decided that we would make a big meal of the fruits in season.

I cannot remember ever tasting plums until that day in August 1972. When one gets to a new country, one tends to look for the more familiar fruits and vegetables to cook with. Even after twenty years' stay, we Nigerians still prefer to cook with spinach and okra rather than cabbages and Brussels sprouts, so my narrowness in taste was no exception. I had by then eaten loads of apples, got used to eating an orange instead of sucking it, but was still rather reluctant to ask what those attractive brown fruits were. Try and ask a busy London English greengrocer what plums are, and you'll be surprised at the answer you'll get.

Some years are plummier than others, and 1972 was very plummy. The greengrocer in Albany Street had boxes of them on display, and those in Robert Street had them all over their shop fronts, and when I went to the market in Camden Town, they were there as well. They were so plentiful that they were reasonable in price. I calculated the money I had saved for the trip and found that we could pack some peanut butter sandwiches and spend the rest on plums. The entrance fee to the Zoo was expensive, but as my son Jake said, "If we do not pay, how are they going to feed the animals?"

The excitement at having a bath, having breakfast and putting on clothes started quite early because I could seldom afford to go out with my family. The church was almost the only thing that was free then. And whenever they wanted to go to the park or the play centre, I was either doing some housework or reading for my degree. The fact that on this day I could close my eyes to the unwashed breakfast plates and unswept stairs and put away my Social Theory books was to the children a great treat indeed. I noticed this straightaway and promised myself that over the next few years their growing would take, I would try to go out with them more. The time would come when they probably would not need me to go out with them or when I could even become an embarrassment. But it hadn't come yet, and today we were going to the Zoo.

It did not matter to us one bit that the Zoo was just across the road. Looking back at that time, I feel that people who deliberately choose not to have children do miss out on a great deal. Children have a way sometimes of multiplying one's happiness when they are young, although when they start growing into young adults, their different personalities begin to intrude into their earlier innocence.

We packed sandwiches and I dashed across the road and bought five pounds of ripe, juicy plums. I washed one and tasted it in my kitchen and it was as I expected. The Europeans in general and the English in particular are not so adventurous in food. If something does not taste sugary, juicy and nice, they won't rush and buy it in the quantity I have seen plums sold in markets like Camden Town and Queen's Crescent.

"Ah, Mum, you bought clums, I love clums," Christy said. She was at that age in which she loved everything and everybody.

"It's plums, I am sure they call it plums," I said mildly.

"That's what a – a – a said Mum, a said clums!"

I turned round and looked at my little girl with a still wet and dribbly mouth and smiled and agreed with her that if her ears and mouth could make the sound clums instead of plums, who was I to argue? So to her we were having "clums" and she was going to love them and eat lots and lots.

It was in the middle of all this excitement to dress, pack sandwiches and sort out plums that I suddenly realized that my oldest daughter Chiedu was very quiet and not making any attempt to get dressed. So I went down to her room and was surprised to see her lying in bed reading a big romantic novel written by Doris Leslie, who for months now had been her favourite author. And I knew that whenever she got immersed in one of her titles, to get her out required a Herculean effort. So I took a deep breath in a big effort to control my anger and fear, because I suspected the answer I was going to get.

"Are you not coming to the Zoo with us?"

"No I am not," she murmured.

"But whyever not?"

"Because it's silly and I have been there twice already and I'm not going there again," she said with determination as she turned her attention back to Doris Leslie's *The Enchantress*.

"I don't think it's silly, after all it is a kind of celebration. I passed my Part One Sociology exams, aren't you happy for me? For us?"

She got up, sighed, and her eyes blazed in anger. She stood squarely and dug her heels into the floor. "I am not going."

That daughter looked so very much like my mother. She had her teeth and at that time I thought she was going to be tall too because she grew very much faster than the rest. Again like my mother, she seldom lost a fight, judging from what her teachers in primary school used to tell me. She was very intelligent and, like me, sought her relaxation from books. I was much bigger, but hated physical violence of any kind, a heritage of my background. I have a very strong brother who inherited my mother's way of settling any dispute – fighting it out, of course. I used to be frightened of them all and now I had that fear of my daughter Chiedu, especially as I knew that she used to beat up her two brothers who were then very much smaller. So we had learned to "respect" her.

She did not go but we did. And what a lovely time we had! I have never seen such huge snakes, monkeys, tigers, lions or giraffes. I was so fascinated by the animals with their little silent ways, doing most of the things we humans do but lacking the ability to tell us all about it. The frustrated growl of the lions was terrifying and as for the elegant giraffes and those exotic birds, I could have stayed simply watching them for days and not got tired.

"Come on, Mum, let's go and eat sandwiches and plums," cried Ik impatiently.

I hurried up to them and then he asked in his low voice, "But you came from Lagos and from Ibusa, Mum, and you must have seen loads and loads of tigers and elephants in your streets.''

"Who told you that? I have seen smaller snakes, dead ones in Lagos but not like these huge ones, and as for elephants and things, this is my first time of seeing them.''

"But Mum, Miss said you came from the jungle.''

"Your grandparents came from places with smaller houses and huge forests, but not huge or thick enough to be called jungle. I have been there several times and loved every minute of my stay, but I have never seen tigers and elephants except here in London Zoo.''

"So London is a jungle, then?''

I had to laugh here, at Ik's logic. "Well, London is a jungle in a way. It has all those captured animals in an artificial jungle and not far from them is our concrete jungle. You are right. London is a jungle too.''

"Yeah, Mum, jungle is where you have elephants and tigers and London has elephants and loads of tigers, so it is a jungle. I will tell Miss tomorrow.''

"You're not going to school tomorrow 'cos it's holiday time still . . . ''

We selected a tree and sat under it and ate our sandwiches. I encouraged the children to act out the Africa of their imagination. They thought Africans ate under beautiful trees like the cultivated ones in London Zoo and had animals wandering around. Since I could not completely erase that impression from their minds, we pretended we were in old Africa. So I told them that some parts of Africa I do not know used to be like that, but not any more.

"Is it because all the animals have been captured and put into zoos?''

"Partly that, Jake, and partly because lots of them have been killed. Also, as more and more people are born in Africa, there is less and less food for the animals.''

"How selfish we are,'' Ik said thoughtfully.

Jake made it clear that he was not selfish and he was going to feed the animals with the rest of his peanut butter sandwich, even though we all told him not to feed the poor overfed animals. Luckily he saw a boy drinking Coke and he tore back, forgetting the animals but declaring that he was thirsty. We proceeded to buy some orange drinks with the money I would have used in paying for Chiedu's Zoo tickets.

The sun shone and it was hot. The boys took off their shirts and having seen all there was to see, we made our way home through Regent's Park. There seemed to be such a relaxed happiness everywhere, a feeling common in late August afternoons in England.

We saw a couple of teenagers kissing and cuddling near the Rose Garden in the park. I saw the couple before my children did, so I smiled at them indulgently and kept on walking, thinking my children were right behind me. I did not have to worry about them because they knew their way home. Then suddenly I heard young voices singing the wedding march and throwing assorted picked flowers at the embarrassed couple. They got up, laughed and chased the children and other children saw the fun and chased the couple until they left the park. It looked as if most of the children in Regent's Park that day were determined to make them husband and wife. We crossed the road into Albany Street and went home.

I then made my family another promise. "If I get through my finals next year, we will all go to Madame Tussaud's." This was greeted by a shout of "You'll pass, you'll see, then we'll go to Madame Tussaud's to see Jack the Ripper and eat plums."

15

Mock Reconciliation

Judging from the way I celebrated the passing of my Part One, one would have thought that I had received a PhD or something. My passing the exams coupled with the fact that *In the Ditch* was already published and serialized were making me into a minor celebrity, so I was surprised at the two major events that threatened to rock the semi-firm life I thought I had established for my family and myself.

The first incident seemed to lead to the second, but looking back now, almost ten years later, it looks as if they were both planned. I came out of them shaken, but learned never to apologize for my single state.

One afternoon in the middle of that summer, a cousin of mine who seldom visited me came with his already pregnant wife to say that he was going to get married. They were already married the Nigerian way and living together. This may sound strange, but at all the Ibo weddings I have so far attended in London the bride has been pregnant. The one I attended in November 1984 in Harvard, Boston, beat the whole show for the bride was not only pregnant, she also had two howling babies in tow. All that is part of our way of life.

It all started, I was told, a long time ago when people used to take church weddings seriously. The fact that a man was condemned to marry one woman was bad enough. But what would happen to the man if his wife could not have a child? So it was safer to taste and see. If she became pregnant, then the husband would risk taking her to the church; if not, he would have to think again. I don't think it ever occurred to our people that childlessness could come from the husband. And to think that, scientifically speaking, about a third of infertility originates with the man!

In any case, my cousin Ugo and his wife Obi came to my maisonette in Rothay to say that they were getting married. Nigerian weddings in England are big social events. I have heard many English friends claim that to know what an English wedding could become, one should attend a Nigerian one. At weddings one meets old friends and relatives and if you do not have either, you invariably acquire some. At this wedding, my two little girls were going to be flower girls and Chiedu was to be the chief bridesmaid. It was left to me not only to make dresses for sixteen little girls but also to buy all the material myself, because Ugo was a relative and that was my contribution to his wedding. I had so much fun running around, going to John Lewis in Oxford Street, buying the patterns, matching the materials, making little head bands and all the little bits and pieces that are needed to make a wedding glamorous.

Ibusa people are very conservative. One always hears statements like "This is how our fathers used to do things." It's of no use telling the person that those fathers lived a long time ago in agrarian communities, that we now live in industrial ones and that this is the twentieth century. You always get the same reply: "If this was good for our fathers, it must be good for us." In short, for my daughter to be fully uninhibited at the wedding, I had to dig out her father! My cousin and the other relatives did not say it as plainly as that, but there was a word here and a hint there and a "How lovely it would look if we could have Mr Onwordi at the wedding", murmured in low tones.

Suddenly matters were out of my hands. Relatives set to work and went behind my back to negotiate the willing hands of my mother-in-law, who sent a delegate from Ibusa to beg me to forgive my husband and take him back. This was at first unbelievable. But when Ibo people are determined to make things work, they really are determined.

My brother Adolphus wrote and asked, "What horrible sins did your husband commit that are so unforgivable? He beats you, but most men beat their wives; he never worked, but many women cope with that, so what is so bad about him?"

For a while they almost succeeded in making me feel hard and guilty. Then a day was fixed for the family hearing. Some relatives even came from home. It was a ridiculous situation. They made me speak first – and where, pray, will a woman start categorizing the wrongs of a fully-grown man who has refused to shoulder the responsibility of his family? He hid behind his Nigerianness – that in the end, whether I worked myself to death or not, the children would always bear his name. He did not even have to pay a penny for their maintenance. They allowed and encouraged me to talk myself dry. All he had to say for himself was that he had committed all that I accused him of and more. That he was guilty and would I please take him back now. "My wife is such a nice lady, she did not reveal half the things I did to her. Some of them are unforgivable."

He was right. There are some mental tortures that go on inside families that women would find degrading to reveal. Sometimes I used to think that he was really sick. But whatever it was, he could no longer hurt my children; they were still young but they could talk to teachers, to their friends, to social workers. And they were embarrassingly cheeky to their father.

"Let him move in straightaway," somebody suggested with enthusiasm. "Our wife has forgiven her husband."

"Ah, not so fast," I put in with caution. "He'll stay exactly where he is, get a job and learn to visit his children once a week as the English court stipulated years ago."

All eyes were suddenly on me. People expected me to be happy and jump and sing Halleluya simply because my children's father might come and live with us. They were surprised at my answer, an answer which I was going to use to gain time to have a rethink, to study him and find out if he had really grown and had learnt like me to put the wants of our family alongside if not before his own. Something told me that I was pushing my luck too far and that if I was not careful I was going to offend these people, who had taken it upon themselves to try and put order into my life. So I added, "Well, the children have not seen him for five years, they will have to get to know him gradually, and not just have their father forced upon them."

"But he is their father, they must accept him, they have no choice," said one irate relative.

Mr Ejoh, who was then married to an Englishwoman and had lived long in London then said, with his eyes fixed on my face as if reading, "Children do have rights here, you know."

So began the most bizarre arrangement I have ever seen. Sylvester was to come and see us every Saturday around noon. And since I did not particularly wish to see him, I usually made excuses and went to the library at Senate House to catch up with some studies. As soon as I had left, Chiedu and Ik would take their younger brother and sisters and go and stay at the play centre. I tried so hard to force my family to learn to love and accept their father; I told them how blood is always thicker than water; yet my kids did not buy it. Maybe I was forgetting one important factor, that these children were now English children and were brought up in England, a country in which they had been taught at a very early age that parenthood is not simply biological. One has to give emotionally, spiritually and without reserve to another human being before one is qualified to be a parent.

I caught myself buying Sylvester a beautiful suit for the wedding, and took the trouble to nag him into cutting his hair to make him look presentable. All my efforts were beautifully superficial, so much so that we put on a convincing front at the wedding. The boys looked smart in their new suits which I had bought from my family catalogue. But after the wedding, that very evening, when I was driving my tired family home, I felt deflated. I asked myself several times what I thought I was doing. Inside me I had stopped caring whether we were a full family or not. What is a full family, anyway? Is it one with a symbolic man who does not contribute anything and still insists on taking the lion's share of everything simply because he is a man?

The children still resented him, but I kept telling myself that this would change with time. But how long was it going to take? My boys had got used to being consulted on many things and did not welcome someone who kept telling them to be quiet because they were still kids.

All that was nothing compared with the exhaustion I was feeling. Could I cope? Could I cope with looking after Sylvester? He was one of those people who wanted women to run around him while he sat down, too busy just being a man. That part of him had not changed. Where would I find the energy to finish my degree, continue writing, feed five growing kids, and earn our living? I could see that he was not only going to find it difficult to get a job, but even more difficult to keep one. He had got used to getting up exactly when it pleased him.

My cousin's wedding was a success. The little girls came to my house to get into their little blue dresses and to have white roses arranged on their heads. Chiedu wore a pretty orange-pink dress. She was in a really good mood that day. She smiled and smiled, and made fun of us mothers fussing over our little girls, but after all the fuss they, too, had a lovely time.

The reception was held in a place in Manor House. My boys were overwhelmed to see so much food and so many people dancing the way they felt. They went out of the reception hall, saw some white boys of their age, and when those boys asked them what they were doing they replied, "We are at a wedding, a Nigerian wedding, and everybody is invited."

"Are you quite sure?" one of the boys asked Ik.

"'Course," Jake replied for his brother.

Soon we saw white boys and girls who looked as if they came from nowhere dancing with us, eating *moyin moyin* and *jollof* rice. I am sure those young people are still wondering about Nigerian people. To Nigerians, weddings are happy times for everybody.

As for me, I wished the day had never ended. But I felt like someone who had deliberately tied her hands and feet in knots and was shouting for others to help her out. It had been a lovely show; I had dressed the father of my children in a blue suit which I paid for with one of my credit cards; I had dressed our sons in flashy suits and our daughters in pretty dresses and had worked myself to a state of near exhaustion, all for what? So that people would applaud me and the father of my children and say how lucky we were to have such a nice family. But I could sense that underneath all the congratulations and prayers, it was my husband they were praising. Why? Because he was the *man*. No one would like to offend him, because with me to work and boost his ego, he could one day be very powerful. Mine was to be the reflected glory. But then, is that not the lot of most women? Why was I feeling differently? Why should I not be satisfied and pleased about what most people of my sex were looking for and thought they were created for?

I sighed as I put my head over the steering wheel, waiting for Sylvester to get out of the car when we neared Kentish Town where he lived.

"Why don't you let us go home together? The children look so lovely today, let us go home together," he said, almost pleading as he sensed my reason for stopping.

"We are both intelligent adults. Playing mothers and fathers is a game for kids. It was a lovely show today, we still have to work hard at making it real."

"Then drive me to the door," he commanded.

"No, this is my car, and you are getting out right here."

"It is very late."

"You're still afraid of facing men on equal footing. You remember how my teenage brother beat you up on our wedding night and you ran to call the police . . . ?"

He got out of the car. He stood there looking at me for a while. As soon as I started the car, I began to hate myself. Had I become insensitive? unfeeling? hard?

No, I was being realistic. I could no longer look after a grown man who would not lift a finger to help me. I no longer had the energy for it; I knew that I had only just enough to cope with my children, my degree and my writing. If he could come back and help in the smallest way in making lighter all these responsibilities, I could learn to live with him for my children's sake. But if he was going to come and saddle me with his own burdens, I no longer was prepared to shoulder them and I said aloud, "May the good Lord forgive me."

Being me, I was still waiting for a miracle, especially as a few well-meaning relatives started applauding my efforts at reconciliation. Then I noticed that suddenly the children started to be difficult. Ik wanted to know why his father started sitting on his seat whenever we were going out together. Chiedu wanted to know who gave him the right to order her about without saying "Please". Jake started calling him Sylvester instead of Daddy as soon as he suspected that doing so annoyed his father tremendously. Jake always called me Buchi and I did not mind. Sylvester said I was raising the children badly, as children who did not even know how to respect their parents.

What could I say? I have encouraged my children to speak their minds about almost everything. I have consulted them on where we went and what they wore. This I knew was very un-Nigerian, but I thought I was bringing the children up to be confident people.

A few Saturdays after the wedding, Sylvester came in looking as pleased with himself as someone who has had a big win at the pools. Whenever he looked like that, my heart would miss a beat. His smile was akin to that sickly one I now see on the face of JR in *Dallas*. My mind raced back to the last time I had seen Sylvester smile like that; it was when he was burning my first edition of *The Bride Price*. With this air of confidence, he came into the kitchen where I was washing up after lunch.

"You'll never guess who has now become my full wife," he announced by way of greeting.

"Your full wife, whatever do you mean?" I asked rather suspiciously.

He ignored my question and instead started to come closer to me. My first impulse was to strike him hard with the wooden spoon I was using for making ground rice, but all I could do was to give him an uncomfortable push with my elbow.

My husband was taken aback; I was too. This was a new me! I never used to hit back in the old days, to say nothing of striking first. When overcome, I used to bite and cry. But then I had not been through Pussy Cat Mansions, neither had I fought the rent collectors nor learned to challenge "fate or my Chi", instead of accepting it all or leaving it all to "God in prayer". The depth of my rebellion surprised me and so did the intensity of my sense of self-preservation.

Sylvester was a very intelligent person who gloried in the fact that he could pretend to be unintelligent whenever he wanted to. As the society in whch we both lived sometimes demanded that from the educated blacks, he found this attitude more useful than I. During the days of *In the Ditch* I used to take refuge in pretending not to know much, but not any more. So it was refreshing to come across somebody who still used that method.

"Is that your new way of encouraging men?" he asked, hiding behind a stupid and cynical question.

The fact that I did not bother to answer him, not even when I knew that he was trying to insult me, woke him up somewhat. He seemed to be getting the message that for me it was over. I think that did hurt. He opened his hands as if about to hit me, resorting to his old ways, but then Ik was at the door.

"What are you clutching your fists for?"

Another voice piped in, "If you hit me mum, I'll bash yer head in with this chaiyer!" That was my cockney-voiced Jake.

Then I realized that I had not asked him what it was he wanted to tell me. I really did not want to, for if Sylvester was that pleased about something, it was bound to be at my expense. Also, I had this unhealthy feeling that the independence I had achieved so far within our tradition was going to be taken away by a man who had never really changed.

But he told me anyway, rather mournfully, on his way down the stairs. "My mother has paid your bride price. Your people asked and accepted more than five times the normal price and I think you should be pleased. Not many families are willing to pay that much on a woman. Not after the recent war at home, so you should be very pleased."

"I should be pleased, I should be pleased!" People still expect me to feel honoured because like my mother a price had been paid on my head. Had I really progressed? Readers of my book *The Slave Girl* would read how my mother was pleased to be changing masters because her bride price was paid. I should therefore be pleased, like her. Suddenly my eyes became blinded with hot tears of frustration. Here was I in England thinking that the African woman had really progressed, but had she?

Then the voice of my Chi came and said to me, "Of course she has progressed, a great deal. When your mother's bride price was paid she was happy, very happy, because she was pleased to be owned. When it came to your turn, you were crying because you valued your independence, and it was paid not by your husband but by your mother-in-law, who in her ignorance thought she was doing you a favour. Your mother-in-law is buying you independence inside the family to claim all your rights through your children. How many years are you going to live with them? By paying the bride price all your rights are preserved for you to hand over to the next generation. Never forget that your husband is the first son of the family and, please God, Ik, Jake and the others are the future generation. You can work your independence through the system. It is left to your generation to re-educate your daughters into a new kind of independence and re-educate your sons into a new kind of awareness. So why are you crying frustrated tears? You don't have to live with him, why should you? You don't even love him."

Although my Chi reasoned with me like this, I did not write to say "thank you" to my mother-in-law. Years later, when I had little difficulty in claiming my land and that of my children, when she started making sure I bought more land of my own, and when we two became strong allies in the family set-up, I realized that in me Mrs Christiana Onwordi had seen a great ally. It was a pity none of her daughters were exposed to the type of life I had had; their mother was stronger than any of her children. Someone had said in Umuedem Ibusa, maybe that is why God gave her a mentally strong daughter-in-law.

All that was still in the future. My immediate problem was how to get her son off my back. According to our custom, I would not now be permitted to get our children another father even if I wanted to. Some women however ignore this in England and carry on with their lives; and I could do this too, even though many Nigerian mothers-in-law have longer tentacles than any women I know of.

"Christ, why did my brother Adolphus accept the money?" cried my heart.

"So you now want to come and live here?" I asked, my voice going small.

"Yes, I have to."

"Then get a job."

He turned and said that he had not finished his accountancy exams, the same story he had told me years back.

"It does not matter, you can still get a job – you got more than half your papers even before I left, and I'm sure you must have got a few more since. So get a job. I am fed up with living with an eternal student."

I talked to the bread-making firm I worked for during the previous summer holidays, and Sylvester was interviewed and taken on. They were pleased with their luck because on paper he was well qualified. He was offered the grand sum of £3000 per annum when the average pay in 1972 was about half that sum. However it was cheaper for the firm to employ him than a white qualified accountant in a professional job. So there was happiness all round. His title was Assistant Chief Accountant, and the bread firm knew that with his qualifications, he was a bargain.

Now I did not know what other excuses to give for his not moving in. I had told him several times that I no longer loved him, but he said most wives don't love their husbands and that even in the Western world most women stay with their husbands for economic reasons alone. I was really tempted by the latter: then I shouldn't have to worry about whether my £900-a-year grant would feed us; or if I never earnt a penny as a writer or became a graduate. But then what would I be? I answered the question myself. A wife and mother. Things I had wanted badly only ten years ago. Why did I not want them now?

I did not want him, I did not want him! Was there no law to help a woman say No to a man who was previously her husband and was the father of her children? Sylvester started coming regularly every Saturday as the law stipulated. The children still ran away on seeing him and at best became cheeky and abusive. He was determined to have the ready family which I had built back, simply because he was a man, not because he wanted *us* that much – even the children knew that.

My friend Chidi? Men! He simply stood back and watched. He wanted me to make up my mind. He was playing the role of a black Englishman.

His attitude was, "You got yourself into this, then get yourself out." He was not going to force me: "After all, Sylvester is the father of the children", as if being a biological parent is all that we need to be fully human.

I prayed as I have never prayed before: God, send all these men away, so that I can have the peace of mind to raise these kids in a calm atmosphere the way kids should be raised. With Sylvester in the house it was going to be fight today and fight tomorrow. We were doing that already; each time I returned from Senate House thinking that he might have gone he would be there, wanting to know where I had been and why I should be studying during holidays when all students took a break. I found myself on the defensive, explaining that I had to do it because when college opened, with housework and everything I did not have as much time to catch up with my work as the average student. His silence indicated that he was not going to have that when he moved in.

The few women friends I had at the time kept telling me what I did not want to hear. They were so keen on my entering into matrimony again that I became suspicious. They could not have been enjoying themselves that much, and I later realized that the facts that I got myself published and was reading for a degree were too much for some of my female friends. With a man like my husband in the house to make me unhappy I probably would not have time to open my books, to say nothing of writing again.

My favourite hymn is "O love that will not let me go". God's love did not let me go. For what happened the next Saturday was really God working in a mysterious way. Sylvester earned his first pay! He marched in, took my car keys from the side table and went down and started to examine the car, knowing that he could not drive. Then I heard Ik's raised voice: "But that's my mum's car! It's not your car, leave it alone."

"It's my car. Your mum is my wife. She wants money, now I have started earning money, so she is mine and everything she owns is mine."

Something coiled inside me on hearing him say that to our ten-year-old son. What he was saying made sense to me, despite the fact that he knew I did not care much for people giving me money, but saying it to a ten-year-old London boy who had hardly seen his father for six years was just too much.

I shouted at them both to stop washing their dirty linen in public. Neighbours were already wondering who this man was who always came in a pale blue suit – the suit I had bought him for Ugo's wedding.

"I have got my first pay. We now have to decide how much you will be contributing. I won't mind feeding the boys, but the girls, well, you can feed and look after them."

I stared in amazement as he brought out what I now know to be a calculator and started to do "book keeping" on the children and me.

He smiled as he came to the conclusion he wanted. "Yes," he announced, "you can afford to look after fifty per cent of the kids and I will take care of the rest."

"You mean I have to financially look after 2.5 children and you look after the other 2.5? So which of the children are we going to cut into two?" I asked as I pulled Alice who was then three to my side. "Should I cut her into two, because she is a girl and the baby you never learned to love?"

I comforted the frightened child, gathered all the dangerous coolness in me and said in a low voice, "Sylvester, Nduka Onwordi, you have lost your second chance to show the world that you could be a real father and husband. Please go out of my life forever. Don't you ever come back. If you have anything to pay for the children, pay it through the court. Don't you ever come near me again."

He made his way down without protest, because now that he had a job, he felt he could get any woman he wanted and reshape his life. I really wished him luck.

Still feeling limp and like someone who did not know where she was going, I went to Clerkenwell the following Monday to tell them that my husband was no longer a student and could now afford to pay for his children's maintenance. Again I was hoping too much. Weeks later, I got a letter from the court to tell me that, yes, he now swore the kids were his and the court now asked him to pay the big sum of thirty pounds a week instead of the eight shillings (forty pence per child) he was paying when he claimed to be a student.

This was something, I thought. At least I could look after the children better. I could afford someone to be with them if I had to stay late at college. We could even afford those cheap holidays Camden Council arranged for one-parent families; I could afford this, I could afford that.

We waited and waited but the money never arrived. I went to the court with Ik in the car; I had already raised his hopes. I told the children what the court had decided. Chiedu knew many one-parent families but none of them was getting eight shillings per week, most of them were getting seven pounds per week per child. People had asked her how it came about that her father was that poor. I used to tell her that it was because he was a student. She had already bragged to her friends that her father would now be paying six pounds per child and they would no longer be eating free dinners.

Well, Ik and I waited and waited until the clerk dug out our file. He came out of their office and called me in. "There is no money, Mrs Onwordi," he said, looking guilty.

"But why? Did my husband refuse to pay?"

"No, he's back to being a student on Supplementary Benefit."

I went to Queen's Crescent and waited for him at the Indian shop where he normally bought his food, to find out why he gave up his job. He told me in a tired voice that he was not created simply to work his guts out for my comfort and that of our children.

On my way back I said to myself, "What a narrow escape."

In October 1973 I went back to college, renewed my grant, looked back at that summer and laughed. What a narrow escape I had had! I did not see Sylvester again for a very, very long time. His children simply got back into living without him and I did not have many problems with them after that. I shelved my African relatives but kept in touch with my mother-in-law, because in all her letters she said how much she wanted to see her grand-children. After all, she breastfed the first two for me. She had not asked her son to be the way he was, but I was too sorry for her to tell her that she had contributed to making him into what he later became. She was getting old. And I am a woman and a mother of sons. So with the same yardstick with which I forgave my dead mother, I forgave my mother-in-law too. To think we raise all these men who later suppress us!

With a clearer view of the world, I rejoined Brenda, Faye, Sue, Meriel and all my other middle-class friends in battling with our Sociology degrees. And I was now more determined than ever to get a good one.

16

Graduation

I have been trying for the past ten years, ever since my graduation, to puzzle out what those people had in mind when they devised the ten subjects students were meant to master before becoming a sociologist in those days. Each of these subjects was in itself a full discipline, yet students were expected to know them all up to degree level. They ranged from such tight and nearly scientific subjects as Statistics or Applied Economics to ones like Comparative Social Institutions. One could fail one subject and that would bring the student's degree level down to a Second or even less. What kind of job would one expect to be considered for after a good grounding in Political Sociology, Comparative Social Institutions or Social Theory? But while we were in it, it was very important and we took it seriously.

We worked hard on our projects, attended lectures, and copied page upon page from other people's books in an attempt to make their ideas our own, ideas which we were expected to regurgitate for class essays, seminars and eventually for the exams. By the time I reached this stage, I had mastered the art of being a student in Social Sciences. I could not cope with it earlier on because I wanted to understand everything. Now I knew that I did not have to understand what Marx or Weber were saying but simply to remember what they said. If one understood too much, one might start putting in one's own ideas and most lecturers were not ready for that kind of student. Who could blame them? There were too many of us per lecturer. It was easier to work to a set pattern, to remember what each theorist from Marx to Keynes, Amis, Kant and all the rest of them had said, and to put it all down on paper using as much of their very own words and phrases as possible. Maybe that is what higher education is meant to be. It helped me to know that people like myself did not thrive spiritually or educationally in such an atmosphere. People like me belong to the open road: I prefer to go to the African farm to watch the termites and ant-hills for hours, or sit around in my London kitchen with plumbers telling me about a type of Englishness I've never read of in books, or marvel at the smog of San Francisco or simply be around Hanover, New Hampshire, in the autumn and watch as the leaves change colour from shades of green to pale yellow and then to brilliant red, making one feel as if one was walking in a flame of fire. Well, all those pastimes were part of the future. For the time being I was confined behind my desk, poring over books and trying to puzzle out what G.E. Moore was implying when he said that "good is like yellow". I still do not see the logic in that statement. But then in England, especially in a classroom situation, I was never one of the clever ones. Not like my early schooldays in Nigeria. Here I had to get a good degree or sink, or so I thought at the time.

We studied in groups; our group consisted of Brenda, always nervous and tending to do too much; Roberta, a very calm person who knew exactly what she wanted; Sue, anxious and yet confident, always richly dressed; Meriel, large, noisy and happy – and myself, uncertain and too scared to show my determination to do well to others. Since we realized that there was no way a student could read all those books and articles recommended for each project and make any sense of them, we decided that the best way was to allocate each branch of a project to one person. That way, we lessened the amount of work done by each one of us considerably. We did not even need to attend boring seminars. One person would go, photocopy the notes she had made, and distribute them to us all. But even in a situation like that, one could detect some flaws in the human make-up.

I did not know much, but somehow felt good when telling others all I knew. Maybe it was giving me some sensation of power – an apt antidote for my chronic inferiority complex. My friend Brenda was even worse than I; she spent so much of her money posting all her essays and notes to the rest of us. Unfortunately, some of us, including me, could not read her writing, and it used to pain her if we told her not to send any more. She simply wanted to help, and you could not stop her. I used to accept them even though I knew I could not read a word. I am glad Brenda made a good grade, for she was so worried about her success that she became ill towards the end of the exams. It was during her illness that I felt guilty and told Roberta that I hoped Brenda had put her best in her papers, because she worked so hard. I was amazed when Roberta simply laughed her calm sure laughter. "I hope so too, because I did not read much, I simply took the trouble to transcribe all Brenda's notes; they were perfect and her essays were first-class."

"You mean you did not read much?"

"I was getting ready for my wedding, so what time had I for revision? I'm sure your friend will be all right . . . "

Then looking back in my mind's eye, I realized that Roberta was right. She was always going about with this lanky, dreamy blond man, so much so that at one time I thought they were husband and wife. It looked as if I was the only one who did not know that Roberta was draining our brains. Meriel did not think it was wrong and she said she knew all the time; nonetheless we enjoyed ourselves. I was one of the few who took life too seriously, so seriously that I refused to attend her wedding, not knowing why she should invite me and not the rest. But as someone said, "Maybe it's because you wrote your 'poverty book'."

My colleagues always referred to *In the Ditch* as "Buchi's poverty book". I had chosen to specialize in poverty and race. I was always quoting Peter Townsend and Sami Zubaida. My seminars, when I came to give them, were always interesting and well attended because for both subjects I took examples from life, rather than set books. It won me the nickname of "Champion of poverty". However, when it came to putting all these ideas together on paper in three hours, my hand almost went limp. I received a fairly good degree, but some thought I could have been given a better one. The examiners did not come into the classrooms to see each student's performance in those days. They have changed the system now. I know that in many colleges of education, if not in universities, examiners now take students' class and daily work into account.

Roberta, who achieved a better result, was taken straightaway to do a managerial course for one of London's biggest stores. We, meanwhile, did not let that worry us. First Brenda had to get better. Thank God she did. I had to recover from a much more subtle illness. Before the exams, I worried and worried that if I failed I could no longer go to the British Museum to start life all over again as a librarian. I was determined not to repeat, as I would not wish even my worst enemy to go through Sociology revision twice! There were seven subjects for Part Two, some of which had two papers, each of three hours. I completely forgot how to sleep. Only God knows how I coped with my family. I think I made a big pot of Nigerian stew akin to an English casserole, and froze it. I defrosted a block for the children's supper every evening, to be eaten either with rice or potatoes.

In those days a portion of chips was five pence, and about four times the size of what they now dish out for six times the cost. My daughter Chiedu did the laundry across the road in Albany Street. The kids had by now learnt to seek their enjoyment from books. They would all curl up with *The Wizard of Oz* or one of the Tolkien books, except Chiedu who had acquired a strange taste for large romantic novels. When the boys needed some action, I would always pack them off to our local cub centre.

Now, when my children are revising for their "A" levels I try to imagine what they are going through and I feel so bad that society can never guarantee its young decent and rewarding jobs after making them go through such an ordeal. I regard my situation as slightly worse, though, because even though I was in my mid-twenties, I still had the five of them to worry about. When I had a few spare hours in between, which I should have devoted to relaxing, I would work on my second book, *Second-Class Citizen*.

To work on this book was an important lifeline for me. If I did not get a good degree, I would take up any clerical job and write in my spare time – after all, I still had my "A" levels and library qualifications. Now that *In the Ditch* was more than a year old, I felt I had to write *Second-Class Citizen*. If I failed I could not go back to Sylvester, after throwing him out, and say, "But I am sorry, let us try again." I was not sure whether I would even wish to marry again. I did not know where my early trust of men had gone; I just did not fancy living with a man. Although many of my Nigerian friends would do anything simply to make a good marriage – a marriage in which the man would take almost all the financial responsibilities – that type of marriage did not appeal to me. I would rather have a marriage in which we would be companions and friends, a marriage in which each member would perform his or her own role, and in which neither role, least of all the kitchen one, was looked down upon.

I could not say that I had read Sociology for pleasure's sake or to make me a better and more cultivated woman. Who wants cultivation when you have five children to feed? All these worries had made me put too much into my revision.

I used to indulge in one thing, though I don't know how much it helped. On Tuesdays I did not have lectures and would not do any revision. Instead I would collect the Family Allowance when the kids had gone to school, cook my favourite soup and have it all alone with ground rice. Then I would spend about an hour in the bath, take my copies of *Woman* and *Woman's Own* and go through all the serials, agony columns and letters in bed. If the weather was cold, I would tuck a hot water bottle among the sheets. When the kids returned around four it was always a happy, cheerful me that they met. I discovered this by sheer accident and it helped me during those four years I was a student, mother, writer and a person.

After the exams, I was given some drugs to make me learn how to go back to sleep. The side effect was that when walking down the street, my feet would suddenly fold themselves under and I would fall flat on my stomach. For a time this became so frequent that I changed to completely flat shoes, and stopped going to doctors for anything. Some of them have a way of making one worse instead of better. This tendency to fall in the street, or anywhere, persisted for about five years. I have my degree in Sociology to thank for that.

When I received my invitation to go to the Royal Albert Hall for our graduation ceremony, it never occurred to me to refuse, although I suspected others would not like it that much. I remember that when I told some of my colleagues my sons were to be confirmed in church, they said I was a "petty bourgeoise". We had by then stopped seeing each other anyway, and most of my classmates had left the country for places as far away as Mexico and the United States.

Sue wanted to go on further to a Master's degree, and had got a place at London. I enrolled to do an MPhil and got a place at the London University Institute of Education. So the two of us kept in contact. Before looking for work or starting on my new degree, I had to return my library books. It was then that I met another colleague, Phyllis Long. We talked and she confessed that she would have to go to the Royal Albert Hall and wear that ridiculous gown for the sake of her ageing mother. "My mother wants to see me in one," she said enthusiastically, very unlike her normal self.

This woman used to live along the same road in Regent's Park as myself. When I was still an evening student, we used to take the same bus, but she would never talk to me. She wouldn't even smile at me when I tried to catch her eye, for after all, were we not in the same class? Then one night the bus conductor asked her for her fare. Raising her voice she said, "Gloucester Terrace." These are expensive terraced houses off Albany Street. She must have thought that I was going further, to the poorer parts of North London. I knew her game – many Englishwomen are good at this. So when the conductor came to me I said "Three pence", which was what we used to pay in London those days for a mile's ride. She turned round and flashed me one of those joyless smiles one had learned to take for granted after a long stay in Europe. "You live quite near." It was a cry of How dare you!

"Yes, quite near." I did not say goodnight when I got out the stop before her own. It did not matter to me that night that mine was a council flat. What mattered was that I lived in the same area as her. Towards the end of our degree course she started to talk to me, especially when *In the Ditch* came out in our second year. She even took me to tea in our last week. She was such a perfect human being. Her hair was always parted in the middle, and fell dark and limp down her back, her suits were always of silk. She lowered her standards a little when we all became full-time students, but she always remained her perfect aloof self. Her talking to me about our graduation was enlightening. I knew that whatever she said, I was hearing it from the horse's mouth, the mouth of the Establishment. All I knew was that I was going to the graduation, whether the gown looked ridiculous or not – and I was going to take a photograph for myself and for my brother Adolphus at home.

I telephoned Brenda and she told me that her 79-year-old aunt who brought her up since she was little had already bought a hat for the occasion. "Aunty" was coming all the way from Wickham Market in her wheelchair to attend her graduation, and she had been talking of nothing else: she had told everybody in the church, in the park, even her doctor, that Brenda was taking her to London. "Buchi," Brenda said in a resigned voice, "I know it is a petty bourgeois affair, but Aunty will not understand, so I have to go for her sake."

As for Sue, the only child of nice Jewish parents, not going was out of the question.

We chose the May graduation, hoping it would be sunny. It was. What was I going to wear? I did not think gowns looked good on women with their legs sticking out like spindles. They looked better on men wearing trousers. I wanted something long to wear under my own gown. I had a long woollen skirt, but to sit at the Royal Albert Hall for hours in such a long woollen Marks and Spencer skirt in that heat would be purgatorial. In the last-minute panic, I pounced on one of my old African lappas. It must have looked a bit odd because when on the way there I asked a very *chic* lady, the type one sees along Park Lane walking her dogs, where the Royal Albert was, she asked me if there was going to be an African dance there that day.

"No," I replied proudly, "I am going for my graduation in front of the Queen Mother."

"Oh," she said nicely, "well done, well done and congratulations." She pointed out the building to me, and somehow she made me feel as if I had really achieved something.

I did not have the money to buy my gown, so I had hired one. What a rush when we arrived at the robing room! The fact that I was not the only poor student in London was not only comforting but reassuring. (Sue's parents had bought hers for her, I think Brenda's Aunty bought one for her, and I am not sure about Phyllis Long – but it did not matter very much.) Were we not proud when we had donned our cap and gown and were walking round the Royal Albert Hall's grounds like penguins? Everybody kept saying "Well done and congratulations". I could see that typical young English students might go about wearing tattered jeans and old shirts, yet they, like Nigerians, like to dress up and love family affairs.

For that split second, I wished my parents were alive. My father would have been just about sixty-five. My brother? He would not understand why I had to read for a degree after having five kids, in the first place, and my children? They were at home telling their friends and teachers that "Mum is going to be gowned today."

I did not want to invite Chidi just in case it turned out to be boring. I wouldn't want a friend to be bored on my account. Many people invited friends and relatives, but obviously those people came from families who knew what it was all about. In my family and in my husband's family I was the first one to get a degree. This made me sad. I saw an ice cream man standing in the middle of the field, and I ran, my academic gown flapping like wings about me. I bought a huge ice cream, and Sue joined me. She had left her parents and relatives safely in their seats and we had to wait outside until our Chancellor, the Queen Mother, arrived.

I saw many people turning their faces towards us. "Now we are the proletariat," I said.

"What?" Sue asked as she licked.

"We are in academic gowns licking ice cream," I said.

"It's hot and I like it," Sue said pragmatically,

I looked around and saw a man in a pinstriped suit holding a red gown in his hand (maybe he was there for his doctorate or was one of the deans – he had said "Well done" to me earlier on) looking at us in disgust, especially as our ice cream started to melt and run down inside our sleeves. He gazed at us for a time, his face looking sad, then he turned away so swiftly and stiffly that I almost choked in my laughter. I could not stop laughing because Sue kept asking, "What?" and licking. "What?", then a lick; "What?", then a lick. Maybe that summed me up. I can never be completely for the Establishment. I always do something that shows me up.

The Queen Mother arrived, in her lovely purple dress and matching hat, a real lady. She wore a smile for four hours, during which I chewed through two packets of gum to prevent myself from falling asleep. I, with my vivid imagination, kept wondering what would happen if the Queen Mother wanted to go to the toilet. And she stood up most of the time. I noticed as I had to slow down when I came to her that her smile of congratulation was slightly wider as her eyes saw the lappa I had on under my gown. I had this urge to tell her that I was a single mother with five kids and that I had really worked hard to get this degree. But thank goodness fear did not let me do it. It might have made her day. Instead I curtsied like the rest and moved on.

Mr and Mrs Kay, God bless those Jewish parents, decided to give us our graduation tea. Other people were returning their gowns or getting into their cars, but I was not going to return mine yet. Sue and I walked down the whole of Marble Arch until we got to the restaurant which her parents had booked. We had tea, still in our hat and gown. Although I did not belong to that family, that little gesture did not make me feel the loss of mine. After that I folded my gown and carried it conspicuously as I made my way back to Albany Street.

The following day, Chidi brought his camera and took my picture. This time I wore the long skirt, and he took the photos in different parts of our flat. The children refused to be taken with me, because Chiedu had said that people who go about in uniform look silly and it's all very Victorian. I did not mind, for somehow I felt I had achieved something.

Two days later, when I returned the gown, the robing officer said I was to pay a pound instead of the fifty pence we were asked to bring. I told him I had no more money and asked him what he was going to do. He said he was going to report me to the dean of the faculty. "Who is he?" I asked as I left the gown there for him along with my fifty pence and walked proudly down the road. When I was about to cross the road to the other side, I met a Nigerian girl who had come to register for Law. I told her proudly that I had just finished my Sociology degree and I had just returned my gown. She was happy for me and congratulated me. We had not gone a few steps when my two feet gave way as we were crossing a side road. I tried to get up but the suddenness of my fall had hurt my ankles. A man ran across to help us and my new friend told him, "She has been doing too much studying."

"Now you try and take some rest," they both advised. "And rub yourself with Vick and Deep Heat every night after your bath," my new friend added.

I was shaken, but somehow the joy of passing my degree and going to the graduation and having my photograph taken in an academic gown made me will my illness into the background.

I no longer fall in the street, I simply willed it away and somehow it went. But I always call it my Sociology and graduation syndrome.

17

Second-Class Citizen

After the intensity of coping with exams and the excitement of graduation I went through a period of anticlimax, almost a kind of inner gloom and bewilderment.

It was a feeling which must be experienced by long-term prisoners. When imprisoned, some inmates accustom themselves to the predictability of life. It is monotonous, but nevertheless some of them are so used to this kind of life that when finally given the freedom they have probably yearned for in the privacy of their hearts, they face it with a degree of reluctance for they have to solve the problem of how to deal with it. Many have to be taught how to live outside the prison walls again. Others simply commit another crime in order to get back to the security albeit predictable monotony of life within prison walls.

I remember my friends at the Mansions. Most of us were happy to leave, although underneath we suffered an inner turmoil. How would we cope with a new environment, new financial demands, new schools for the children? The fate of those with relatives at the Mansions was gloomier than mine. How would the young mother who had been used to enlisting her own mother's help now cope with her demanding children by herself?

On leaving college and being faced with the outside world, I felt like that. I wanted to go back to continue studying Sociology, but to what end? I had convinced myself originally that I went into Sociology to equip myself with ideas about human society or communities. Surely after a first degree in it, I should have had a vague idea what communities are all about. Why go further, to a second degree? I was simply not ready to face a world not ordered by lectures and seminars.

So I registered with the Institute of Education. But I needed finance. I needed money to feed the six of us whilst studying for my MPhil and writing in my spare time!

Soon after the exams, I still had plenty of time which I used in writing the latter part of *Second-Class Citizen*. But as I boarded the bus from the Royal Albert Hall that night these worries started to nag me all over again. How would I cope now that I did not have to dash in and out of lectures, walk from Albany Street to the Euston Road and then to Malet Place into the Senate House Library? That life was so tidy, so predictable. One disciplined oneself to read for at least three hours at a stretch, then go to the loo, brush one's teeth and have a bit of rest, then back again to do another hour, then down to a salad lunch at the Students' Union, back to the library to read for another two hours and then home, shopping on the way. I used to fill my head with so many facts that at one stage friends remarked that I spoke like a textbook.

That life was all over now. Yes, I knew that nothing was permanent in this world, but how could I face the new stage? It was back to *Second-Class Citizen* and the search for a job, before thinking seriously about my MPhil.

Second-Class Citizen was nearing its end, but because it is an autobiographical work I did not know that then. I was not quite sure where to stop. That I had to write the book, there was no doubt. I had to reply to those critics who felt that women did not live as I had described in *In the Ditch*, and who felt that any woman with a little education should be able to make a living, even though she had a number of children to bring up alone. Writing *Second-Class Citizen*, I thought, would give a rich background to *In the Ditch*.

Having previously thought that I had not learnt anything in Sociology, I realized after writing the early part of the book that I must have got something out of those long hours at Senate House. Without my being aware of it, my writing was being shaped sociologically.

The first part of *Second-Class Citizen* is about how Adah initially left her poor family background. Her parents were not farmers or peasants, but were among the first wave of Africans who had left their exotic background in search of a white man's job. Being partially educated, her father had the type of job that would have brought the whole family into contact with the likes of those she later met at Pussy Cat Mansions. The fact that she gained a scholarship and went to the Methodist Girls' High School changed her life, but not to the extent that she forgot her modest upbringing. What originally shocked her was that a situation like the one in which she found herself in *In the Ditch* should exist in England at all. England, which her father had told her was the Kingdom of God.

What many people still do not agree with me about is my claim that falling so deep into the ditch is not necessarily a black thing. In Adah's days in the 1960s, England could afford a full welfare state. Now the plight of all Adahs, white or black, is more grim. The only difference is that now women are more informed about birth control and one does not have to tell one's husband before going on the Pill. The Pill was still in its embryonic stage when Adah came here, as was the profession of social worker.

The message in the second part of the book is much more subtle. I found myself writing more and more about my life, my bitter experiences in England and my desperate attempt to be a good wife and mother. The more I wrote, the more I felt like strangling myself. How could I have put up with that life? I explained that Adah came from a culture where a woman had to be married at all costs, that she did not have many friends to confide in, and that there was nowhere for her to go. Maybe it was a combination of all these, because I can't imagine any of my daughters in such a situation. Maybe Adah lacked confidence; maybe I lacked confidence, and had never shaken off the hold my early traditional African life still had on me.

Nonetheless, I came out of it after the burning of my *Bride Price*, but could not bring myself to go on after the terrible experience I had at Clerkenwell Magistrates' Court when I was eight months pregnant with my last child, Alice. The more I tried to go beyond this and join it neatly with *In the Ditch*, the more impossible I found it. So I stopped the book, telling myself that I would continue it by and by. I did not know then that that was going to be its end. Apart from getting across the theory of the conflict of two cultures, the book had no plan as such, and I was becoming disillusioned with the people I had to deal with in the field of writing.

Who was I to give it to? It was still in a shambles, a page here, another there, this one written in the Senate House when I was tired of reading, that one written when I wanted to write in the early morning. I wrote parts of it after Sylvester's visits, when we had had our usual bad Saturdays with him, and I would go into details. Some parts are so detailed that I thought that no publisher in his senses would print it. After all, most publishing houses have editors, and I was sure one's editor would cut a lot of it out as too emotional. I thought that all editors spent as much time on books as John Bunting did on *In the Ditch* – that man, it took him almost three months of twice-weekly visits to our flat to edit my first book.

I later found out that all the poor lonely man wanted was the noisy warmth of my family. By the time I was doing *Second-Class Citizen* I had fallen out with him, with all of them, because they kept referring to me as "that intelligent African girl with little self-control". I saw this accidentally in a note written about me, and Mr Bunting kept calling me "little Buchi" – I was then twenty-six!

Again, this is a cultural thing, but in the Western world people in general and women in particular like to claim to be young forever. For us it is the other way. When things are shared in the village, the older people take the lion's share. The dregs and the not-so-good parts are left to the young. A young woman is seldom listened to, but when she has given birth to sons and daughters she regards herself as a full woman and does not welcome people referring to her as a child.

This man, John Bunting, was fond of buying me a single red rose each time he came to our house to drink my Nescafé and talk about his army life till late. I thought, "How stingy the English upper class is. Why give me one red rose, which cannot stand alone in an empty coffee jar?" I had not by then started to buy flower vases. Years later people told me what a single red rose meant, and I laughed. Poor Mr Bunting, I had not understood what he was trying to say, and I encouraged my agent to get rid of him. I did not escape from my husband to fall into another prison, however platonic.

Now I wish I had not been too rash with them all, all those people who helped me with the first book. I just did not like being treated as somebody's property. I poured all my heart into *Second-Class Citizen*, telling myself that no one would ever publish it.

Then I too learnt another lesson. Those people at the top stick together. A few months before, most of them were saying how clever, how promising, but now, it seemed, because of telling one of the clan to go home with his red rose, the rest seemed to clam up on me. When I tentatively sent bits of *Second-Class Citizen* out to those very publishers who previously praised my work, they said it was unintelligible, they could not pronounce some of the names nor understand such writings. So I packed away *Second-Class Citizen* and faced the job market.

Luckily the job situation in those days was not like now. Most graduates did get jobs, especially those prepared to take anything. All I wanted was the type of job I could fit in with my way of life – taking my second degree, my writing, and my family.

In my naîvety I was forgetting so many things: that I was engaged in writing a book I was going to call *Second-Class Citizen*; that, although the work was fictitious, it drew heavily upon my personal experiences; and that I was becoming more and more the black woman in the book, Adah. I *was* a second-class citizen. Maybe I became temporarily carried away: because I had got a middle-class job when I first came to Britain, coupled with the fact that for the past four years I had been going around with so-called enlightened, middle-class whites, I had a feeling of what I now see to be false security.

When I found that the likes of John Bunting, though meaning well, was nonetheless too patronizing for my sense of freedom, I suddenly found all doors slammed in my face almost overnight. I was told that *In the Ditch* was no longer selling, even though Pan had just issued their paperback edition and called it a best-seller. They now wanted to pulp the rest. Barrie and Jenkins, who published the hardback, said that although I might not agree with Mr Bunting, there was no one else in the firm who would be interested in editing and working on *Second-Class Citizen*. My agent, then Mrs Alexandra of Curtis Brown, shunted the manuscript from place to place but the first question was always, "What happened to your first publisher?" So I locked the tattered manuscript away, and bought about three hundred copies of *In the Ditch* to save them from being pulped. I did not expect to get any income from my literary efforts for a very long time. Maybe I started too early, I told myself again – after all, my big mother must have been about forty before she became the champion story-teller of my imagination.

Now I was not just an eighteen-year-old black girl looking for work, but a twenty-seven-year-old woman who, as well as being a graduate with some library qualifications, five kids and no husband, was also a failed writer. I knew my position was grim. I could no longer call Sue, Brenda or any of my college friends. I knew that Brenda had gone back to her nursing and had become a lecturer at the School of Nursing in London rather than an ordinary nurse. So her degree had helped her. Sue was going to go further; being an only child of a Jewish family, I was sure her parents would help to see her through. They were proud of her. Faye and Dennis decided to go back to the West Indies with Chioma; they both got jobs there.

But I could go nowhere. My children were all established in English schools, many of my people at home were still taking a low profile after the civil war, and my going home would have meant my having to live with Sylvester. In England I had learnt that one did not have to live with a person one had stopped caring for. I could put up with people I did not care for for a while, like at college or at conferences, but if I was forced to live with such a person, I would do everything wrong. I would shout at the kids, forget to start the car when the lights had turned green and some days prefer to roam around parks rather than go home. And I would dread bedtimes so much that I would rather sleep in the afternoons and start washing up in the middle of the night to avoid any nightly demands made on me.

So I had no choice but to look for a job.

18

Job-Hunting

Although the 1970s was a belt-tightening decade in England, there were plenty of jobs for graduates, and if one had a good honours degree one could afford to make a choice. If one was black and a woman, however, things were different.

It was just a year or so after the Powellite vision. He had suddenly woken one morning with a vision of the River Tiber bubbling with blood. And he claimed that if the blacks were left to stay in England, the streets of England would be flowing with blood too. He did not explain whose blood it was that was going to flow, whether that of the whites or the blacks, but he successfully injected anxiety and insecurity into the minds and homes of blacks, and made some liberal white British rather uneasy.

There were strikes, there was unemployment and the usual balance of payments deficit. But Enoch Powell implied that most of these troubles were caused by blacks. They all should be sent home, he cried, forgetting that only a few years back he had welcomed the black nurses from the West Indies with near hysterical enthusiasm. Those workers from Africa and the West Indies had been referred to as "willing hands". The press said black people had fought gallantly to help save the mother country during the Second World War, and now they were here to help rebuild her industries. Everybody wanted the black people then. As most of the ravages of war had by now been repaired, the willing hands became the root cause of all the British ills. In Enoch Powell's vision, they were going to cause blood to run in the streets.

My daughter came home from school one afternoon and started to cry. "We will have to go home soon," she sobbed, "and I will miss my friends Belinda, Michelle and Sacha and the rest of them ..."

"Which home are you crying about? You're home, silly," Ik retorted.

"No, home to Africa."

"Africa is home for mother and father, not ours. I have not even been there yet, so how can it be my home?" Ik continued to reason with his heartbroken sister.

"Enoch Powell will make us go, whether we like it or not. My teacher said so this afternoon. She said that the Tory party will win the next election and that Enoch Powell is the most popular man in the party, and since he'd been saying that blacks cause all the trouble, he is going to force us all to go home."

"Your teacher said that?" I cried, imagining what it must have been like for her. She was the only black child in her class and to say this in front of all her friends was a bit thoughtless of the teacher. But who was I to say the teacher was wrong when Enoch Powell had given every white Tom, Dick and Harry a big whip with which to beat black people? If I went to school and told the teacher off, what would I do about the press? Powell was always being interviewed for this and for that. His opinion seemed to be sought for everything going on in England. I said quietly to my child, "It is not going to be like that," knowing perfectly well that it could be like that.

When Enoch Powell had made his "River Tiber" speech, it had given me a sinking feeling. I knew of a lady who had got rid of all the dark clothes in her wardrobe in a futile effort to be white. I kept writing about Powell in my essays and howling abuse at him during seminars – I was almost as hysterical as he was. I felt as if I was doing something against this man who thought he could ride on the backs of black people in the race to Number 10 Downing Street.

By the time I had left college to look for work, the Powellite vision was no longer so hot, but one could still feel the effect of the heat, and he was very much alive, injecting his poisonous vision into the media whenever he feared people were beginning to forget his existence. That man really did try to get to Number 10; his not ever getting there was one of the miracles of English politics. He appeared to be so sincere in what he was saying, until I saw his wife being interviewed. It was she who explained that all that heat was simply a ploy to get into Number 10. One of his daughters even said that he was not a bad man.

Edward Heath was now in Number 10. If we blacks were vulnerable before, we became more so after Mr Powell's outpourings. So, although I now had a degree, I was not hoping to get even the type of job I had before my studies. The Sociology degree had brought me to a new kind of awareness.

I made a few attempts which failed, either because the working conditions did not suit my family life or because I was not accepted after the interview. I must say that I was called for an interview for most of them because I had taken the trouble to say that I had written articles for the *New Statesmen* and I was the author of *In the Ditch*, even though it was being pulped at the time.

Then I saw one job advert in very tiny print in *New Society*. They were looking for a youth worker at a centre called The Seventies, somewhere in Paddington. I told myself straightaway that if I was accepted, this was going to be it, for several reasons. The hours were flexible enough to allow me to see my children to school and back; to see my then postgraduate research supervisor, Professor Basil Bernstein, at the Institute of Education; and the job would provide an ideal situation to allow me to be a participant observer for my research. (I was then toying with the idea of doing a doctorate on the plight of black youth in London.) I prayed very hard that there would be some young black people at the centre.

The application forms arrived, I filled them in and returned them that same day. A lady's voice phoned me only two days later asking me to come for an interview the following Thursday at six o'clock in the evening. "You know where we are, don't you?" the voice said, sounding matey and almost plebeian. I did not know where they were or who they were, but I said yes, of course I did. I had by then been through many interviews, but had never had one at six o'clock in the evening when everybody would have finished their day's work. Nonetheless I was determined to go, and nothing was going to put me off.

It was in the height of summer, and having read from one of the women's magazines that a woman who went to interviews in trousers was asking for trouble, I took pains to buy myself a very reasonable summer dress from Marks and Spencer – it was short and navy blue. Throughout my student days, I had always worn trousers. Now I had to wear a dress and a very short one at that, exposing my not so thin thighs, because everybody else wore mini-skirts. I felt very uncomfortable. I could have gone in my African lappa which I had used for interviews on arriving in Britain ten years before, but Enoch Powell had succeeded in almost making me feel conspicuous about my Africanness. I even cut short the hair that had taken so long to grow. In short, I did not look my age, but like a seventeen-year-old in search of her first job.

That made me feel even more ridiculous. I was sure that all the people in the street were pointing at me and saying, "Look at that woman, she's wearing her daughter's dress." This culture conflict was going on inside me as I walked up from Albany Street to Great Portland Street to wait for the Number 18 bus to take me to Harrow Road, where the centre was. I kept pulling my dress down and asking myself the logic in the Western attempt at making women always aspire to look younger than their age. Why oh why can't we allow each age to have its beauty? My ancestors worshipped and glorified old age, and we found people claiming to be older than they actually were. In Africa it is regarded as insulting to tell a woman than she looks younger than her age. Here, it is a compliment. The world, the world and its people.

I noticed the length of the queue at the bus stop and noted also that we were waiting for a long time. I was unused to that bus route, so I asked a harassed-looking lady who seemed to be returning from work how long the Number 18 bus normally takes.

"Too long," she said. "Yesterday I waited for fifty minutes. And this strike doesn't help either."

Well, strikes, strikes in England. You always had one type of strike or another. In summer, when London was full of tourists keen on moving from one part of the metropolis to the other, the bus drivers or the conductors or even the bus cleaners would go on strike. In winter it was the Electricity Board, the miners, the Gas Board, and much later in 1978/9 the rubbish men's strike, which made London almost unbearable. So my interview journey that would have normally been only about thirty minutes was going to take me an hour and a half. I would consequently be late, even though I'd reserved an hour for the journey.

As I waited those long painful minutes, my feet in my best shoes started to hurt. Though it was August and the day had been warm, evening was approaching, and as the wind blew over my near hairless head and around my exposed thighs, I felt like running back home and putting on my familiar cord trousers – I was going to be late anyway, thanks to London Transport.

The situation was made worse by the fact that I was caught in the rush hour. People were still coming from their offices and their other places of work and almost all were in a mad hurry. I stood a little apart, watching them, rubbing my aching feet, and wondering why people should hurry so much. Yes, there might be one or two cases in which hurrying in this way was justified, but why almost all should do it on this mild evening in August beat me. In London, hurrying is part of living. So is queuing. People queue for everything under the sun, standing there immobile with faces as long as your arm, clutching at bags, etc. Seeing them standing there, one gets the impression that people like these would patiently queue for death.

It was a different story when a Number 18 bus groaned through the evening traffic to the bus stop. The queue became very disorderly, people rushing from the back to the front. There were talkings, not in low voices, but in harsh, tired ones, one or two of which were actually raised. People were simply just too tired of waiting to be civilized. There was so much pushing and jostling that it suddenly occurred to me that if I did not join in the fray, I would miss my interview altogether and that would be sad indeed because I had set my heart on this job in Harrow Road.

The conductor, a black man with wrinkles on his face, raced down the bus stairs from the upper deck where he probably had been collecting fares and started to push down those of us still hanging by the door, saying, "It's full now, no more room."

I ignored him because I needed this job and no conductor was going to stop me riding on that bus and many more passengers were behind me. But he seemed determined to get me out of his bus, and I think he would have done so had not a timely quarrel broken out between a black woman and a tired-looking white man very near the door of the bus. The white man swung his rolled umbrella dangerously in the air in a vain attempt to ward the woman off. He said the woman had jumped the queue but the woman denied this, saying that she had been standing leaning against the cream wall that formed part of the International Students Union. The man said that she shouldn't have done this, that she ought to have stood in the queue, not leant against any walls. And the woman replied, "Me feet pain me, man." It took the conductor a while to sort this out and to ward off more tired people from his bus. He decided to give his bell a push, otherwise he would have been there saying, ''Full, no more room!'' all evening.

An old lady with a square hat on her grey head said, ''They should put more buses on the road. This is shameful!'' She was a good woman, for she was speaking for everybody, and she set people talking again.

''It's this bloody strike,'' put in the plump black lady who had been fighting the white man with the rolled umbrella.

''Well they want more pay, who doesn't?'' cried a man's voice. Meanwhile these little fights meant that the bus conductor had forgotten all about me. I was safe and the bus lumbered on towards Baker Street.

Before getting there, the bus was forced to wait at a traffic lights. To my left, in a little square surrounded by cream walls, stood a bust of the late President Kennedy. At the sight of it, my mind went back with a pang of sorrow to the night we heard of his assassination in 1963. I had just returned from working late at Chalk Farm Library when there was a news flash on our slot-in-the-meter television. The man on the TV told us that the President had been shot. I stood there by the cooker staring at Sylvester who stared back at me. We noticed one thing: the pub in front of our house in Willes Road was quiet. The street was quiet. We were all waiting. We did not know what we were waiting for, but the terrible news flash came again . . . the President was dead. I have hated TV news flashes ever since. I don't care whether they bring good news or not.

The bust in the square looked so young, too young for his forty-six years, but that was how he was when he was alive. The day following his assassination, a colleague of mine at the library said to me, ''The world is destined to be ruled by old and ugly men.'' I was still thinking of the Kennedy family when the dome of the London Planetarium glided into my view. The building was like the mighty umbrella carried by staff carriers of chiefs in Lagos, the only difference being that this one looked so much bigger, as if sheltering the greatest of all giants.

I often wonder why there are so many head offices along Marylebone Road. It looks as if they were all built there to guard one another. Woolworths' head office stood there glistening in that summer sunshine. Almost opposite it stood the Marks and Spencer building with its name written in letters of gold. The British Home Stores stood near, solid, square and unchanging, the epitome of all that is traditional. Yet not far from there stood an ultra-modern building with open verandahs, belonging to the Polytechnic of Central London, and almost opposite this was a little building that suddenly brought me down to earth. It was a little red brick house squashed among all the splendours of the road. So traditional was this building that you expected its little windows to fly open and a person from the Elizabethan age to come out, beckon to you and say, "Welcome ye to olde England." That building was a great symbol of the England that was passing. It was one of those little establishments called grammar schools that trained and produced the boys who opened doors for ladies. At that time they were still producing little Pitts and Burkes, and what a shame it was that those boys would come out and face the plastic age of the 1970s.

Soon after leaving that part of the road, we went underneath a flyover that seemed to have sprung out of the middle of it. One road joined it from the right and another from the left, making the place look like a tree with many huge branches. Our bus had stopped inching; now it rolled because most of the private cars climbed up over our heads, leaving the slower traffic like the London double-decker to moan its slow way along. Soon the solid ground seemed to be giving way for a tunnel, a real tunnel, all concrete, but before you got used to it you emerged again into the open sunshine – this time not into Marylebone Road, but into Harrow Road.

The number of the centre was 470, so I still had to sit for a couple more stops. I noticed one thing immediately. There were people of my colour all over the place. On the bus, in front of shops, walking on the pavement and in front of the new council flats that had now taken the place of the big buildings along Marylebone Road. Things were so different here from the Regent's Park area where I lived. Maybe I had lived there far too long, cocooned in the bogus idea that I was "making it". Had I forgotten that many people of my colour still lived the way I used to live when I was "in the ditch"?

I followed carefully the road numbers with my eyes, whilst listening to the conversation of two West Indian women behind me. It was like being in another world. To think that Regent's Park and Marylebone Road were just a few minutes away! The bus stopped in front of a building with bright, almost Rastafarian colours on its façade. This was a place of amusement no doubt, because in front of it was a cartoonist's impression of Nina Baden Semper, and they were showing the series that made her famous, *Love thy Neighbour*. I wondered whether showing that series in this predominantly black neighbourhood was wise. The writers of the script had thought that they would make fools of the racists by laughing at them and showing up their follies, but in doing so they had to show us most of their thoughts and what the racists call us, a Sambo, a nig nog . . . I came to hate the series, even though I loved watching anything on TV that had a token black face on it.

Involuntarily I turned my face away. I did not like that cynical show in this area which was reminding me of my Africanness and making me feel at home. There was no doubt now that the centre would have some black young people in it. That made me glad.

At the next stop, I looked at the other side of the road. It was Number 470 Harrow Road, and I got off.

19

The Interview

The front of the building had been modernized. It had previously been a terraced house like all the others on the street, but The Seventies had been given the modern plain, geometrical facelift. The front was now square, with factory-like windows running across the ground floor. The first and the second floors still looked like the other old houses in the street. The front of the ground floor was painted in three bright colours, grey at the bottom, bright grey at the top, and running through the centre a portion of deep blue. The top part carried a placard announcing "Seventies Coffee Bar" in black. Near it was stuck another signboard, bearing the words "Coca-Cola" in the traditional white flowing writing on a red background. The door was square and trimmed in white, but painted deep blue to match the blue centre. The whole frontage looked very cheerful, much like one of those gay caravans one sees at holiday caravan sites. The difference was that this one was standing in a busy street, and on solid ground, not on wheels, but it looked inviting, The Seventies, and I walked in.

The interior was cool – a coolness forcibly brought home to me by the repetition of the deep blue colour, this time on the ceiling, even though a quarter of the blueness was peeling, revealing a creamy undercoat. The walls were bright orange, and on one was a brown hardboard with notices of football matches and of young people's legal rights in Britain. In front of you as you came in was the picture of a young black soldier fighting in

Vietnam. I did not know why this was stuck there, since the young members of The Seventies could not go and fight in Vietnam – maybe simply as ornamentation. If so, it was not too much out of place. Pinned adjacent to this was a picture of the head of Angela Davis, her mouth opened in bitterness. She was apparently making a speech during her trial in the United States when the photograph was taken. She looked young and vulnerable in her big Afro hairstyle that was rather too large for her head. She was sincere, and could carry any listener along with her, with her mouth open like someone crying bleak tears. If I had had any doubt about this club not being a multi-racial set-up, it was banished from my mind. If there were to be any white members, they would be rejects from their people.

The whole ground floor was like a big open hall, the front part scattered with wooden chairs painted brown. Two or three tables stood in awkward places. Against the wall stood four other chairs with cushions on them. Almost in the middle of the hall stood a coffee bar. This, too, was painted deep blue with a black formica top. At one end of the bar was a Coca-Cola machine and at the other, a till for money. I had never before seen the inside of a youth club but if The Seventies was typical then there isn't much difference between a youth club and an ordinary ice-cream bar in a summer settlement. Behind the bar stood a black young man, who welcomed me.

He had a square, open face, with deep black beard running from one ear to the other. It seemed as if the back of his head was completely cut off by this beard. Not only could you not see the back of his ears by simply looking straight at him, you could not see his ears at all. His face looked like a mask standing out in relief amidst the bushy black surroundings. Even though he was indoors, on his head was a checked cloth cap, the type that had a part of its front sticking out. He had on a creamy open shirt revealing a very hairy chest, now moist, because though it was nearing six o'clock, the day was still very hot. In summer in London, unless if you were by the River Thames or somewhere, you found the whole atmosphere dense, sticky and airless. There are so many houses stuck together, so many people rushing about, that the air seems almost used up and the little air that's left is heavily polluted by car fumes. As I watched him, he smiled at me and I noticed that he had a front tooth missing.

"Are you here for the interview?" he asked me politely and in perfect English.

I nodded, my fear disappearing. If all the young men were going to be as nice and friendly-looking as this one, my work would be easy if I was accepted, I thought to myself. He offered me coffee which he made in a mug so big that I could not drink it all without swelling my stomach in my tight-fitting mini dress. I wanted to ask him about the job, who he was, whether he was a youth worker or whether he was one of the youths, but could not. I did not know which question to put to him first, so I waited impatiently.

Soon another very young man came in. He was white, tall and looked well educated. No doubt a university product. He had also come to be interviewed. He sweated in his light brown suit and we caught each other's eye as we waited. All of a sudden the young man behind the coffee bar told us that he was sorry for the delay, but the committee was waiting for a very important member. He would soon be here, and we would be interviewed. We both laughed nervously and silence reigned again.

I thought to myself, "What will a committee look like? How many people will be there? How many people usually form a committee – ten, twenty?" I had never been interviewed by a committee before. One thing was certain, the committee was not going to be composed of only one person. My nerves rattled at this, and I could see my legs shaking. I always had the ill luck of showing myself in a bad light when there were lots of spectators. In any case, it was too late now to go back. I had gone this far; I had to see it through.

A portly man in his early forties rushed in and shouted to our friend with the cap, "Sorry, Trevor, to be so late! Have they been waiting long?"

"Not very long," he replied, smiling again.

That, I thought, was a lie. We had been waiting for what seemed to me like centuries with our hearts beating like mad drums, and he was now saying that those other members of the committee, wherever they were, had not been waiting long. Of course they had been waiting long, and so had we. The portly man gave us a nice bow, rushed through a small door by the side of the coffee bar, and raced up the stairs. We heard a door open and some voices, and then the door was closed again. We were once more left to our fates. Soon my companion was called.

My stomach began to make funny noises, and my hand began to shake. Trevor saw these nervous signs and asked if I would have more coffee. I thanked him but refused. He then glanced at the clock and said, "They are not bad people, the members of the committee. I am one of those who are supposed to be interviewing and I suppose I should go up now. But don't worry, it may turn out all right.'' He patted his cloth cap into shape and disappeared through the little door and up the stairs, his feet echoing through the house.

I don't know how long I sat there, but not long after Trevor's retreat my friend with the university air came down the stairs. Funnily enough, he did not wish me goodbye but simply opened the glass front door silently as if there was a dead body lying in state somewhere, and moved out, like a ghost, his tall figure stooping forward. I did not have much time to think about him because Trevor soon raced down, his heavy footsteps pounding on what sounded like old stairs. "You can come up now,'' he invited, and I followed him.

The stairs were pretty old and very narrow. The house was not custom built. The inside, the first and second floors still had all the rooms intact. Somebody had tried to add glamour by using as much deep blue as possible. Even the now dusty and faded stair lino was the same colour. I would not have been surprised if the room in which I was to be interviewed was also deep blue.

I was wrong, it was pale grey and the carpet on the floor was a mixture of blue and green. A rag-like net hung from the two windows, looking like the rags Ibo *juju* men hang in front of their shrines. My eyes wandered over all this because I could not bring myself to look at the rather funny-looking group that formed the committee. I was expecting a long polished table with a group of well-suited individuals sitting around it with a clean paper pad in front of each. But this was an ill-assorted gathering. There were two women – one very elegant and efficient; the other younger, very thin and very pretty and apparently even more nervous than I. She was chewing her nails and stealing glances at me. At one end of the room stood my new-found friend Trevor, leaning against a huge table that stood in the corner, his eyes glued to the pieces of paper he was holding. I soon realized that they were all holding identical pieces of paper, which they consulted from time to time when the interview got going. I then guessed that these contained the whole history of my life, as I had filled it in on the application form. There were three other men. They and two white women were sitting round an old, battered table, with mugs of cold coffee in front of them. The mugs were the big functional type you buy from Woolworths, not at all fashionable. One of these three men was black like Trevor, but I could tell that unlike Trevor he was an African. Trevor was a West Indian, judging from his brand of English which, although perfect, still had a touch of patois. The other black man was very small and had a long neck like that of an ostrich. He kept stretching this long neck towards the window. I kept wondering what it was he had lost in the street that made him stretch over so often. He was very orthodox in his dress. He had on a light brown suit, a polo neck sweater and polished black shoes. He was very clean, unlike our Trevor, who did not seem to care much about his appearance.

The other two men were very English. One was the portly noisy one that rushed past me in the coffee bar downstairs. He was enthusiastic about everything and quite human in the sense that he broke into cockney every so often. Whatever post he was occupying, he looked and spoke like those nice Englishmen who started life on a council estate.

The other man was a contrast to the first. He looked much older, he was slow in speech, very methodical, and had a thorough way of wanting to know everything. The type of man who would be a good manager but not such a good friend, he gave one the feeling that one was being watched all the time by a headmaster. He looked like the chairman; he spoke to me first and I knew the interview had started.

The others watched as I answered his questions. I could not recall exactly what they were afterwards, nor could I recall the full answers. When all those present took it upon themselves to ask questions, I thought to myself, "Bloody hell, if I ever get out of this place alive, I shall never smell the place again." I talked and talked with careless abandon, throwing caution to the winds. I stopped caring. They could do what they liked with me. One or two things added a sense of reality to the whole show. One was the skinny girl who, I was told, was leaving The Seventies because she was going to be a detached youth worker. I did not know exactly what a youth worker did, to say nothing of a detached one. She never stopped shaking. She only asked questions when she had stopped eating her nails. I thought to myself, "God have mercy, did The Seventies make her into such a twitchy female?"

The other feature that brought reality to it all was the other man – the African. They told me he was from the then Rhodesia (now Zimbabwe) and that he had been trained in college here as a youth leader. He had only been employed a month before; the twitchy girl was handing over to him. I would have to work with him, if I was employed. He never stopped saying

"Hm, hm, hm" all the time and each set of "Hm, hm, hm" was followed by a stretch of the neck, a wrinkle of the brow and a nervous ruffle of the paper he was holding. He looked like a man who had lost something. But he burst into terrific laughter when I was asked if I would accept the salary offered to me. I said something like "Not bad", and the Rhodesian man with the funny little face and long neck thought that very amusing. It was a solo laugh, because everybody else either did not find what I said very amusing or was too nervous to join in. He stopped very quickly.

I was then asked to ask them questions. I said I had none, because my mouth was dry from talking and mentally I was drained. I needed some fresh air. I was then dismissed and told to wait for their reply in a day or two. Since I hated suspense of any kind, I told them there and then that if I was eligible for the job could they please tell me in time, because I was going on holiday with my children and did not want to go in a state of uncertainty. The efficient-looking lady smiled, a highly professional smile, and told me that they would let me know as soon as possible. The skinny girl twitched her bony body. Trevor patted his cap and the man from Rhodesia went "Hm, hm, hm" as he craned his giraffe neck towards the window.

I walked out with a big hollow in my stomach.

20

The Wait

I stepped out of the building into Harrow Road. I was going to walk as long as I possibly could. That way, I would have time to think of all the thinkables about this job, this project, and the members of the club. I did not want to face the barrage of questions my well-meaning children would be asking before I had had time to think up the answers they would like to hear. My mind was in a muddle and my head was reeling as if I were drunk. I needed the walk.

The hot day had given way to a cool evening. It was still bright, and you could still see your way about quite clearly without electric lights. That day was a very long and summery one. People too had stopped hurrying. It seemed as if everybody had done all the rushing that had to be done and was now taking it all very easy. Again I noticed that there were blacks everywhere, even at this time of the evening. In our part of London the day population is very different from the evening population. People, the middle class in particular, live in the suburbs and come in to London during the day, and then you see the streets jammed with cars, some moving, others stationary. It is always difficult to know who actually lives in London at this time. But in the evenings, the streets are less jammed and parking spaces are usually vacant. It is at this time that you know who actually lives in the metropolis and who does not. Seeing so many blacks cooling it off at this time in the Harrow Road showed that they actually lived there, and did not just go there to work.

There was no doubt in my mind that The Seventies was established in a predominantly black area. So what was its function, I wondered. Just to keep the black youths happy? Can the government of this country be so generous as to give a club costing almost £10,000 a year to run simply for the blacks?

I still did not understand it. Personally, I would never shun a gift given with good intentions, but one on this scale made my mind go back to what I had learnt in Economics. I remembered the phrase "tied aid", which simply meant that the rich industrial countries of the world gave aid in form of money or personnel to the so-called underdeveloped Third World, which in return would buy the technological products of the rich nations, and also sell them their natural resources cheaply at a price dictated to them by their benefactors. So I was always suspicious of such assistance. The recent power crisis had been an example of such tied aid. When the sheiks decided to raise the price of oil, the man on the street in America moaned when interviewed on television, he moaned and said, "After all we have done for the Arabs." What he did not say was, "After all the Arabs have done for us." I still wonder what the reason for the next world war will be. A crusade to drive the sheiks, the Nigerians and many others from the Oily lands? I now wished very much to be accepted for this job, at least to dispel or justify my doubts.

I did not walk for long before I met the woman lecturer who had tried to teach me Statistics at college standing at the bus stop, and fell into conversation with her. I found the whole conversation very strained at first. The last time I had seen this young woman was when she was standing in front of the board, explaining something which I was sure only she understood. You see, she was using such incomprehensible words and phrases as "depression from the mean", "standard deviation", "parameter", "chi-square" and many many other such meaningless phrases. She was not very popular, not because we did not like her but because she was teaching us such an unintelligible subject. Most of us Sociology undergraduates did not see the point of our taking Statistics to such an advanced level when all we needed to know was a few averages, which we had all learnt at school. Still, we had to take it, and to pass it, in order to be awarded a certificate.

It never occurred to me that such a woman as this, intelligent and with a mind that I was sure was working like a computer, could talk of ordinary phenomena like the weather and me. She even went so far as to tell me that she had been reading all about me from her sister. I opened my mouth and shut it again, wanting her to go on and to tell me how come she was reading about me at her sister's, whom I had never met in my whole life. She laughed at my surprise, and look! she laughed like an ordinary person, all the mathematical complications about her dispelling. I even thought she was beautiful. I had never seen her like that.

Then she explained to me how it came about that she was reading about me. Her sister was a psychologist who worked as an administrative assistant for the very project I had just been interviewed for. She had got a copy of those sheets of paper which the other members of the committee were reading, but she could not attend the interview because she had had a baby the day before. Now I understood. But connecting this young female with a sister who could have a baby was beyond my imagination. Maybe she herself had held the baby. I saw her with a new eye. It reminded me what a bundle of contradictions women could be – that from the same head could erupt thoughts of maternal love, and the abstract concepts of highly applied mathematics.

She gave me the background of The Seventies I wanted very much to know. It was a new project, only two years old, very much in its transitional stage. They had had their crisis, but on the whole it was not a bad project to work for at all. I would enjoy it, because the members of the club were predominantly black.

When the Number 18 came I could not bring myself to tell her that I had intended to walk home because I wanted to think. I had to get on the bus with her because she had been so kind, talking to me the way she did, making me realize for the first time that during those years she had been teaching us Statistics she actually knew who I was, and also dispelling my fear about The Seventies – that it was a good project to work for, especially for a woman with a large family. With The Seventies, I could see my children off to school, see that the boys combed their hair and the girls remembered to clean their teeth. But I would not be in when they came home. I did not feel too bad about this because I would always leave them something to eat, and they always did their homework at this time and would not need me around very much. I consoled myself that after all I was doing the best I could for the children. I said to myself, "Think of all those mothers who have had to send their children away to be fostered, think of those children who, though they have two parents, still have to live below the national poverty line. With this job and the salary they are offering I shall not be living below the poverty line, although I will still be in the poverty band, and will forever be caught in what sociologists call 'the povery trap.'" My mind was whirling with the different concepts of poverty, and with the morality of leaving one's children at home to fend for themselves, when I realized that the young woman next to me had paid my fare. I thanked her and she told me not to worry about it. I did not worry about it. As a matter of fact I was glad for the free bus ride.

Waiting for the reply to an interview is an ordeal in itself. You wonder time after time if you have given all the correct answers to the questions you were asked. You blame yourself for the least mistake, which you have by now magnified in your worried mind to such an extent that the little mistake seems to walk, talk, even to have wings of its own, telling you that you have performed so badly that any chances of your being accepted are nil. You hate yourself because you think you could have done so much better, you bite your nails, miss your sleep, skip your food, worry, panic, and then, bang, the result arrives and you are either accepted or rejected, making futile all your worrying and sleeplessness. It is a funny thing, the human mind. Even if you are rejected, you are disappointed for a while and then you rationalize and tell yourself that you never cared very much for the job, or some other excuse. But when you are in a position of suspense, your mind simply refuses to rationalize.

My own worry was intense; although I told myself that I might be accepted because I was black, and that my blackness for once would be a blessing, yet sometimes I admitted that this very blackness might fail me. The committee might decide to take a university young man just because they wanted the young members of The Seventies to have direct dealings with a white person and not an intermediate person like me. Whatever happened, I told myself, this was a job that was going to be based on race.

It was all very well being told that the greatest agent of mobility is education. What then occurs in a society which is multi-racial, and you happen to belong to the minority, the hated and scapegoatable group? Education, then, could never be your sole agent for both social and economic mobility. Other factors would have to be considered before you could ever hope to gain this kind of employment. You have to ask yourself if the particular work is prestigious, because if so you do not stand a chance. You have to think of the reward. If the job is fairly strenuous but very rewarding, your chances are marginal. But if the job is degrading, with marginal reward, your colour becomes an asset. It is not an accident that you see a great percentage of black people on the roads sweeping, or that in places like America the term "shoe-shine boy" is almost synonymous with "negro".

I knew that if I was accepted it would not be simply because of any educational merit. There would be other reasons. No white person with the same qualifications as I would condescend to work in such a job, as not only would the person be bored and not stay very long, but it would be an insult to the superior race. From all I had so far seen, The Seventies was not a place for the really well-adjusted white but a place of attraction for the freak, of curiosity for the Bohemian, and of acceptance for the white reject – the kind of white person who jumps on the bandwaggon of anything black just for kicks, and maybe gets hurt eventually. Such "helpers" are generally attracted by blacks that have already gone off the rails, because in most cases they are off the rails themselves.

As for the curious Bohemian, he is usually in search of his social identity. As soon as this is established, he forgets his funny outfits and his friendliness with the unemployable black, whose social identity has been lost forever. A young lecturer might identify himself with the black students, and might wear an Angela Davis badge, but when the press accused Miss Davis of being an ordinary girl in love, coupled with the fact that the lecturer's own position was becoming established in his college structure, his friendliness towards the blacks would take a more distant dimension. Such blacks are used as curiosity pieces to be discarded as soon as the curiosity had been satisfied.

Two weeks went by with me in this state of suspense, then one day it happened. My telephone rang. It was the voice of the cool professional lady present on the day of my interview. She sounded distant and impersonal, even when saying something she might have guessed would have brought some joy to her listener.

I was about to give a whoop of joy when she asked me to go and see The Seventies, with the members present, to see if I still liked it. I was then to tell her my decision, as she was the secretary. I thanked her, trying in vain to match her coolness. As soon as I put the telephone down I breathed a sigh of relief. This might not be the way I had dreamt that I would serve my deprived and poor race, but at least this was a start.

The fact that the secretary asked me to please go and look before committing myself confirmed my suspicion. It is always essential to me to get the feel of a place, and I knew then that my intuition had not deceived me. The Seventies was only for us black people, but those selected to work there were to be responsible to the almost all-white committee. The committee would tell the workers what to do, when and how to do it, at the same time giving the workers the impression that they were quite free to follow their own judgement. The latter impression was very false: the workers were in fact controlled, and few new ideas were ever welcomed by the committee.

Any face-to-face relationship between the committee and the members was to be avoided as much as possible. The members of The Seventies were free to vent their grievances on the workers, and the committee was to tell the workers the limit of their power in such situations or simply to ignore the members' complaints, as the case might be. It was therefore left to people like me to keep our dissatisfied youth in check.

21

A Peep into The Seventies

The first impression The Seventies and its members gave me was graphic. It was one of those impressions which stands out in the vastness of one's memory as a hill would stand out right in the middle of an open ocean of sand on a very clear day. I shall never forget the way those members, whom I later came to know very well, appeared to me that very first day of my meeting them.

Since I came to England I have never seen so many blacks, and all young blacks, in such close confines. They were like a group of giant bees all shut together in such a small place, many buzzing lazily from one corner of the room to the other, one or two making loud angry noises as if to attract attention, others simply slouching on chairs or tables, their attitude withdrawn and completely negative to the noisy atmosphere.

Those young men were beautiful. I suppose anything young and still unhardened by age is beautiful. One or two were in their late teens, most of them were in their early twenties, and a very few looked around thirty.

They had bodies that hung long, smooth and shiny like those of seals. They hung so loosely, their bodies. The arms were so supple that one or two draggled and shuffled them about, with shoulders sloping down on one side and up on the other. Their arms hung so loosely from the rest of the body that they gave the impression of being quite separate, yet they used them a great deal, in happy gesticulation or in frustrated anger. A few couples were using them to bang some white discs on the naked tables in front of them. Later I understood that the game they were playing was dominoes. They were banging those domino discs so hard and so loud that at first I jumped with every bang. I wondered if it was not possible to move the discs as quietly as you move draughts, but I soon found out that the banging noise was part of the game's excitement.

Their heads sported different hats, hair styles and hair cuts. One or two had on one of those large-brimmed hats made popular by Princess Anne. A great many had the type of cloth cap Trevor wore the day I came for my interview. The same thought that struck me on the first day I saw Trevor wearing a cloth cap indoors struck me now. Why wear a hat when the weather was so hot, and why wear it indoors? Maybe, as with Africans, it is part of West Indian dress. We, too, love head coverings.

The suppleness of the members of The Seventies reminded me again of Lagos, Nigeria, where I was born. In the early 1960s we had many English settlers and they mixed with us at parties. When we started dancing to Nigerian calypso, we used to laugh at the way their bodies seemed to hop about like soldiers on parade. It was in such contrast to the average Nigerian dancer – when he danced, every part of his body moved with him. The older people used to tell us that when a noble man dies in England he is marched to heaven with all the mourners dumb, walking straight and stiff like moving palm trees. All this I had forgotten because in London you see so many white people that you forget the difference. It is a good thing, for who wants to go about the world looking for differences, to the extent of forgetting that we are all members of the same human race?

Here at The Seventies, the differences came back to me with force. Outside, in the London streets, I was surrounded by a sea of white faces, but here after so many years of leaving Nigeria I was surrounded by a sea of young black faces, and all in such a small space. I asked myself whether I too walked like that, moved like that, for after all do I not belong to the same race?

With these young people, their suppleness was a hopeless kind, coupled with a degree of lethargy that had a tinge of apathy. They did not all look drowsy and near sleep, but there was a kind of forced laziness pushed into them. There seemed to be nothing they could do but accept this forced attitude. One did not have to be aware of the frequent bursts of anger and cursing, or even that kind of laughter that shouted for attention, to appreciate that all was far from well with these youths. All they needed was a demagogue to tap those bottled-up and unused emotions to his own advantage.

The institutionalized policy that encourages deprived people of the same origin, the same basic culture, to live together in an area with tumble-down houses, houses where they have to share rooms with rats and cockroaches, is encouraging the formation of a time bomb. It is no use asking these people to go, as most of them have stayed long enough to be citizens, a few were even "born over 'ere". It is all right in a society where all are poor. But in this society, how are they expected to close their eyes to the riches about them when the television brings it all to their doorstep? They do not need to possess a television, all they have to do is stand in front of any shop selling TV sets and watch their fill until they are moved on by the police. Their hopelessness seems all the more intense when they are first encouraged to see such sights, then forced to stop looking, just like a tantalized animal.

How does society expect people to behave naturally when it keeps telling them that they do not belong? Hence the sense of helplessness in the air, the bottling up of incensed feelings crying for room to escape, to fight, to revenge if possible, to destroy. If such opportunity is denied, I still wonder where they will find an outlet. Will they go on accepting such isolation for themselves, their children and their children's children? That would be too much to expect. As I stood there by the door, I could not help hoping that maybe, by the time I was through with them, their lives would have more meaning.

It was now nearing the latter part of August. There were still long days of sunshine, and people going about in pretty and colourful light outfits, as if it were Christmas in Nigeria. Maybe it would not be a bad idea in England to celebrate Christmas in summer rather than shutting oneself in with steaming puddings and overblown turkeys. After all, Christmas is supposed to be a time of goodwill. What time of year is better to spread goodwill than when the weather is warm and comfortable? For who is actually sure of the date and hour of the birth of Jesus of Nazareth?

In England during August everything comes alive, unlike in winter, when almost all living things go to sleep. All the little happenings in human bodies are at their peak in August. The London Underground during the rush hour is a good example of this – so packed and stuffy that you tell yourself that God was not all that perfect: the smelliest things He created are us humans.

At The Seventies, that very evening, I realized that people of different races smell differently. The smell in the Underground reminds one of the rotten corn we use in Africa to make a custard-like food called *ogi*. But the young men from The Seventies conjured up a different kind of smell. Most of them wore very clean clothes, and one or two were smartly dressed – too smart in my estimation just to come to The Seventies. Still, the stuffiness could not but bring out a kind of smell I had experienced before, when I was a little girl.

The farmers from Ibusa smelt that way. There the local farmers used a system of farming known to the people who deal in agriculture as "working with nature". When it rains, the farmers plough and sow their seeds; when it is dry, they gather the dead, useless plants and burn them. Acres of farm were burnt at the same time. Many innocent animals were trapped in the fire, and were later collected for food to supplement the dwindling yams. During this season, farmers smelt like their farms. A kind of burnt animal/wood smell, occasionally found in the men's body scent seen in sophisticated bottles before Christmas in London shops. This bush smell, I do not know why it sometimes awakens a kind of animal sensuality in women, including me. The smell was always sharp, because it came from burnt tropical plants and animals. Our farmers at home in Ibusa smelt like that when they returned to their homes in the evenings.

It was rather strange how the smell that hung in the air at The Seventies reminded me of it. After a while, standing there by the doorway, I noticed a subtle difference. It was not very apparent at first, because my mind was busy recalling my first experience of that burnt smell. Later this difference loomed so large that it almost obliterated my sweet remembrance. At The Seventies, the burnt smell was not very clear, it had a sickly undertone.

Maybe it was because these men were all very young, in their early manhood, that they sweated a great deal; maybe it was because they were in such close confines; or maybe it was due to their frustration, which was evident in their noisy communications.

I could not bring myself to walk right into the middle of the room and announce, "Look, boys, I am your new worker", as there was nobody there to introduce me. The coffee bar was not empty. There were groups of men inside it and some outside, playing different kinds of games. At this point, I was still sceptical about accepting the job. I had not committed myself in any way. Luckily, as I was debating in my mind whether I should just walk out and call it quits, forgetting The Seventies and its problems forever, the man from Zimbabwe, the one I had seen at the interview, ran down the stairs. He saw me and welcomed me (rather coolly and distantly I thought). His greetings were in contrast to those of Trevor the very first time I came to The Seventies; nonetheless, he led me through the knots of young men to the coffee bar, saying "Excuse me" here, and "Mind" there. At the coffee bar there was a group of people playing draughts. The man from Zimbabwe had to shout, "Excuse me, please, I want to get in", as there were young men standing behind the coffee bar.

One of the men turned round and said, "Fuck you, guy, whar 'appen, guy?" I felt like running out of the building. The man from Zimbabwe was eventually able to lead me in, after a great deal of argument and more curses. I was beginning to think very carefully and quickly. Should I or should I not take this job? Would my temperament be able to take such abuse, such language and such bad manners? The man from Zimbabwe saw the look on my face and felt it was right to introduce me to some of the members, the ones nearest to us at the coffee bar who were playing draughts.

In fact only two people were playing the game, but there were about four or five others standing around them, leaning against the coffee bar and watching the game. They were more excited than the actual players. One was busy telling each player what a great fool he was in pushing forward this draught and not that. The others were simply busy shouting their excitement, clutching their hats, and intermittently slapping their friends on the back. Another was just shouting to no one in particular, "Go on guy, give 'im guy, yeah guy . . . " And on and on he went, shouting out in a loud and excited voice.

The man from Zimbabwe made a further attempt to stop the game in order to introduce me to the draughts players. So annoyed were the young men, two of whom swore horribly at him, that I begged him not to bother any more.

He laughed apologetically as if to tell that this was the type of behaviour I was to expect. I did not like his apologetic laugh, so did not bother to return it. Why should they become so annoyed as to swear at him when all he wanted to do was introduce me? Surely some of them could have guessed that I was going to be the new worker? Were all workers treated with such disrespect? Soon the game we were being forced to watch ended, and while they were shuffling themselves into position for another the man from Zimbabwe quickly introduced me. They acknowledged my existence with jerky polite nods. A very nice one said, "Aye." Another one, who had been standing at the other end of the room, marched up to us and said, "I am Peter, right? I am the king here, right?"

I nodded, managing a not very successful smile, and said, "Hello, Peter." He was the young man I had noticed before; one of those who was overdressed, in a cream suit and a large pale blue hat with a wide brim. His tie and shirt were the same colour as the hat. He looked as if he was going to a wedding. As he talked he chewed some gum, and was jangling a bunch of keys in his hand. He must have been about twenty-six or so. As soon as I saw him, I knew he was going to be difficult. He did not disappoint me, for as soon as he had finished his introduction he pushed his way into the coffee bar and took a bar of chocolate, and when asked to pay for it by the man from Zimbabwe he shouted, "Tomorrow, guy, whar 'appen?"

The man from Zimbabwe laughed nervously again, changing the subject. He introduced himself as Bulie. He did this with much neck-stretching and a great deal of "Hm, hm . . . ". I told him my name, and he expressed the wish that he should be called by his first name. This was not only a relief to me, but I knew it would make things easier. I also guessed that he was the type of person who would be offended if his second name, the family name, was badly pronounced. Most African first names are short and easy to pronounce, as are his and mine.

I watched the members for a long time in silence, because they made so much noise that to hold a conversation was impossible. Bulie with his usual grunts, which I was to become used to later, mouthed some words to me in between the noises. I could not make out all he was trying to say but I knew he was asking me, with wild gesticulation of the eyes and the hands, whether I was going to accept the job. He seemed so impatient about it all, as if he was expecting me to say, "No, I am not taking it." In reply I frowned at him, and mouthed to him that I did not know. He laughed again nervously, his neck no longer stretched like that of an ostrich but more like that of a giraffe.

I thought of the young woman whose post I was filling and consoled myself that after all, she had lasted for eighteen months. She was white. If she could stand these young men with their ways for that long, why could I not stand it for eighteen years? I did not ask myself why she had to leave. There were so many things that I did not understand then. But seeing people of my race reduced to banging tables and shouting at each other instead of talking overpowered my other instincts. I must accept the job. I must improve the lot of these young people. I must help.

I was going to teach them to learn to talk in low voices, to show them how to relax with a good book rather than banging draughts, which only stimulated them into a state of high excitement. I was going to introduce them to cultural activities such as listening to music, my own type of music, which in my over-optimistic state I was sure they were going to like. I was going to make them realize that they could achieve things with their lives, lives which were just beginning. I was going to make their visits to The Seventies worth their while and make the centre serve as a place of relaxation and civil education, the type of education that would teach them political and social awareness.

I decided to accept the job, but did not tell Bulie, then.

22

Job Acceptance

When I got home, I became convinced that I could help the members of The Seventies in my noble aims.

How was I to know, then, that all this could be rejected, including me? I was not aware then that I stood for the very type of black image they felt emphasized their failures. They knew that blacks like me who could claim to have made it were a pain to the masses of other blacks who could never make it. They also knew that my type of black suffers from a kind of false consciousness. We think we have been successful in achieving equality with white middle-class intellectuals because we say to ourselves, have we not been to their universities, have we not gone through the same degree of socialization via the educational system? But we often fail to see that we are middle-class blacks or, to put it more correctly, a black middle class.

During my first few days at The Seventies, apart from coming to know about the boys I came to know my colleagues and fellow workers. Amanda, the white girl, was a Londoner. She was leaving The Seventies as soon as we were all settled in. She had told us that she would not be coming to the coffee bar, because the members were so used to her and would tend to make comparisons between us, the new workers, and the old set of people like her and Trevor.

The fact that she was leaving when apparently there was no job awaiting her did not worry me then. I asked her many times during those first days why she was determined to go. She gave the vague excuse of being fed up with staying at the coffee bar all her life. The way I was beginning to see the work, it was not simply a matter of staying at the coffee bar. The bar was used as a meeting place, a place to communicate with the members, to listen to their troubles and to take their abuse or curses. Vague promises were no doubt made to her that she would be made a detached youth worker, and that she would be working from the building next door that belonged to the Community Relations people. It all sounded like a very neat arrangement then, especially as she was promised a desk of her own. This seemed to excite her more than ever, the fact that she was at last going to have a desk of her very own. Such luxuries were not available to her at The Seventies. She was supposed to stay and work with us for six weeks before departing. But she never actually left. She could not. Her soul belonged to The Seventies, the members were her pampered young men. They were not angels – far from that – but she accepted them as they were, she did not see the point of changing them.

It was this attitude that I was not going to accept. They could still lead useful lives even if they had spent a great part of their life so far in remand homes or approved schools.

Bulie was to be the Senior Worker. He had arrived four weeks before I. He worshipped the whites. You see, in his country, the blacks were still second-class citizens, and the only first-class citizens he had known all his life were whites. This made it impossible for him to rely on his own judgement. He had to consult a white person before he made any move at all. He had no ideological qualms about the members. To him, our employers employed us to keep them quiet, and out of trouble, it was our duty to do as we were told. It did not matter to him whether or not they were black, it did not matter even if their lives were being wasted. All that mattered was that we should do what we were told, to ensure our pay at the end of the month. He was the kind of black man that my father used to be. They worshipped the very shadows of the whites. They were the type of blacks the white colonials usually referred to as "faithful and devoted boy in the tropics". I thought that race of people had died with my father. But they live on.

The other worker, Orin, was from the West Indies. He was not so different from the members, but happened to have a couple of GCEs which landed him a job as a youth worker. But our young worker knew it all: he had had experiences with youths in Brixton, in Jamaica, almost all over the world. Green people like me, from colleges, had been "brain-washed", as he used to say to me. A more arrogant young man you could never imagine. I liked him better than Bulie, though, because he never wormed his way in with the whites. He was too proud to do that. What he actually resented was my being better educated and getting almost double his salary for a job he thought he could do better than I.

His relationship with the members was what I failed to understand. It was clear from the outset that I was going to have to work very hard to be accepted at all. They could understand a white person coming to work among them and even having a degree, but a black person, a woman, and an African – it was too much. Orin, however, was not popular either. He too was attacked many times and when you referred a member to him, you were greeted with the gruff answer, "Forget". He gave us some explanation. He came from the British West Indies, but most of the members from that part of Paddington came from the Dutch West Indies. This made many things clearer to me, too. I could understand the plain Jamaican English, which is very beautiful to listen to when spoken by young Jamaican women, but the type of English the members spoke was quite different. It took me a while to make out what they were trying to say, especially when they were annoyed. Maybe that was why Orin was not wholly accepted. Most of our members were unemployed, and a few who had been to prison many a time were almost unemployable. They knew that in terms of age and education, there was little difference between them and Orin. They envied him, his job, his position at The Seventies, and of course the power and authority he often displayed. Almost all of them felt they could do his job and even do it better.

We had another young West Indian, Kalo by name, who was our helper. He was a typical example of the beautiful black male. He was tall and well moulded with a handsome face and very polite manners. He lived at The Seventies, and he was studying to be a youth worker. The trouble was, as I learnt later, he was one of these unfortunate people who, though very bright and well spoken of by their superiors, had gone through the full system of education in England, yet could read very little and write only illegibly. He could have taken the job given to Orin; not only was he accepted by the youths but he used to be one of them until somehow he became friendly with Amanda. When he was homeless, he was housed temporarily at The Seventies, and he worked three days a week at the coffee bar. He and another member who was allowed to stay at The Seventies created quite a problem for us when we had to ask them to move, because the centre needed the room to expand. They resented this and so did all their friends, the members. They, incidentally, could come in and go at all hours, whether the full-time staff were there or not. The result was that even on Saturdays, when the club was not supposed to be open, the place remained filled with members playing dominoes and helping themselves to the food and drinks at the coffee bar, because they had nowhere else to go.

During those early days, Amanda introduced me to some key places associated with The Seventies. She showed me the Cash and Carry, where most of the food for the centre was bought. She showed me another residential community centre which was being organized for the homeless black youths in Paddington. The head of the community was at that time one of the directors of The Seventies, but unfortunately I had not met him in person. The day we visited Dashiki, as this community was called, there was no answer to our knock. But I could see from the outside that though attempts were being made to keep the building in good condition, the area was very grey. The Dashiki centre on Ledbury Road was surrounded by a wilderness of tumble-down and abandoned houses, one of which, opposite, had a red blanket for its window curtain – evidence of squatters at work.

I was very curious to see the inside of this building, especially as I had heard from Amanda that this man, the director, had had the original idea of wanting to set up a separate place for blacks. He also wanted to have the black dropouts re-educated and trained; in short, most of the measures I would have liked to have seen introduced at The Seventies. But, no, the door was locked. They must have been out that day. Whatever noble ideas this man, Vince Hines, had, he would have a great fight ahead of him, because he had chosen a very depressing area in Notting Hill Gate to start his work.

Amanda also introduced me to another black youth club called The Metro. This was everything that The Seventies was not. It was custom built, and had such large resources that they had additional activities for female members. I was shown the kitchen where young females were taught to cook, there was a dress-making apartment and children's sessions. Their members were a much more heterogeneous lot. I liked The Metro, its modernity, its cleanliness, and its different activities.

As we were going back to The Seventies, I could not but wonder why it was necessary to set up three all-black youth centres within a few miles' radius. I had read somewhere about the racial tension in Notting Hill, but thought all that belonged to history. Why was it necessary to cater for so many black dropouts? I understood that sometimes Dashiki was so full that they had to turn many homeless and unwanted black boys away. What was wrong with the area, the society and the people themselves that contributed to such a large number of unsocialized and rebellious youths? Were people encouraged to be that way?

After studying the methods of my predecessors at The Seventies, I came to think wrongly that some of the youths were being encouraged to be delinquent. Firstly so that the workers could keep their jobs, and secondly so that they could be used as scapegoats. This may sound a little extreme, but what conclusion was left for the observer, after seeing how many young people broke the law?

Amanda was a very attractive and intelligent girl. A university girl who would do anything in the cause of "black". We read of such middle-class female products becoming victims of the very people they originally set out to help. Amanda really meant well, got herself attacked many a time, but was able to accept it longer than I. Maybe because she held the old ideas of the missionaries who came to Africa in the early days, hoping to bring Christianity to the savages, when in fact the black natives were being prepared to meet their doom either at the hands of the slaver or the colonial officers.

Here is a typical example of an attitude I could not then understand. Most of these young people at The Seventies had been brainwashed into thinking that England was their mother country, that England belonged to them. At the time when the myth of the "mother country" was being perpetuated, it was beyond the imaginings of the white colonials that one day the blacks would turn round and say to them, "Fulfil your promise." It did not seem feasible at the time, because every imaginable artificial barrier was being successfully imposed, especially in the field of education. In Nigeria, for example, one had to go through the nursery class, even if you were eight years old, then a class they called the kindergarten, then infant one to three, then standard one to six, before you could sit the equivalent of what was called the eleven-plus in England. Few African children started school at the age of five, and by the time our fathers left so-called primary school, they were already in their late teens or early twenties. How then could they compete with an English person of the same age, who by then had got through secondary school and perhaps university? These colonials helped to perpetuate the myth that blacks are low in intelligence while they themselves made sure that the myth held true.

The colonial masters had not calculated on the possibility of such a system bringing out a large number of educated blacks, large enough to man their own local administration and to spill into London in search of middle-class jobs. History proved them wrong, just as they were proved wrong in the case of the Ugandan Asians. Those groups of Asian traders were not only promised the myth of the mother country, they were given British passports. When it came to fulfilling those promises, the poor Asians found themselves countryless. British diplomats found themselves running helter-skelter in search of homes for those with British passports. Many went to Canada, some were admitted into England and others remained in Uganda. But they were on the whole better off than most of the blacks in that at least they had some kind of wealth to start with. The black immigrants into England had nothing but their dreams.

One member of The Seventies said to me once, at the very early stage of my work there, "When I was a little boy and have done anything good, my ol' ma used to say to me, 'You know, you be England boy, boy. You are growing into such a big strong man, boy, you be England boy, man, yeah man!'" On the day that particular boy landed in England about fifteen years previously he felt his dream was coming true. What a great shock it was to him to find that at the end of the day, after going through the educational system in the land of his dreams, he still could not read. He was as ignorant of his whereabouts as he was when his ol' ma was patting him on the back and telling him how good he was in his island home.

Many educational workers asserted that they found the black youth living in a fantasy world. When an English boy found himself in a secondary modern school, he knew, and the educational system helped him to accept the fact, that the chances of his getting an élitist job were very very slim. He could be a good bricklayer, a building site worker or any other kind of manual worker without losing his self-respect. He would accept this because he had been taught to be proud of his job, and he would be paid accordingly. He would have to be trained for his job, and after his long period of training he would be promoted according to merit. He would have nothing to be ashamed of.

With the black boy, the story is different. All those who contributed towards his arrival in England would be hoping that one day they would be repaid, if not in money, in knowing that the little boy they had helped years ago had now made good.

He would be fully settled and put into a school, but it would never occur to his people here in England to ask what kind of school it was. To his parents, all English schools are good schools (for are the children not being taught by white teachers?). For the child, there would always be a further problem. His first social promotion was coming to England; having achieved that, he would tend to rest on his laurels. He might find the school rather hard going, and the teachers unintelligible. Truancy would follow but the English teachers, who are usually liberal in their approach, would let him be. Except for the occasional reports to his parents of his truancy, they would be too busy making good to pay much attention. The boy would gain nothing from school.

The big trouble now is that though he did not work hard at school, he will never abandon his dreams. When asked what he wants to be, he will say that he wants to be a doctor or a lawyer. One educationalist, flabbergasted by this attitude, said to me once, "Your people chose professions that even the middle-class English boy, with all the necessary cushioning, would not dream of mentioning." What other short cut is there, since the educational hope has failed?

By his being told to go into manual work, the black boy sees the end of his dream. He is no better off than his poor parents or the people who helped him to come to England. He has to be in an élitist position to rub shoulders with the whites he sees around him, the whites who tell him on the one hand that this is his mother country and on the other, that he cannot reap any benefits from her. He will soon learn also that the darker his skin, the meaner his job. These are not salubrious experiences for a young person. But these young people will carry this hurt and humiliation in their hearts.

In 1985, at time of writing, a new survey has shown that a great number of black children born here do not regard themselves British. Things have not changed that much. But in 1974 I took it upon myself to change them, just as I had done with my husband Sylvester a decade before. In neither case did I know what I was getting myself in for. I did not know that Sylvester, having been brought up in a family where there were too many girls who were willing to serve his every whim, would never respect women, nor did

I have the slightest idea of the depth of the damage that had been done to the members of The Seventies. Sometimes I asked myself, "If I had known, would I have hesitated?" The answer would probably be no. Fools rush in where angels fear to tread. The black boy still clings to his dream, so much so that when all looks grim and hopeless he turns to crime instead, because all the successful people he sees around him have a great deal of money to spend.

23

The Seventies

My honeymoon with The Seventies did not last very long. How could it? How could I ever hope to change people to my way of thinking when I did not understand them and they did not understand me?

We were all black, yes. But my black experience was not the same as the type weathered by the members of The Seventies. We all came to Britain as economic refugees, but the experiences and expectations of the African were different from those of the Caribbean. I had to struggle and fight my way through libraries, colleges, universities and grant departments, while all most of them wanted was simply a good job. Most of the Africans in those days would take any job, however dirty, because they knew they were here to work their way through college. Most of them hoped to go home after their studies. The Caribbean wanted a good job, which he would hold just as if he were in the West Indies. I remember a friend of mine who came from Ghana who always prefaced any ill she experienced with, "This is not our country." That kind of sentence I would never utter to the members of The Seventies.

Despite these differences, I was going to try, and I was going to succeed. I was going to make them all respectable, lower-middle-class people exactly like myself, because in my ivory tower I felt they should all aspire to be like me. My argument was always, If I could get a university degree with five children, why could not other people, who had fewer responsibilities, do the same? Reading all this now in the diary I kept in those days, I feel like dying of shame. How egotistical I was! How they must have hated me! Well, I was then twenty-eight, and it was all thirteen years ago. I hope I have grown a lot since then.

I did not understand why a handsome, well-dressed young man like Peter could regard it a triumph to con me into making him a ham sandwich and coffee without paying. This was one of my earliest shocks. The satisfaction on his face when he had succeeded in doing this was amusing to watch. I put up with it at first, then I found it too pathetic to ignore and I was overcome by this feeling of anger – anger at the waste of such handsome young bodies, anger at them, anger at the fate that brought them there, anger at myself for being too soft and for trying to shrug my shoulders and pretend that the situation did not exist.

Peter would walk in slowly, managing to make one shoulder higher than the other and at the same time shuffling one foot. He would then bang on the counter and cry, "'am sandwich, chocolate and coffee."

If one told him that one was busy, he would become irritable and start cursing and swearing. Eventually, he would get his order and if asked for money he would cry, "I 'ave them because me fancy them guy, whar 'appen, guy?" And other members of The Seventies would tell me that they paid their taxes or that their fathers or mothers paid taxes, so why should they not have the food free? He would then take his order, shuffle back to his friends at the draughts table and enjoy his tea.

Peter and a lot of his friends dressed most expensively, but their elegant and beautiful outward appearance was invariably ruined by the way they behaved; the language they purposely cultivated and spoke was a far cry from the lovely and musical patois Caribbean English. Then there was the strange smell that gathered around them as the evenings wore on. I usually left around six-thirty, and Bulie or Orin would take it up after that. But before I left I noticed that a kind of giddiness would almost overwhelm me. I always put it down to the noise or the brand of cigarette they smoked. I learnt later how wrong I was.

We, the staff, had to report the progress of the project to the committee at regular intervals. The members of the committee, who were mostly volunteers, were not always in the mood to be burdened with our tales of woe. They met once every three months or so in the evenings after a tiring day at work. Tales about the members who refused to pay for their food were the last thing they wished to hear, and I later found this very annoying: they were free to complain that the bar was losing money and not making the profit they thought it would make. I wanted to put my pride and dignity in my pocket and *make* them listen to me. This, I guessed, surprised them not a little, and I knew they resented it, because Amanda never complained. But Amanda was white and single and had no family to bring up and was willing to accept the members as they were. She was a very liberated young woman who could afford to invite most of the members to her flat after the centre had officially closed. She would let them have as much food as they wanted and would make it up with her own money. It was very noble of her and I would have loved to be the same, but I could not afford it, and being black, I did not wish these young people who I felt could still do a great deal with their life to be dependent on me. They were mostly unemployed and on Social Security and, apart from the fact that the committee expected us to show some takings from opening the coffee bar, I felt a sense of the patronizing in Amanda's attitude which I thought was not quite right, however well she meant. Would she have been that indulgent in an all-white youth club, I wondered? To be fair, she did not see anything wrong in this and I probably felt it just because I was black.

The committee listened to me politely even though I could see that I was boring many people when I suggested that we made The Seventies more rewarding for those coming there. We should encourage them to read magazines and newspapers, especially the black ones like *West Indian World*. We should encourage them to come to us with their Social Security problems. One committee member, who was completely out of touch, reminded me that all the members of The Seventies had social workers and she had to be told that few of them would take the trouble to talk to their social workers, whom they all saw as social police.

Apart from that minor objection, they encouraged me by agreeing to most of my ideas. Subsequently, we had money allocated to buy some glossy black magazines and started to take in the local Paddington rags. There was not in those days as much black reading matter as we have now.

As soon as we started to place magazines and dailies on the tables, I noticed that a few boys around the ages of eighteen and nineteen started to read them. But some of them tore the papers up and strewed them on the floor. When they got terribly excited they would use the edges in rolling up their cigarettes.

We tried to ignore this. Bulie and I managed to get a lawyer to come and talk to the members about their legal rights, and they behaved well and asked so many intelligent questions that they confirmed what I had suspected: that inside that "Don't care" exterior there were frightened, law-abiding people struggling to get out. The very next day, however, they went back to tearing up the papers and not paying for their food. I became angry, demanded money first before preparing anything for anybody, and threatened that they would be forced to pay for any reading materials they tore up. I did not know how I was going to perform such a miracle. The result was that they did not like me: if Amanda, who was white, could let them do what they liked and not report anything to the committee, why should I who was black do more? When they hinted or said things like that, I almost wished we could afford to give the food away free. But then giving free food away was never the aim or purpose of The Seventies.

One evening, just two days before Guy Fawkes night, they showed me the depth of their resentment. I was so absorbed with the piles of sandwiches I was cutting that I took little notice of the unusual silly smile on the faces of many of the members. Peter and two or three of his friends came in and asked for food. I asked him for his money first but instead of shouting he started to laugh. It was probably that unexpected laughter that saved my eyes. I could have been blinded, for at that instant a big firework exploded on the counter right in front of my face, very near the sandwiches I was cutting. At the same time others, strategically placed, started to explode in all parts of the room. I was too far from the door to dash out for it would have meant running through them all. The place was like hell – young men shouting and jumping in childish excitement, like the scene in a football stadium when a group of fans attack those of their opponents.

I still to this day do not know how I managed to keep my cool. I picked up the phone that was hooked on the wall behind my head and dialled 999. Before the firemen arrived, just a few minutes later, I thought I was going to be hurt. I stood firmly behind the counter and bolted it, so if anyone wanted to come nearer, they would have to jump over the top.

Luckily, they were still too happy at my confusion, the noise, the smoke and the pandemonium they were causing to think of jumping over the counter. The sandwiches I had been cutting were scattered all over the floor, the Coca-Cola fountain was smashed, somebody had turned off the light, sparklers and fireworks were flying about the room, and I was dodging this way and that when we heard the bells of the fire engines. The firemen kicked the door open, then I saw The Seventies in a new light: "She's call the law, she's call the pigs, the woom'n's call the f... pigs... Oh guy!"

This I knew instantly was the cry of fear. These young people feared everybody white and in uniform. I had wondered why.

The firemen on their part worked as if they were deaf and dumb. They probably knew the place well. They soaked the whole place in water, took away all the remaining fireworks and opened the windows to let in air. Four policemen came in their wake. It was then that I saw my mistake.

The young men hated the sight of policemen even more than firemen. We read about police harassment of the young blacks when I was a student. Then it was an academic thing. I was still one of those who would rush to the London bobby for help if I was too lazy to read a road map, I went to the policemen in Holmes Road, Kentish Town, when I was having a really rough time, although I stopped going to them when they told me that they did not take part in family quarrels. I did not fear them, neither did I find them intrusive, so I did not understand why the members of The Seventies looked at them with such horror. The officers pretended not to notice, of course. They tried to maintain the proverbial "stiff upper lip", but I knew from their accents that most of them came from places like Pussy Cat Mansions. They probably thought I was just a sandwich seller or something. The one who spoke to me tried to be rather too nice, too patronizing – a male chauvinist.

"You're new here, I see," looking down his nose at me. "You're lucky the explosion didn't blind you – they gave the other girl two broken ribs and a black eye so that she stayed in St Mary's Hospital for days. They used to have some male workers – where are they?"

"They come in later, when it gets very busy," I said, shocked and frightened to learn why Amanda resigned.

"Risky job for a woman, especially with the smell."

"Yes, it's the smell of their cigarettes."

As soon as two of the officers began to smile, and another to rub his nose, something clicked. I think I looked into the eye of one of the older members, and saw him dropping white packets the size of tea bags behind him. My feet suddenly became wobbly with fear. "Oh good Lord," I screamed inwardly, "are we all going to be arrested? My poor kids."

But then the policemen did a funny thing. They simply said "Good luck" to me and left. They made no arrests, they searched nobody. I could sense the air of relief that went round when they left. So that was why I always felt giddy in this place. But why were these young people not stopped from taking these drugs, however mild?

From then on, I opened my eyes more, and saw to my horror that the place was used as a drugs centre. I noticed that the older members who had lived around Maida Vale for over twenty years or so always brought drugs and sold them to the younger ones; I noticed that around six every evening, two hours after the centre opened, the screams and excitements would start; and I concluded that it was the effect of whatever they were taking that was making them behave the way they did.

Stupidly I pleaded with the committee to do something about this and told them how I almost lost my eyes. My complaints about drugs were ignored completely, but there was concern about my safety, so much so that a younger youth worker by the name of Malcolm was told to work in the early evening as well, so that there were two of us.

It was an example of what one educationalist calls "institutional inertia". As long as those young people did not go onto the streets to smoke their grass, or inject heroin or mug the old, it was all right with the authorities. The female members of the committee said to me once, "But all your people smoke marijuana, they say it's part of your religion." How could I tell her that I had never seen any before, except on *News at Ten*?

Fear started to wriggle inside me after that day. I knew I would leave eventually. Although I was undoubtedly failing with the members, they on the other hand were opening my eyes the more. We blacks were employed to face our unhappy blacks. And oh, how I wished in those days to reach Peter, Delroy, Aldwyn, and many of the others. They were too far gone to be saved by the likes of me. More commitment on the part of the Establishment was needed to effect any change. I could see that, most of the members of the committee could see that, and some of us workers could see that, too. I hung on, however, and reported everything that was happening there on the academic level to my supervisor at the University, Professor Bernstein. He used to listen with sympathy.

My description would be so detailed and graphic that he would say, "Look, Buchi, reading for a PhD is fine, but I think you would do more for humanity by being a writer. I wish I had your gift."

I thought he was just saying that to put me off, especially as the rows of books he had written could fill several library shelves. I was not going to listen to him. I would dig into all the sociological theories I knew in my frantic efforts to explain the members of The Seventies, and why some of them kept going in and out of jail for the same offences like shoplifting, breaking and entry, and GBH.

After the firework incident and due to all Professor Bernstein was saying, I decided to book an appointment with the new lady that had taken over my work at Curtis Brown, the literary agents. I took this step just in case the academic goal was going to be out of my reach for a while. I knew that if I left The Seventies, it would be difficult to find another place to base my research on "The Plight of the Black Youth in London".

This new woman was very mild and never showed much emotion, very unlike Mrs Alexandra, with whom I had worked when the contract for my first book was being prepared. This new woman, Elizabeth Stevens, promised to read *Second-Class Citizen* and said that since it had been rejected by many publishing houses she was going to try a new one by the name of Allison and Busby, and that she was sure they would like it because they were mildly radical, just like the manuscript.

As soon as she said that, my imagination soared. So I probably could write and would write! I probably did not need to be patronized. She complained about my rough work and asked if I could rewrite a little. I told her definitely that I could not. That was the way I wrote, pouring my heart out non-stop, and if I started to rewrite and correct my mistakes, it would be too artificial. She said she liked it but that she was sure it was this roughness that was putting publishers off. It was the first time somebody had said they liked *Second-Class Citizen*. I was going to hang on to that. I still refused to accept the fact that I could not be fully academic from Professor Bernstein. After all, the writer of the famous *Love Story* was a lecturer. So who said that one could not be a creative artist and an academic at the same time? If I could not make a living from writing alone, then I would have to be both.

"You can still be a novelist and not a sociologist. There is nothing bad in being called a novelist," he had said to me once during one of my tutorials.

"But I hope, sir, to go back to Nigeria," I cried. "In Nigeria, everybody has a title. You're either a Professor or a Doctor or a Chief. I have no money for chieftaincy so I would like to be a Doctor of Sociology."

How patient those poor supervisors are. I feel now like burying my head in the sand when I look back fifteen years and remember the things I used to say. But if Professor Bernstein was amused, he did not show it. In fact he took everything I said seriously, because though my remarks now sound naïve and stupid, I was serious about them.

"Why can't you just be Buchi Emecheta? It's nice and musical, I quite like the sound of it, Buchi Emecheta."

Yes, but that was because he could pronounce it correctly. He should have to come to hear my new agent at Curtis Brown call my name. She made me sound Russian – Bukki Emeketa. I corrected her, but right up to the day I decided that I did not need her services any more, about ten years later, she still called me Bukki, much to the amusement of all my publishers.

For the moment, whilst I was walking back from that first interview with her, my mind kept darting from her to my supervisor. Was Professor Bernstein patronizing me, I wondered? I did not feel so. He said I was a good student and that supervising my work was not so difficult because of my easy style, which he found interesting and refreshing. But I would be wasting this good experience I was having at The Seventies if I did not turn it into a novel instead of a research piece which would be read by just a handful of academics. A novel based on The Seventies would be read by thousands of people. He had a point there, but I still went to him. Now this woman at Curtis Brown who did not smile very much was saying she liked *Second-Class Citizen*.

Well, maybe I would take Bernstein's advice and start another story based on my research. I was going to call it *The Scapegoat*. If the University was indirectly telling me that I was too wordy to be a social scientist, then I would write it up as a documentary novel that would be half academic and half literary. Maybe my whole writing career should be like that. Little did I know then, on that walk home, that I was mapping out my life. I remembered that walk when in spring 1985 my American publisher said on the phone, "Your books don't go so fast in the book stores but they go like mad in schools." Like most Americans, he calls universities "schools".

When I got home, I went happily back to my typewriter and started to turn my research pieces into a documentary novel. As the days went by, I found that the more I wrote, the less I worried about the members of The Seventies. I started seeing them as a means to a kind of end. If I could not help them, I could at least write about them and let the world know that some black youngsters went through that phase in the mid-1970s. At the same time, my mental detachment from them warned me that I would soon be leaving the centre.

What was I going to do for a living? There were still six of us to be fed and clothed on my one income. I was also paying full university fees for my postgraduate course. The thought of filling forms and going back to the dole did not appeal to me, not after Pussy Cat Mansions. Although it was beginning to look as if *Second-Class Citizen* would be published, I had long stopped labouring under the happy delusion that Literature was a profession in which self-support was really attainable. I watched Somerset Maugham, Jimmy Baldwin and the rest of them on television and regarded them as stars. I could never be like them: they were writers of the first grade, and the best I could ever achieve would be the lower bottom of the second grade. I could never be like them, because even then I knew I was going to write about the little happenings of everyday life.

As if all that was not enough, the London Borough of Camden decided to charge me full rent. I guessed they had got fed up with a mother with five children claiming to be a student all the time, although I was still a full-time student who had to work because it was part of my research and because I did not get the First Class Honours that would have qualified me for an SSRC grant. To start writing petitions would take up three quarters of my time, and there was no guarantee of winning. I was therefore in the poverty band. I knew from readings that this band is the trickiest social class in which to be. Most people with lower-middle-class jobs were in this band. In this category, one was not poor enough to benefit from all that the welfare state could provide, yet after paying for everything, including full rates and full rent, one was poorer than those in the poverty trap. The only way to escape was to look for a sympathetic building society and start buying one's own house. At least the forced mortgage repayments would serve as savings for the future. The amount of rent that Camden was demanding would just cover mortgage repayments for a modest house.

The Seventies came under the umbrella of the Inner London Education Authority. I quickly asked them to give me a statement of my income, even though I had not started looking for a house. I was doing all this just in case I had to leave The Seventies suddenly, as I was beginning to dread going there. I could never predict the mood in which the members were going to be, and did not like to think that I was breathing in air which had been heavily polluted by "grass".

The University was very kind, allowing me to pay my fees by instalments while I got myself mentally ready to look for another job that would relate to my project.

Peter and his friends at The Seventies took my decision to leave out of my hands. It happened one evening in March 1974. Again, if I had not been so mentally detached and had taken more notice, I would have suspected that something was wrong. Peter's clothes were unusually rough; he and his friends were very quiet that evening. When they came in they usually took their "grass" at the centre and then would proceed on to whatever took their fancy after that. I knew that one of the group had been jailed only the day before for breaking and entering and from their bragging I gathered he was simply unlucky and too slow. The others escaped but he did not tell on his friends. Perhaps I mistakenly took their quiet as a result of their guilt. Most of them were already "high" before they came in, and when they were this high they would withdraw only to explode at the least provocation. I knew all this was so – why I said "No" when Peter demanded free food I do not know. I had by now got so used to the committee's moans about the budget for The Seventies that I no longer felt threatened, but did my best to make the majority of the boys pay for the food they took. On an evening like this, it would have been better to let Peter have his way and take free food and go away. But I knew that if I allowed that, most of the members there at that time would also not pay. Maybe that was why I refused.

The word "No" had scarcely left my mouth when Peter, baying like a dog to the moon, shot out a hand and struck my face. I saw my glasses fly across the room whilst he pushed the sandwiches, crisps and chocolates all off the counter and trampled over them, shouting all the time. Bulie rushed from upstairs where he had been asleep, no doubt. He was there just as I got carried away and was about to fling a saucer at Peter's face. He caught my arm, and started to argue with the members. It was the same old argument: they wanted to know why they should pay for anything in a club which the local council said belonged to them. They paid taxes, their parents paid taxes . . .

I'd heard all that before. They all knew that The Seventies was being run like a youth club. It had started as a youth club for everybody, white and black, living around that area. The white youths stopped coming when they found they were in the minority and when they saw that there was no love lost between them and their black co-members. Hot tears temporarily blinded my eyes, and I knew that for the sake of my family I would simply have to give up this job.

I packed my things and left. Again I walked home to give me time to think, and I felt sad in a way for having failed. I failed in everything I tried to do, I told myself. I tried to be a wife and a mother, and look at me, a mother and not a wife. I tried to be an academic and they said I would never make it; I even tried to help my fellow blacks, but my type of help was not wanted. What was I good at? What would I do? Was there any job left for me to do?

Children and responsibilities have a way of stabilizing one. If I had not had kids, I would have harmed myself that evening – jumped in front of a car or something. It was tolerable to know that one was failing, but to be told so in such a vicious way was more than humiliating.

I knew it would be difficult to get another fairly well-paid job as a youth worker that would give me time to do all I was doing. The Seventies job was not demanding academically, it was a nice change from the University and from my writing. The Seventies was supplying me with my raw material, yet after the fireworks episode, I knew that my going there was a great risk.

I got home, having walked off all my anger against humanity, and the phone rang. It was Vince Hines, the director of Dashiki. He phoned to apologize for all the black youth in London. He phoned to say that he understood what I was trying to achieve. He phoned to say that yes, those young people were not reacting against me but against the society that had sent some of them to prison many times for stealing much-needed food. And now he was saying that, after I had recovered from this shock, could I come to Dashiki and set up the education scheme he had heard me outline at the committee meeting? Vince was one of the few token blacks on the committee. I could do exactly what I wanted because the boys at his centre badly needed the type of individual attention I wanted to give. I could choose my hours. The boys were much younger and I would not have more than five at a time. The pay would be a little less than that of the ILEA but the atmosphere was so much healthier.

One of our thoughtful members had dashed out after I left The Seventies to tell Vince Hines. Though most of the members could be violent, there were a few who needed The Seventies. Some of these worked, and went there in the evenings to play draughts and chat with their friends; some of them were even thinking seriously about their future. There were some good, thoughtful boys there, but they were not as loud as the likes of Peter. By doing the right thing and phoning me as soon as I got home, Vince Hines without knowing it softened for me the blow of failure. So, someone thought I was right because I refused to tag the young men of my race as "picturesque problem people": "That is the way they are", as Amanda used to say.

I went in the kitchen to make some coffee and Jake brought me a squashed letter from Elizabeth Stevens of Curtis Brown. Allison and Busby liked *Second-Class Citizen* very much; the contract and advance payment would soon follow.

"Maybe I'm going to be a writer after all," I murmured, as I took some headache tablets and tried to avoid Jake's inquisitive eyes. He saw that mine were swollen but I was smiling at the letter and the phone call too. He did not know what to do so he compromised by asking, "Was it a bad day, Ma?"

"No, Jake, the day was a bit bad, but the good part of it was bigger than the bad."

"Tomorrow will be better," he assured me with his wide grin and cockney voice.

24

The Bride Price

Westminster Council was very generous to me after the attack at The Seventies. I was allowed a whole four weeks to get over the shock; I was really shaken and it had probably only just occurred to them how dangerous the job could be. I did not want to go back there, but I was not going to let them know until I had used my holiday to cover my notice period. With my holiday, I would be away from work for a whole eight weeks or so. This was an unexpected bonus. I was going to use it well.

When the heat of The Seventies was taken off my back, I started to look at the whole concept of my *Scapegoat* again. Was society responsible for all that was happening at The Seventies? Did God not give us a little free will? Doubts started to set in. I knew I was going to shelve the work and finish it when I had started at Dashiki. But I was not going to Dashiki until after I had had my long-deserved holiday. I was going to write during that holiday.

The contract for *Second-Class Citizen* arrived from Curtis Brown a few days after I left The Seventies. Soon after, I was invited to lunch with the publishers.

Lunching with publishers used to be such a big event for me. I would plan what to wear, and what to talk about. I would have done so with this new group that formed Allison and Busby but for the fact that they sounded so ordinary when I spoke to them on the phone. The publishers I had had previously were John Bunting, and later one Christopher

Maclehose who took over his job at Barrie and Jenkins, and of course I met people like Corinna Adams and Mr Crossman of the *New Statesman*. When those people spoke to you over the telephone, you could feel their detachment. Allison and Busby, however, allowed their interest to show over the phone. I noted in my diary for 1 April 1974 that I asked Chidi what I should wear and he asked me to describe how I thought they looked, judging from their voices. I said, "They sounded like a couple of hippies to me." And he said, "Wear your trousers."

To him, asking a woman to wear trousers was the greatest insult he could think of. What he was telling me was that they were not worth dressing up for. I did not take his advice. I went in a skirt and blouse.

Noel Street in Soho, where their office was, was not too far from where I lived near Regent's Park, so I walked. The building was in a narrow street surrounded by sex shops and Indian shops selling jewellery. Inside it was like the old curiosity shop, with stairs curving in and out like the body of a snake. The publishing house was only one room. Allison and Busby, my two publishers, were sharing one huge table on which were piled all sorts of papers imaginable.

What struck me was their youth. They were both around my age. I had thought all publishers were huge worldly people in their late middle life with pots of money. If these people had money, they were good at hiding it – The Seventies, which I thought was a bad place to work, was much, much cleaner than this. They shook my hand; the man's name was Clive Allison and the woman was Margaret Busby. Another lady with a different accent was Mrs Allison. It looked as if Mr and Mrs Allison were working with Margaret Busby. Margaret was very beautiful with a close haircut, and Clive had dark brown almost reddish fizzy hair. There was a lot of hair on his head but it was all in curls, he had a beard to match. They were all in jeans! Now I wished I had listened to Chidi and gone in trousers.

We went to a nearby Indian place to eat. The place was filthy. I remember thinking, "What a come-down." My first publishers had taken me to eat at the Scotsman, the Savoy, and places on that level; now I was sitting in a dirty Indian restaurant. But the food was delicious. Clive ordered everything on the menu, saying we should mix them all up. He said they tasted better that way and he was right. We had hot Madras and not so hot Madras. We had rice fried and boiled and one lady who later joined us commanded us to drink beer because "We always have beer after Indian." This was because I said I had never eaten Indian before.

First impressions can sometimes be right. In my diary entry for 1 April 1974 I wrote, "Margaret Busby looks younger than myself, she is very beautiful and agreeable and seems to agree with all the suggestions made by Clive Allison. He is young too but talked incessantly about a magazine for writers he was going to start. I still do not know what to make of them. Food was Indian and the place filthy." Not a very promising impression of the publishers I stayed with for exactly eight years.

The good effect they had on my life was quite different. Here was a group of people around my age who were talking of what they were going to do in the literary field. They were not rich or too sophisticated like my early publishers. Those early ones were too far above me. To meet them on their level, I would need a giant leap.

These people who took me to a dirty place to eat nice Indian food in Soho were not talking or worrying about "the plight of black youth", or children, or whether they qualified for a mortgage. They had all been through university and were simply enjoying the work they did. Then why, oh why could I not be like them? Maybe because unlike them, I needed money to feed the six of us.

Hearing Allison and Busby talk, they gave me the impression that they would publish *Second-Class Citizen* soon. Those were the days when I used to believe everything a publisher told me. Allison and Busby themselves cured me of that. But I believed them then. All that was needed of *Second-Class Citizen* was slight editing, and the woman editor said she would come to my flat in a couple of days to work on it. I suspected that I had found a publishing house in which I would grow for, like me, they were young and inexperienced in the trade.

Walking back to my council flat, I reminded myself again that I had about eight weeks ahead of me in which I could do anything I liked. I had tentatively decided that I would write, but was not sure what. Seeing who my new publishers were, I thought I would tackle *The Bride Price* again. I would rewrite the book my husband had burned years ago when I was still living with him. It happened a long time ago, but every time I remember the incident I shudder.

Now, in 1974, I was going to use these forced eight weeks of rest to start the book again. The plot would be exactly the same, but now, having read Sociology, it would have a new depth. It would be an improvement on my first attempt. Maybe I was not going to be good at anything except putting my ideas on paper. I love being with people, but writing is a profession that isolates one. The more isolated one is, the deeper the thoughts and the more meaningful the literary products become. Loneliness is one of those things I think those of us who were born children of Africa still do not know how to cope with. The big mother in Ibusa may tell her stories to a group of wide-eyed children, but here in England, people write alone and the books are read individually. I did not then foresee the public readings and talks I now get involved in. I thought then that because I was too sensitive, and felt too easily hurt, I was condemned to be a writer living alone with no one to talk to but the typewriter.

When I got home I phoned Elizabeth, my agent, and told her my impression of Allison and Busby. I don't think she believed that they were going to publish *Second-Class Citizen* within a few months, because she said she would phone them after two weeks to give them a push.

Lots of writers in England must have had one or two brushes with people in films. What time wasters that lot are! I think laws should be made to protect writers from them. They come to you while you are in the middle of a book, and talk you into leaving what you're doing to listen to their project. They get carried away and make you believe that your book is going to make the best film Hollywood has ever seen. A month or two later, you will see neither the film crew, the director nor the project organizer. By then they will have wasted your time, and you will have to return to your typewriter and try to find the thread of the story you have lost during the interruption.

After *In the Ditch* was published, I saw a few of these men with big projects. I simply ignored them when I found that they were going to use my work to make names for themselves. I still see some of them, now established as DJs, their earlier attempts at being film directors having failed. But this man from Silver Screen was very cool and looked as if he was serious. He phoned to book an appointment, and when he came he talked about our collaboration. He was going to make *In the Ditch* into a comical series on black people and on one-parent families. I must have really believed him because I put in my diary for that day of April 1974, "Now I am really going to keep my head above water, all from writing. Pompidou died at 9 pm!"

During the next few weeks, I wrote five pages a day of my *Bride Price*. The concept behind this book is tradition. Although I was then approaching thirty, whenever I failed in anything I always remembered what I considered my greatest failure – the inability to make my marriage work. Sometimes I used to say that maybe I did not pray hard enough, maybe I did not do this or that enough, but when it came to the actual reality of living with Sylvester again, I just cringed. I was still feeling guilty for simply having enough to eat and give my children. I could never shake off my Ibo-cum-Christian upbringing. I had promised to honour and obey, so why had I come to England and disobeyed, when all he wanted to do was sit at home enjoying being a man whilst I did all the work? In Nigeria there were still women who were happy to have a man in the home at all costs, whether or not he worked, or dragged them and their children down, whether or not he beat them daily. Oh, why could I not be like those women? Why did I want a man whose ideas I could listen to and who would listen to mine, who would regard me as a person, a companion, a wife, yes, and would do his own share of the housework? Maybe I was ahead of my time. I decided that people like me who go against tradition must die!

In *The Bride Price* I created a girl, Akunna, who had an almost identical upbringing to mine, and who deliberately chose her own husband because she was "modern" but was not quite strong enough to shake off all the tradition and taboos that had gone into making her the type of girl she was. Guilt for going against her mother and her uncle killed her when she was about to give birth to her first baby.

Akunna died the death I ought to have died. In real life, due to malnutrition and anaemia, I had a very bad time with my first daughter, Chiedu. I was in labour for days, and became so exhausted that when she was actually born I knew I was losing consciousness, but was too scared to say so because I thought I had caused everybody enough trouble as it was. But one thing was certain: right from the moment Chiedu was born I was delighted to have given birth to a baby girl. I was not going to listen to all the stuff about girl babies being inferior to boys. And those nurses at Massey Street Dispensary knew me, and had seen me only a year before in the khaki uniform of the Methodist Girls' High School. They knew I was going to treat this baby like my own doll.

I could not hold the baby because I was too weak. Suddenly the labour ward, an open one in those days, was growing darker and I thought that evening was approaching, even though Chiedu was born at 2 pm. Mrs Ndukwe, one of my mother's friends who was then a staff nurse at the

Massey Street Dispensary, came in, recognized me and took charge. She screamed at the nurses, she ordered them to get blood ready because I had lost so much, and I think her quick thinking saved Chiedu and me.

In *The Bride Price* Akunna did not recover. She died because she had gone against our tradition. The original story ended with husband and wife going home and living happily ever after, disregarding their people. But I had grown wiser since that first manuscript. I had realized that what makes all of us human is belonging to a group. And if one belongs to a group, one should try and abide by its laws. If one could not abide by the group's law, then one was an outsider, a radical, someone different who had found a way of living and being happy outside the group. Akunna was too young to do all that. She had to die.

In life, I was too young to go against all that, but what I think saved me was coming to England when I did. I doubt if I would have been able to survive emotionally all the well-meaning advice from family and relatives. I left the husband for whom all the sacrifices had been made. Maybe that was my death. Then why in real life was I enjoying my independence? I could not answer all that in *The Bride Price*.

The story was tenderly written because I had watched a lot of Ibusa men looking for their women. They are very romantic until the woman comes to live in their house. Chike, Akunna's husband, maintained that romance because of their slave ancestry and because he knew that he and his family were outcasts. I rushed the book, because writing it was like reading a story.

After the fourth week, Vince Hines kept phoning to find out whether I still wanted the job at Dashiki and if so, please could I come and take it. I was beginning to fear that working in such a place would mean another emotional involvement which would sap all my mental energy. I knew I could never be detached from the people I work with. The Seventies had taught me that.

Consequently, I applied for a teaching job in ILEA, and the County Hall phoned to say that I would be considered as a Social Science teacher for GCE classes in the ILEA secondary schools.

This was very comforting news, but I had not by then finished *The Bride Price* and Allison and Busby still had not sent the editor who in April had promised to come to my flat "in a few days". And the enthusiasm of the Silver Screen man seemed to have cooled. In short, the malady of the one-parent family hit me again. I needed money. Although I was accepted by

ILEA, the job would not start until after the summer holidays. They were going to take three months to sort out my papers and check me medically.

I had to sell my car in order to buy enough time to finish writing *The Bride Price*. As the children could now go to school on their own, I had plenty of time to work on the book during the day.

I finished it in June, and Elizabeth Stevens did not know what to do with a writer like me. She was sure that Allison and Busby were not even ready to send the long-awaited editor for *Second-Class Citizen*, and here was I saying that I had finished another novel. She did not waste time in reading it, and suggesting some rewriting in parts. By late July, however, the final edition was with her.

I was there in her office when she phoned Allison and Busby, and when they told her that they would deal with *Second-Class Citizen* in a few days, I realized that for some publishers contracts are just pieces of paper which, though binding for the author, are not so for the publisher. In desperation, Elizabeth said she would send the manuscript to Heinemann instead and was sure they would snap it up since the story was based in Nigeria. Another of my dreams was coming true. I had always dreamt that my books would be read in Nigeria.

I then felt mentally ready to tackle Dashiki, and if it did not work I would go and teach, do anything until I started earning enough money to make me a full-time writer. I knew that this would take a long time. If somebody else had been contributing to the welfare of the children, I would not have needed another job.

That is the lot of one-parent families like ours. The lone parent is the bread-winner, the mother, the father, the counsellor, the comforter. I knew I had to shoulder the burden. It was one's cross, which one simply has to carry. In my own case, it was not all gloomy. I enjoyed the endless chats I used to have on the phone with Brenda and with Elizabeth, and even enjoyed eating out with agents and would-be publishers.

It was at this time that the BBC External Services started inviting me to make comments on current affairs. I think I was paid £3 and a free lunch at the BBC canteen per visit. It was then that I came to know Florence Akst of the African Service and African presenters like Sopiato Likimani.

If I had had a little outside help, these earnings would have been sufficient. But I needed more to feed six mouths. So, reluctantly, I had to become once more committed to "the plight of the black youth". This time it was to be at Dashiki and not The Seventies.

25

Dashiki

Dashiki was one of those self-help projects that educated Afro-Caribbeans set up to correct some of the scapegoat myths attributed to the blacks. It was started by Vince Hines to house some of the homeless black youths who wandered round the streets of Paddington.

These young people had failed or had been told that they had failed everybody and in everything. Most had passed school age, and those that were under fifteen had long failed to see the relevance of the boring lessons they had to sit through. Their parents, who had originally brought them into this country with high hopes for the future, now had their own lives to worry about. When most of the boys failed to reach their parents' expectations and started becoming difficult, the bewildered parents did not know what to do. This was a new experience for them. A harassed mother, after listening to a graphic description of what her sixteen-year-old son had done to a tired old lady in her home, broke down and cried, "I curse the very day you were conceived. I don't ever want to see you again for the rest of my life!" She was later taken away suffering from mental exhaustion, while her son, so condemned, took to the streets.

It was for this type of young people that Vince gave up his journalistic career to try and set up homes. It was to be a self-help project. But how does one set up such self-help establishments without funds? The boys needed to be fed and kept presentably clean while they fought for their rights of livelihood either from the Labour Exchange or the Department of

Social Security. To make these claims would be impossible if they had no address and wandered through the streets sleeping at some hidden corner of the London Underground, in old garages or in some abandoned cars. Vince provided this much-needed address for them.

At first he used his flat but he did not realize the extent of the demand. His flat soon became too small and Dashiki, though still a self-help project, had to become a charity organization. It became necessary to acquire a building and maintain it, and the huge Georgian house in Ledbury Road was found, and housed eleven to twenty boys and about five girls. Some of these young people went out to work, a few at government training centres and some at colleges of further education, but the majority of them stayed in all day.

For those boys who stayed at home, a kind of education programme was to be set up. It was to achieve this that I was hired. It had been in Vince's mind for a long time, but where then would he get a black graduate or a black qualified teacher to undertake it? Those were the days when sociology was still a glamorous subject, and most of the qualified sociologists were looking for equally glamorous jobs such as university lecturers or heads of big management firms, but not getting themselves involved with the type of young people I dealt with at Dashiki.

As I walked down to Ledbury Road, right in the middle of Paddington's grey areas, my mind went through the different jobs I had had. First at the American Embassy in Lagos, driven there each morning in a friend's Mercedes, then as a poor mum working in North Finchley Library, as a Civil Service librarian at the British museum, and now, so reduced as to have to walk through this horrible part of London to take up my next appointment.

I was not feeling bad about it. I felt I was tasting reality. These jobs were affording me the kind of opportunity I needed to see at first hand the way many of my own race and people lived. I might have lived like that too, if that great miracle had not happened – the miracle of finding myself a pupil at the Methodist Girls' High School.

I was happy to do what I was doing – at the variety in my life. I was a mother and an education liaison officer, even though it was at Dashiki. I was fast becoming a writer and on top of all that I was still a postgraduate student. All these, I calculated, were much more interesting than just being a cataloguer at the British Museum.

Yes, Vince was right. Dashiki was cleaner inside. It was decorated taste-fully by the boys themselves. Expensive-looking curtains hung on gold-plated rails; the carpets on the floor looked deceptively plain, but I could tell that they were expensive. Most of the walls were white. The inside was a vast contrast to what one would have expected to see, looking at the rest of the street.

I had a large room, a large desk, a video recorder and my own telephone. I had to share the secretaries, whose rooms were on a floor above mine, with Vince. The girls were so well dressed and proud of their jobs that they soon made me feel proud to be there. Vince, a quietly spoken man from Grenada, had been very modest when he said that Dashiki had a cleaner atmosphere than The Seventies. What he had done was successfully to create a very "home from home" atmosphere where one would least expect to find one. Now I saw why there was a waiting list of young people from their different boroughs. It looked as if I would have no reason for not wanting to stay here until my research was finished, now that I had finished writing *The Bride Price*.

I was not at first quite sure how to go about my educational programme. I knew I could teach, but I had never taught without any sense of direction before. This was one of those situations where you came, you saw, you planned and then carried out that plan as best you could, because you knew that you were trusted to do the right thing, and that your plans could be implemented without each one having to be discussed by this or that com-mittee in three months' time, and then approved or disapproved by those unconcerned people at the Town Hall.

My first impression of the young people at Dashiki was that they were quite different from those at The Seventies. The Seventies was an ILEA project where young people were expected to be bad because "that is the way they are made". Even when they were not bad enough, the atmos-phere would encourage them to be so. We were simply employed to watch them go from bad to worse until the law decided to put them away for a very long time.

Dashiki was different. The atmosphere was like this, "Yes, we all know that you had a rotten time in the past, your parents have rejected you, the school you have been shuffled through has declared you uneducable – now we want you to forget all that. Turn over a new leaf and let us start all over again." That was exactly what I was determined to do.

The young people at Dashiki dispelled all my doubts. Maybe it was because there was a fairly rigid discipline, maybe because they saw that real efforts were being made on their behalf, I do not know. They soon taught me not to brand any boy or girl as completely bad. The strange thing was, even the social workers who sent their very bad cases to us found that those "cases" were now beginning to work to acquire a new level of self-respect.

My typical class was a far cry from the orthodox. I allowed everyone in class to do exactly what they wanted at that moment. Some simply wanted to talk and argue with me about English politics, or those of the Caribbean; others wanted to draw or paint pictures, most of which we stuck onto the walls of the office-classroom, some would be reading aloud whilst others were going to write stories. To teach basic mathematics we used our daily Dashiki accounts, and made good use of the calculators provided. The youths loved the calculators, because then they were still new toys and luxuries. For books, we chose those written by black writers about this society, because I felt they needed immediate people to identify themselves with. We studied my first book, *In the Ditch*, in detail, not so much for literature but more for its sociological implications. For literature and relaxation, Savon's *Lonely Londoners* was useful.

The result was dramatic, even to me, who had started to lose hope for my race. The young people started to attach importance to reading; it now took on a new kind of meaning, and Vince started to talk about having a small library of about thirty titles or so.

There were two boys who were learning to drive in the hope of becoming either taxi or coach drivers, or simply of owning their own mini-cab company. The two of them, who were both eighteen, felt that no institution could help them any more. Vince forced them to take reading and spelling lessons. I found the case of one of the boys very interesting. He had gone through school in London, but when he left he could hardly write his name. He took to driving because he thought that he could bluff through his test.

He came to me one day and asked, in his shy way, if I could please teach him alone when no one was present. Why did he not do well at school? I asked. He said that when he came here his accent was strange and when he pronounced certain words even his teacher could not understand him. I started this boy on the alphabet, and in eight weeks he could join his friends in reading the first few chapters of *In the Ditch*. A few weeks later, we had managed to read the book from cover to cover. Then his friend exclaimed, "I didn't know you read books from cover to cover! I thought you read a page, or the teacher photocopied a page for you – I never knew you read a book from beginning to the end." His shy friend agreed with a nod.

To think that at the age of eighteen those boys were for the first time finishing a novel, when my much younger daughter Chiedu read five a week! Something was wrong somewhere. I was to understand this much later when I taught in a London school. Here at Dashiki I was still baffled by it.

The project was not without its hitches. The first and the greatest menace, I noticed, was that of the police. At The Seventies the police left those big boys alone, because they would fight with anything. Here the boys were younger and some of them were brought to Dashiki as cases. So if something got lost in Portobello market, any of our boys would be stopped in the streets and searched in the most degrading way. Sometimes they chased them in, looking for this and that. Throughout the time I worked in Dashiki, from June to the end of October, boys were harassed this way. The police did not find anything but they managed to make the boys hate them, and some were even arrested resisting search and arrest. Whenever it came to "talking time" in the class, next to girl problems the talk was always about the Paddington police.

The boys told me some unbelievable stories about police brutalities, especially at the police station in Harrow Road. I, who still believed that the English bobby was the best in the world and would not hurt a fly, found all this very disturbing. I found it even more so because I was raising two black boys as well. Unable to bear it any longer, I invited an Inspector from the Paddington Metropolitan Police to come and talk about all the complaints.

The Inspector was the image of politeness. He personally had nothing against the black youth of the area, but of course he could not vouch for all the policemen under him. Some, he said, had been employed at the early age of nineteen. These young ones were invariably frightened of black youths because of the erroneous myth of lawlessness that was then attached to the Paddington area. There were bound to be clashes, but he would see that everything possible would be done to rectify this. The evening ended with him inviting our boys to come and have a game of football with his boys of the police force. One of our boys said to him by way of saying goodbye, "See you on the pitch, Inspector."

Alas, it did not go that way. Within a week, our boys had a clash with the police in which not only were the boys beaten up, but Vince was punched and his car smashed by some white youths. I think this brought out most of the residents and they were charged for resisting arrest. I still do not know the details of this case because it happened on a weekend when I was not there, but what did happen was the boys became so bitter that they refused to play football with the Inspector and his boys.

I was always absent when these incidents happened, but I witnessed a minor one which could have become a really big event had I not been there at the time.

The whole concept of Dashiki, especially the educational side, started to attract attention. Many social workers came to talk to me about the project, I got invited to give talks about it. I remember Alan Little of the Commission for Racial Equality coming to the centre one day and being so impressed that he wrote about it in one of those innumerable pamphlets the Camden Council for Community Relations and the Commission for Racial Equality are so good at producing. We became so well known that a Swedish film company came to film us. We and the Swedish National Film Company were very happy about it. They told us they had filmed the Notting Hill Carnival and were horrified at the demonstration of the National Front. I did not know what the National Front was at the time and, though I had heard of the West Indian carnival described, had never yet seen one.

The film company wanted an educational scheme sandwiched between shots of the noisy and happy Carnival. They covered my class in detail, intrigued when the boys called me "Mum", and interviewed me to ask what I thought the future of the place would be. Of course, I was hopeful for Dashiki.

For one of the scenes, it was necessary for the boys to walk down Westbourne Park Road near the Portobello Road. I was following them slowly in a car, when I saw a police Panda car drive straight up to the boys. The cameramen were hidden so that everything would be as natural as possible. The policemen came out wanting to know why the boys were walking down that road in a group of six. Of course the boys were annoyed and became abusive and I was quite sure a fight would have resulted if I had not come to tell the officers what we were doing. What was wrong in walking down the street in a group of six or even ten, as long as they were not blocking the road? They were not fighting, just walking leisurely along for the cameras.

I took this up with the Inspector and his assistant who came to see us. They told us that the boys were being protected. Personally, I did not know what they were being protected from; surely the embarrassment caused to innocent people stopped by uniformed officers in a public place and asked where they were going and what business they had in walking down the road was not all in the name of protection! Thank goodness I was there and trouble was avoided.

I was happy working at Dashiki, especially when we started having a few good results like taking boys back to school to re-register for another couple of years, or introducing some to Paddington College of Further Education.

Vince reminded me very much of the Americans I had worked with in Nigeria. You could claim to be this or that, they wouldn't dispute it, but all they would like you to do was to prove it. My unorthodox programme was beginning to look as if it would answer the educational problems of the black boys brought to Dashiki.

I had not then got a PhD and never did get one, but it was flattering to see universities sending their PhD research students to work with us. They were looking closely at my alternative educational programme, which I had originally started when I wanted my own children to pass their eleven-plus and go to grammar school. With the exception of Jake they all went there; he got into St Augustine's in Kilburn. I saw the progress young people could make, with individual attention and determination on both sides.

I usually left home as soon as my children had gone to school or play centre, going into Paddington through Westbourne Grove. Sometimes the boys would still be asleep when I arrived, but as soon as I raised my voice and let out a bellow, they would all run down the stairs for fear of being told off by Vince or one of the other workers. We had three or four other workers doing different things: one did the accounts; another wrote off for funds; there were the secretaries, the cook, the detached youth worker.

I made the boys work for about three hours until lunchtime. As soon as I noticed that their attention was beginning to wander, I would let them go off for lunch. Since my pay was about a quarter short of what I had been earning with ILEA, I could have free lunches if I wanted, and if I stayed late I could have tea as well. The lady cook – the boys called her "bigger mother" – was a typical West Indian woman; I still do not know how she managed to fit all she did into one single day. She had a stall at Portobello market where she sold beads and trinkets. She cooked the food in Dashiki, did all the shopping, and would not leave Dashiki until she was sure everything was cleaned and set ready for another day. In between cooking and shopping she sat at her stall. She also had seven cats.

I did not have to take part in all of the evening's activities, although I arranged most of them; however I made sure I was present when we had important people coming to talk to the boys. So I tried to be there by ten o'clock, and leave around three in the afternoon to be home in time to welcome my kids home from school. It was such a good arrangement: they saw me in the morning at home, and they saw me when they came back from school in the evening. "Just like a mum who never worked," Christy told me once.

Dashiki was beginning to solve most of my problems. Money was short, but I did some broadcasting fairly regularly and knew that *Second-Class Citizen* would soon be out. Allison and Busby were still promising to publish it in a few weeks – I suppose I was expected to be thankful it was accepted in the first place.

What actually broke Dashiki was our rapid growth and success. When the authorities saw what we were doing they approved of Vince's application for a £49,000 grant, but he had to set up a committee to help him, and us, to cope with Dashiki and all the money now invested in it. There Vince made a very bad mistake.

He invited his friends, or people he thought were his friends, onto the committee and these friends started finding faults with Dashiki. Some of them told me they could run it better than Vince, and that my salary should be raised to ILEA level. I knew of the latter, because it was included in the grant.

I hate unpleasantness, especially when we blacks do it to ourselves. I did not attend any of their meetings. I don't think Vince attended one either. The committee wrote to the council to stop the grant and not only that, they also wrote to most of the boroughs from which we used to get our small fundings, to ask them to stop sending money for the boys in our care. Those on the committee were all West Indians, most of whom needed jobs, and were not aware that Dashiki needed so much money to survive. I am sure they thought Vince was making a fortune from running the place.

I came one morning, called the boys as usual, but I saw the hopelessness on the faces of those who came down. Their faces were accusing me, accusing us, the so-called black intellectuals, for letting our young people down once again. I suspected what had happened, but did not wish to voice it. I went into my office and saw Mr Birmingham, one of Vince's friends who worked with us, smiling there sheepishly. The committee had now appointed him as the new director, because Vince did not attend the committee meetings. I could go on working, they loved what I was doing and it would not affect me at all.

I did not know what to tell the man. I worked the whole of September and October, whilst Vince tried to pay me whenever he could raise the money, as he knew I had a large family. The council did not give the grant, because the members of the committee could not agree among themselves.

The place had to close down and many of the bright boys went to colleges of education. Social workers started to come to collect their charges because they had been told the boys would not be paid for, but the saddest part of the story was that some of the boys simply had to go to borstal because there was no place for them. Two of my very shy and rather simple boys – they would rather talk most of the time, yet one could make them useful in the garden, in cleaning the kitchen and the toilets, in doing any manual job – were sent to a mental hospital. These boys were not mad, they just did not look intelligent enough for some.

A small number of the committee knew all this, but they had scored their goal; Vince and Dashiki were becoming too well known. Vince went on fighting legal battles with the committee, but by this stage, I had stopped going there. If Dashiki had not died the way it did, I probably would still be working there. At the end of the day, the boys suffered simply because some of us niggers are too damned greedy! Those men remind me of Nigerian politicians!

I was glad, though, for those boys whom we helped to get places at Paddington College of Education. Eighteen months later one boy got his two ''A'' levels. And to think that when I first met him his greatest ambition was to kill a white policeman!

The boys were not hard like those at The Seventies; I'm sure that with money, some kind of alternative intensive education can work with most young people. Women should try it more with their own children during school holidays. One never knows, it could work, because one is better at teaching one's own child to read than a million teachers.

I know that now, in the 1980s, a good degree does not necessarily mean a good job, but those hours spent in intensive education at polytechnics or universities usually sharpen one's eyes and senses for all the alternative employment available around us. Success in life does not necessarily mean a nine to five job, but a young person who cannot enjoy a good book or is not taught how to make himself useful has been robbed of his full humanity.

I was sad to leave Dashiki.

26

The Black Teacher

The only great thing about my next job, as a supply teacher at Quintin Kynaston in St John's Wood, was that I met Mr Luke Enenmoh. He was from Asaba, a town only six miles from Ibusa. And of course we talked about nothing else but home.

I was in London while the civil war was fought in Nigeria, but that did not stop me from wanting to write a book about it. I had by late 1974 collected bits and pieces from relatives and friends. But until I met Mr Enenmoh, I hadn't the opportunity of hearing a detailed account from someone who was not only in Nigeria but in our Ibusa-Asaba area at the time.

Our lazy boys at Quintin Kynaston could not pronounce his surname, so they called him "Mr Luke" and behind his back "Black Kojak". This was because he was beginning to go bald. Having a curious sense of humour, he did not mind in the least.

Mr Enenmoh made me enjoy my brief stay at QK. And when, weeks later, I met his young wife, I was able to add them to our friends at the time. We spent most of our lunch hours talking, or should I say he talked and I listened. Like a typical Western Ibo man he liked women to listen when in his company and he to do the talking in his low African voice. He had been teaching for a very long time, and he would tell anyone who cared to ask that he was one of the masters of the old school. His subject was Mathematics, a subject which many teachers still shy away from. He was a wizard at it.

There was another Ibo man, one Mr Anakwe, also in Mathematics. He was then finishing his teaching practice. He stayed with us for only one term.

It was the first time I had worked with someone of Asian origin, one Mrs Patel. She was, like me, a supply teacher, but she had been trained in the profession and I had not. I was there to teach, not because I particularly wanted to but because, apart from at places like Dashiki, working as a teacher meant I could be at home during the holidays.

A supply teacher in the real sense should go from school to school. The ILEA realized that they could get honours graduates to teach on the cheap by calling them supply teachers yet attaching them to one school to do the work of an established member of staff, minus all the privileges. We were not covered during holidays or during sudden strikes, but our daily wages would work out slightly higher than those of an ordinary teacher. After about a term a supply teacher could apply to become a permanent member of staff.

It was here that the supply teacher could be led a vicious dance. The school Head literally held the life of such a teacher in the palm of his hands. You were invariably sent to the worst classes; you had no free periods, and yet you were expected to prepare lessons, write reports, mark papers, do all the things other teachers do in their free period; you often had to work on after you had done your full quota of teaching for the day. So for someone who wanted to get on, the next stop after becoming attached to one school was to remove the label "supply teacher" from one's name. Mrs Patel wanted this very much.

At first she sat with us, the blacks, and we talked about our work, our backgrounds, and our families. I came to know her very well, and thought she was a friend. Then suddenly she stopped sitting with us, and wouldn't even answer my "Good morning". I kept staring at her, not knowing what we had done. A few days later she walked over to Mr Enenmoh and myself and said that she wanted to be an established teacher and she would rather be seen to be getting on with the white teachers. She was sure the white teachers got upset when they saw us sitting together and talking, even though we all spoke in English. We laughed about this throughout the term and I personally admired her frankness. I was even more amused when I noticed that she would call it to the attention of the head of Social Studies, the subject which I taught, whenever I had done anything wrong, such as rushing out to do some shopping whenever I had finished teaching for the day and had no class to dismiss. Most of us women did this, even though we were supposed to stay in the staffroom until the school officially closed. I stopped this as soon as I knew that my friend, Mrs Patel, really wanted to be an established Social Science teacher. The irony was that she was led on, she really believed she would get the post, poor Mrs Patel – I saw her on the last day of term, sitting there in the corner of the staffroom looking forlorn. She did not get the job, and the ILEA did not ask her to come back. The pupils said they could not understand her brand of English. That was an experience I never forgot.

I had gone reluctantly into this teaching job, and would not have bothered if Allison and Busby had published *Second-Class Citizen* when they promised to. I delayed joining the school until the last day in October 1974. If Allison and Busby had published *Second-Class Citizen*, I was going to stretch the publication money until I got a contract fee for *The Bride Price*. Here again I was living in a dream land. When a contract for a book is signed, most publishers pay half the advance on signature, and the other half on publication. But when they say ''on signature'', one can wait for months.

I went to Quintin Kynaston as a last resort and after a few weeks of teaching there I knew that I would never become an established teacher, and would not even stay if they allowed me to. We were all required to apply for the position and would be considered the next term. I applied halfheartedly and when, during the next summer holidays, the ILEA asked me to be a full-time established teacher in another school, I did not even bother to reply. This was because I did not understand the way pupils were taught in this school, nor did I understand why teachers should play up to teenagers. I *was* beginning to understand then how young people could go through five years of schooling and not learn anything.

Quintin Kynaston was a very, very large comprehensive school. My first surprise was that the teachers had to provide pens, pencils, paper and duplicate copies of the book that the class would study. Most of the boys came to school carrying their sports gear in their Adidas bags and very little else. Some of the really tough ones did not bother to bring a bag at all, so when one saw them in the streets they looked like junior clerks going home from work.

The school reminded me of The Seventies, whose main purpose was to keep boys off the streets. Each lesson lasted about an hour and twenty minutes. You would have to spend the greater part of the night before preparing what you were going to teach, but when you got into the classroom the first twenty minutes were spent in settling boys down – they shouted abuse at you and called you names. I remember the black boys born here in England were fond of making Tarzan sounds whenever they saw me coming. They laughed at the Africanness in me, because they thought the West Indies was better than Africa, and they had nothing to do with the latter. Hence, much later, I was to support the group founded by Dorothy Kuya in Paddington to encourage black children to understand and like the Jewish child, by being taught the history of their people.

The first clash I had with the school was when I ordered a boy out of the class for misbehaviour. The sixteen-year-old had stood on his chair and then decided to go to look out of the window. When he was fed up with that, and knowing I was doing my best to ignore him, he turned round and started to throw paper kites at everybody including me. The rest of the class, not wanting to do any work at all, were pleased with the diversion this boy was creating. So I asked him to go out.

I saw the look of horror on the faces of the other boys as soon as I said this. They were suddenly quiet, as if readying themselves for a bomb. I thought the boy in question would feel deep disgrace, the way I felt when Miss Humble ordered me out after I told her I wanted to be a writer. I still laboured under the delusion that a school was a school, no matter whether it was the Methodist Girls' High School in Lagos, or Quintin Kynaston in St John's Wood, London. I forgot that at the Methodist Girls' High School we paid fees and sat very stiff exams before we got in, and when in, felt very privileged. I was forgetting that at QK, the ILEA paid us an extra stress allowance because they knew the type of children we were dealing with.

The boy went out, not before he had thrown all the pieces of paper on his desk at us, and banged into everything as if he had no eyes. Suddenly the rest of the class became noisy too because for the next five minutes he banged at our windows, made funny faces at us from the corridor, and went down to the other classes smashing everything as he went.

The Head was not amused. I was even expecting him to call me into his office and tell me that these were not the type of pupils one ordered out of the class. He did not, but he must have reported the incident to the Head of my department who later remarked casually that some of us teachers came from the type of schools where being sent out of the class was considered a disgrace. I knew then that I was not experienced enough to teach in a school of that size.

I must say that after this incident I taught at QK only as a dutiful, not a dedicated person. Most of the other teachers were really dedicated. We were all in an impossible situation, and some were trying to do their best. I could do nothing: I was the supply teacher who had little power and little respect, and my being black did not help, so I simply watched.

Out of about a hundred or so boys who entered the school that year, very few got enough GCEs to qualify them to go further. The teachers were so proud of these boys that for weeks their names were printed on the staffroom's notice board. To think that a few bus stops away was St Marylebone Grammar School where the average boy achieved between nine and eleven "O" levels at a sitting. The Labour Government closed the school because the Headmaster, who I understand had taught for years in one of the British colonies, refused to let it go comprehensive. Closing that school was a shame, because for most of the boys their topic of conversation was, "Which university are you trying for?" I remember phoning the school in panic when I thought my son had failed his "A" levels and would not get into his first university choice. The voice of the Deputy Head came over with assurance: "Ik will have no difficulty at all. If you have any difficulty, let us know. He won the first prize for Physics for all the schools in the London area last year, you know! The results are not out yet, so don't worry." And he was right. Ik went to university.

This was not because he was particularly clever. He ought to have done well in Physics because he was being taught by the master who wrote the textbook! There were only fifteen of them in class. In places like QK, most of the teachers' time was taken with basic discipline. In primary schools like St Mary Magdalene, where all my children were educated, and in secondary schools like St Marylebone, one could tell that given adequate attention few children are really uneducable. I was then living on a working-class estate, but because I knew that my family would probably live and work here in England, I had to utilize everything society could provide to help me raise them. They may not all be top academicians, but a parent likes to feel he or she has done her best. Schools like QK should have more teachers, more libraries, more money to run them, so that the pupils can then leave school with more hope.

Packing young people into large comprehensives, or dumping them in places like The Seventies, is like condemning a child before he is born. An uneducated person has little chance of happiness. He cannot enjoy reading, he cannot understand any complicated music, he does not know what to do with himself if he has no job. How many times have I heard my friends say, "I want to leave my boring job because I want to write, because I want to catch up with goings on in the theatre, because I want to travel and because I want to be with my family."

The uneducated man has no such choices. Once he has lost his boring job, he feels he's lost his life. That is unfair!

27

Women's Year

The year 1975 was one of those years on which I now look back and wonder where I got the energy to do all that I did.

I had a full-time job almost the whole year, I rewrote *The Bride Price* for non-Nigerian readers (as Heinemann of Nigeria did not bother to reply to Elizabeth's approach), I finished *The Moonlight Bride*, worked a little on *The Scapegoat*, and finished writing *The Slave Girl*. By the end of the year, I had written and had approved a BBC play, *A Kind of Marriage*.

Looking back, I knew that I had promised myself several things. That Rothay in Albany Street was to be my last council flat, that by the time I was thirty-five I would stop working outside my home. I love people but was beginning to realize by 1975 that I could never reach my full potential when there was somebody breathing down my neck.

For me the year opened in March, when Allison and Busby eventually published *Second-Class Citizen*. I had expected and spoken about this book for so long that when it eventually came out it was an anti-climax. I did not feel the type of excitement I felt with *In the Ditch*. For a start, the cover of that first edition of *Second-Class Citizen* was more than awful, it was insulting. An artist drew Christy, Alice and myself like the caricature of the Black and White Minstrels. However, I was grateful that it was published at all.

That same evening I had a small party to which I invited Mr Enenmoh and his family, my friend Sue Kay and her boyfriend, Chidi, the Olufunwas and my friend from the BBC, Florence Akst. Florence Akst had broken one of her feet, and she came with the plaster on. She has never lived that image down in my family – ten years later they still refer to her as "the lady with a foot and a half"!

Mr Enenmoh shocked my guests when he took a copy of *Second-Class Citizen*, poured half a bottle of whisky over it, broke kolanut on it, and commanded our Western Ibo gods through prayers to make me the greatest black writer Britain has ever seen, and to make the names of all my children greater still. I watched Sue Kay's face, and could see that she was really shaken. She said later that she thought we were doing voodoo. All Mr Enenmoh was doing as the oldest male present was to represent my father, and knowing that I intended making writing my career, was thanking our ancestors for revealing my vocation to me, and praying to them to make me use my gift responsibly.

It was a nice evening during which we danced to African and English records, and the children enjoyed being made so much fuss of by all present. I enjoyed myself as well. Months later I heard one of our lecturers at the Institute of Education, where I still pursued my postgraduate programme, talking about the big party I gave. Sue had said, "It was a greater show than many people put on at weddings." I'm sure she meant Western weddings, not Nigerian ones. But somehow *Second-Class Citizen* gave me the confidence to invite all these very close friends to my flat weeks before London and everybody started telling me that I had written a good book.

London did. The press did. Everybody started phoning me for an interview. A teacher waved the *Guardian* at me and said, "Look, what a long review", and another said, "The book was reviewed in yesterday's *Sunday Times*." I take *The Times*, but was so busy feeling sorry for myself about the book's delay that it never occurred to me that anybody would take the trouble to go beyond the awful jacket. When everybody started talking about it in the staffroom, I could hardly wait to get home and unearth my copy of *The Sunday Times* to read about it.

At home, my lot had thrown our *Sunday Times* into a bin. I phoned Chidi and he brought his, and we rushed and bought a copy of the *Guardian* and read Carol Dix's review. When everybody had gone, I took out a copy of *Second-Class Citizen* and read it again. I had forgotten half the things I had put in there, and somehow when I was writing the original script I thought no publisher would publish such personal nonsense. When the lady from Allison and Busby said she was going to edit it, I thought she was going to cut parts of it out. She did not. She corrected the typographical and grammatical mistakes but left the whole book as I had done it.

My first reaction was to be angry with myself. Why did I allow my feelings to be so transparent? Why did they not tell me that they would not edit it, and why had I not read it again myself? The manuscript had been lying about for so long that I hated the sight of it. Then I consoled myself, saying that like most mistakes I would just have to live with it. I had put more of me into that book than I intended, but then as the Cyprian Ekwansi told me in Nigeria in 1981, "That is creativity."

I did not have much time to feel sorry for myself. I was again becoming famous. Sandra Harris of Thames Television was to talk to me about it – my first television appearance. I thought we would all die of excitement.

The children told Mr Harper at St Mary Magdalene, and the whole of the school, teachers and pupils, watched. I dashed home from my own school since I could not use the school TV. Some of my boys at Quintin Kynaston never came back after lunch, because "Miss" was on TV. Oh! it was madness. One would have thought that I had written a masterpiece. How fickle public opinion is! The book you do not think much of, they come to like. Writers simply have to write, and not worry so much about what people think, because public opinion is such a difficult horse to ride.

Second-Class Citizen was reviewed by so many papers. Everybody had something to say about it. *The Times Literary Supplement* commissioned me to write an article about youth education in London when they heard that I studied as well as wrote. I didn't think the Head of Quintin Kynaston liked the idea, as he did not know what I was going to come up with. I however wrote a piece called "Time Bomb", drawing my material from The Seventies, Dashiki and QK. Somehow, that piece in the *TLS* foretold what happened in Brixton and Toxteth years later – that when people are not educated enough for the job market, it is like a time bomb ticking away which could explode in the streets. I knew that by writing the way I did, I was writing myself out of the orthodox educational system, but I was determined not to go back to teaching after the summer holidays anyway.

After the TV appearance, people made me look at myself in a new light. I could talk humorously – even though it was a desperate attempt to cover chronic shyness – and even though there was little sense in what I was saying, I could talk. Only God knows why other women, married, single and widowed, were all interested in hearing about the boring way I coped with five children single-handed. Well, I won't say quite single-handed, because in 1975 I got the first payment from my husband in three years. It was £6. I was told he went to Clerkenwell, and swore again that the children were his, that I was his wife, and that he was tired of studying. He got a very, very low paid job. The type of position I helped him get in 1972 was now out of his reach. Lost opportunities! I personally thought that he must have read *Second-Class Citizen* and felt guilty somehow. Most of us have a conscience after all.

I had stopped thinking about him, however. My life was so full that the pace of it sometimes frightened me. I would wake at about 4.30 am and write till 7.30 before getting everybody ready for school. I had to be at Quintin Kynaston at 8.30 and would be there till four in the afternoon. On my way back, I shopped in St John's Wood. Home was usually very quiet, because with Chiedu at Highbury and Ik at St Marylebone, evenings were devoted to homework. Those two schools kept their pupils really busy in the evenings. The younger ones simply had to follow the elders' example. I banned television on weekdays, and the kids went to the library, to Brownie meetings or to tap and dance classes. I think I had the time to do all I did simply because I filled the children's time with activities. We were lucky in Rothay. Everything was within five minutes' walk. The school was only a few streets away. The tap dances took place in the big local Tenants Association building next to our flat and the local Brownies used the Christ Church school building for their meetings. I did not have to take them there myself. They knew where they ought to be each day. As for Mrs Slattery, the children's librarian at Robert Street, her name was mentioned so many times that I sometimes confused her with one of the teachers. Everything she said was quoted and the books she recommended were read. In front of the library was our local Co-op supermarket, where Christy got our daily loaf. We called her the bread woman, and as she was so keen to get a new book to read every day, she didn't find the task too much. I had by now got my own washing machine, so Chiedu could now concentrate on her school work. She used to take charge of the laundry. The boys cleaned the house at weekends, and they washed up after Sunday dinner. I had a great deal to do but I managed to get the family to help, too. All these neat arrangements became difficult when they grew older, but in 1975, when I think they needed me most, it all worked.

Readers must have liked *Second-Class Citizen*, for in late April Allison and Busby gave it to an American publisher, and of course this meant more money to be shared between them and my agent. It was for me a big step and the fattest single fee I had ever been paid for my writing: my share when it eventually arrived in May was £322.98. My take home pay from ILEA as a full-time teacher was £223.00, and my rent was £90 a month. Of course by this time I was no longer entitled to free dinners and most of the state benefits because my tax returns were higher than those of the really poor. I felt really rich, for Allison and Busby not only paid the £125 publication fee for *Second-Class Citizen*, they also signed and paid the contract fee of £125 for *The Bride Price*.

Apart from Curtis Brown's percentage, I was paid most of the money. I was beginning to look forward to when I would have saved enough to make up the £4000 deposit I needed for the house I hoped to buy later in the year.

I met my publishers for a meal to plan in detail the talk I would give on Tuesday 22 April 1975. For the first time, there was a pressure on me to leave my agents, Curtis Brown. I saw Margaret Busby's point, but I needed Elizabeth Stevens to bully Clive Allison into paying. Maybe if I was not thinking of buying a house I would have given my agent up.

Allison and Busby are not by any means the ideal publishers. Clive would never pay one's royalties on time, but I never felt intimidated by him. As for Margaret, at one time I was beginning to see her as the sister I did not have. The relationship we all had in those early days was funny. It was like a hurricane. Always fights over money, but everything had a way of ending well.

I could not say the same about my agent. Maybe it was because she was typically English and behaved that way. One could shout at Clive on the phone or in his office, although it did not mean that one would win. But when I visited my agent in Craven Hill, I was invariably kept waiting in a beautiful very American-looking reception hall, just as one waits for a dentist or job interview. To cap it all, Allison and Busby found me the American publisher who is now a very good friend of the family, and much later I found the OUP, BBC and Granada Television myself. Why then have an agent?

After I had agreed to the advance on the phone, I would then phone Elizabeth to sign the contract, and of course by doing that her firm would claim ten per cent and charge the VAT to the author. One sees in films of writers' lives the agent visiting the writer and the two planning out their line of campaign, but in real life Elizabeth visited me only once, to see my first house in Crouch End. I remember that she was so nicely mannered, as she sat in the same seat and sipped her tea, that she left me feeling as if I had just invited my Headmistress to tea. When Margaret and Mrs Lyn Allison came, we three toured every room and speculated on the prices.

The talk that I gave at the Africa Centre, the first formal talk on my book, was a big success. It was advertised in many papers, even *Contact*, a journal for teachers, so my colleagues at Quintin Kynaston saw it. A. and B. had brought copies of *Second-Class Citizen* to the talk, and I think they sold quite a lot because I saw a faint smile on Margaret's face.

1975 was International Woman's Year. I had never heard the word ''feminism'' before then. I was writing my books from the experiences of my own life and from watching and studying the lives of those around me in general. I did not know that writing the way I was, was putting me into a special category. I had the first inkling of it on 28 June 1975 when the International Women's League invited me to give a speech. My fee was a free lunch.

I did not know that I might have been paid; I was happy to be invited at all. I remember sewing a special blouse from the piece I bought from the remnant counter at John Lewis's and making a scarf of the same material. I tied a lappa instead of wearing a skirt. I felt really chic!

When I saw the people on the panel, Lady this and Princess that, my stomach ached. I knew the only way to beat these ladies was to shock them. And I did. They all came with nicely typed, readly prepared speeches which they distributed to all of us. (I did not know that that was the way one does it.) I carried all my speeches in my head, and ten years later I still do. Sometimes I would take the trouble to write out all I was going to say, only to lose the paper when rushing to catch the plane or my train. Even when I did manage to get everything ready, I found reading out speeches rather boring. So nowadays I take the trouble to know my subject inside out, so that I can approach it from any angle. Thank God for those days' experience.

Before I spoke, the general talk was drifting to women's emancipation, birth control in the Third World, and how the Third World women were suffering. I don't know why I hated people talking about us like that. I still hate it, and because of this I find myself disagreeing on everything suggested by white women, even though I know that some of those suggestions could be quite relevant. I think that like the black boys in the school I taught, one simply becomes fed up with seeing oneself as a problem.

So I got up and shocked all those ladies, telling them to mind their own business and leave us Third World women alone. One could have heard a pin drop. I thought at one time I would be thrown out. But I was not. As if that was not enough, Dr Harriet Sibisi, a lady I came to know much later, a black South African who was then lecturing in Oxford and an eminent anthropologist, stood up and said that the blacks in South Africa were there to increase and multiply, because how did we know how many of them would survive the white tyranny. And all the black women and men present, and some thinking white women, cheered and applauded my speech!

Oh! the age of innocence. I told those women everything I felt, and they applauded me for my sincerity and assured me that steps would be taken to bring the black and white women together. In my blind and stupid way, I did hit on the truth. They were not joking, they meant what they said. A voice asked where they could get copies of my latest book. I had only one copy, which was snapped up, but I told them that after the lunch break, I would bring round a hundred copies.

During the break I phoned my children, and Chiedu, Ik and Jake brought round the books I had bought at a discount from A. and B. only the week before. I knew I could sell my books, because the three hundred hardback copies I retrieved from Barrie and Jenkins when they wanted to pulp *In the Ditch* were all sold within six months. I just sold them to friends and relatives. There are still copies of *In the Ditch* and *Second-Class Citizen* on the bookshelves of most Ibusa people in London.

The children were there waiting for me. I had to call a taxi and took all the books to the hall. I had by then missed the lunch which was to be my pay. But I autographed so many copies, and sold all the books, that a Dutch woman who wanted 86 copies had to be sent to Allison and Busby.

I think that talk really put me on the map as an international author. What I did not realize at the time was that more than three quarters of those present came from abroad. I still don't know how Lucy Kaye, secretary of the International Women's League, found me. Most of the lady members were so rich, one would have felt sick simply just looking at the clothes they wore, the number of chauffeur-driven Rolls waiting outside, the way they talked in whispers . . . Oh! they were different.

And yet they invited me to talk. Was I sorry? No, I was not. I'm still not, because that was the foundation on which I still hold a lot of my beliefs. I am not so blunt now, and have since met many, many really nice women, white, black and pink, but in 1975 and 1976, I was still feeling very bitter. I am glad I wrote *Second-Class Citizen* and that it brought me the minor success it did. Because that book was therapeutic – both writing it and talking about it.

I made over £100 profit that day, and paid Allison and Busby back the following week. I was already feeling guilty at making so much money and instead of asking them to deduct the cost of the books from next year's royalties, I paid them cash. Now that I publish my own books, I understand why Clive always remembers that incident. He told me that a few weeks later the Dutch woman I met at the conference placed her order from Holland. The book was a big success not only for me but them as well. Somehow with its publication and success, I stopped scratching the front of my nose each time people referred to me as a writer.

28

Self-Catering Holiday

When the summer term was nearing its end, I knew that I did not want to go back to teaching. The emotional strength needed to cope with classes of over thirty boys, most of whom did not wish to come to school in the first place and in whom one had no way of instilling a shred of discipline or setting any standard, was beyond me.

I knew it was still too early to pack up work altogether. I wanted a home of my own. I resented having to pay all that money for a flat that would never be mine. The money I was to make from writing would never be enough. I did not let all that bother me, though, not on that last day, when I knew that I would have six to eight weeks all to myself to do exactly what I wanted.

Mr and Mrs Olufunwa, our former landlord and landlady, had by then learned about buying and selling houses in London. I was going to enlist their help. A teacher could get a mortgage easily and in *Contact*, the magazine for teachers, I saw an insurance advertisement for Sun Life of Canada. One had to take up a kind of endowment and if one's income was not quite enough, a mortgage would have to be arranged. The insurance man, a very good-looking Irishman by the name of Mr O'Hagan, called, and was so nice that he made it all seem simple. I could get my agents to give me a copy of my tax returns and with what the ILEA paid me, I could get a mortgage, after I had saved about £4000 and taken up the insurance. Later, I knew that it was an expensive way to buy one's first house, but then that was how it worked. If you were a woman in my position you had to pay more for most things. I wanted a house, and I was not going back to teaching. So before the end of term, I made sure I got my income statement from the ILEA. I think Curtis Brown came up with the statement that I could get between £800 and £1000 a year from writing. But my savings were not up to £4000 yet, and I was not going back to Quintin Kynaston. How was I to make the money?

Buying a house was a really big step in those days. I took up the insurance, and was glad about that because it meant that should I die suddenly, my children would not be thrown out of our house. This gave me so much peace of mind: I had met two Nigerian brothers whose parents suddenly died in a motor accident, and they were thrown out of their parents' house within weeks of the funeral simply because their parents had not taken out a mortgage protection scheme. Those poor boys were sent to Dashiki to continue their education; the elder boy said that he was going to be an artist. I doubt whether they ever made it, as the younger boy was one of those sent to borstal when the project ended.

I always remember that incident. And to imagine my family being forced to go to places like that made me sweat all of a sudden. So although I knew I was paying a great deal, Mr O'Hagan's endowment policy gave me peace of mind. And I also knew that because I paid regularly, he was not going to ask me when I had saved enough, whether I was still teaching or not. And as it happened, he didn't. Although I had butterflies in my stomach many, many times, I knew I had never defaulted, which made me feel good.

All that was in the future. In summer 1975, I simply asked Mr Olufunwa to go on and look for a house for us. The story of the Olufunwas and my family is really interesting. They were the landlord and landlady who persecuted us and later threw us out when we first came to England. My husband never forgave them, but I did when Mr Olufunwa came to our house several times to apologize, and when I saw that they had at last started having children. I don't think Mrs Olufunwa ever forgave herself, though.

In the early 1970s I had never been to areas of North London like Enfield, Crouch End, or Muswell Hill. I used to travel along Muswell Hill Broadway on the 134 bus when I worked at North Finchley Library, but I never got to know the area. I was only used to the elegant grey buildings around Kentish Town and Albany Street. But when I took Chiedu and Alice to see the Olufunwas' new home in Enfield, I was hooked. Theirs was a little doll-like house with red carpets throughout. It had a dream all-blue bathroom and a real garden, not the sort owned by the council. They were lucky. They had to leave their house in Kentish Town where they had lodged, and because they were husband and wife, Camden gave them a hundred per cent mortgage. A single parent with any number of children, even one in a better job, could not get that. And if that single parent happened to be a woman, and a black one, the idea would forever remain a dream in her head. I saw that house in the early 1970s but I never had the courage to say that I would like a house like that. Like the social worker I had then, they would have asked, "But where are you going to get the money from?" I watched, though, as my little Alice enjoyed playing in the private garden, the first time she had ever done so, and for a while I felt my kids were deprived. But I did not worry too much because that was the summer the other three, Ik, Jake and Christy, went to Norwich and stayed with Mrs Walls for two weeks.

Three years later, I had the courage to tell the Olufunwas that I was looking for a house and they believed me. Not before my children insisted that we needed a real holiday. When they said real, I knew what they meant.

My experiences of holidays as a one-parent family would fill a book. But the one that stood out in my memory was the one we took in Deal in 1973. We were told that this place, tucked away somewhere in Deal, was beautiful, and specially chosen for women and their children. Of course there was the usual talk of the seaside, the white sand and the night life. I had published *In the Ditch* by then and could have afforded a real holiday, but since it was cheap, being subsidized by the council and specially kept for parents who could not otherwise go on holiday, I said, "Okay, we will go." We did. And it was hell!

We were packed into one room which had just been vacated by a family that morning, and I think those people had used the blankets for their latrines! Jake was the first person to realize. He jumped on the bunk bed, only to let out a scream – "Ma, Ma . . . wee!" I could not look, it was too terrible.

Chiedu, knowing me, suspected that I would demand we were taken home. She ran and got the students who worked there, who came and collected the blankets. They gave us some they claimed were clean, but they stank so much we never used them. Luckily, we had brought some others, and I came with my ever-useful African cloth in which I wrapped my exhausted children at night.

Later we saw why the former occupants of our room relieved themselves inside. The toilet was useless. One had to tip the flat pan, and it would bring out everything that was there before. Then you'd add yours and tip it back. There was no water system. The kids thought it was curious but fun. I felt it was not only heartless to send women with children there, but inhuman. I was not surprised when four or five women started screaming in the middle of the night and had to be taken back to London. I would have returned as well, but my children had never seen such a large open space in which to do exactly what they liked. We were taken every morning to the seaside in Deal. I soon learned to control myself and use the toilet there by the seaside, which was clean. And we had plenty of sunshine and there were miles of white sand by the sea. It was overcrowded, but we always left our "compound" by eight o'clock with packed sandwiches and returned around six-thirty in the evening. We only returned to that horrible place to sleep, and I was sure that my family enjoyed themselves. I had my bank cards with me and could give them decent lunches when we got fed up with the sandwiches; we had toast in the morning, with tea or coffee, sandwiches in the afternoon, and rolls and humble soup in the evening. But it was a very demeaning experience, and I never forgave myself for exposing my family to it.

I thought I would write about it, and told one social worker so. I don't know whether I could have done, because it was the year I was thinking of repeating my Part One in Sociology, and bad holidays were the least of my troubles. But after the revealing descriptions in *In the Ditch*, I only had to say "I think I may write about it" for people to take me seriously. In short, the council returned all the money I paid, with a letter of apology. I understand the place was closed. That put me off English charity holidays forever.

In 1975 Chiedu said her friends were always telling her what a lovely time they had. We could go to France, she suggested. I thought, no, being another country it would be too expensive. We chose Devon, which was even more expensive than France. But it was a real holiday because we paid for everything, or almost. The train was the best part for me. I enjoyed travelling in England on British Rail. There is nothing like going to my places of lecture by train. Some universities are kind enough to let me travel first class. In 1975 the fact that we were travelling by train and not by coach, as we had done when we went to Deal two years before, was heaven.

This time, because of the extra money from writing, we had radios, sunglasses and very, very smart seaside clothes from Marks and Spencer and John Lewis. The place in Devon was Brixham. We did not have miles of sandy shores, because the place was full of pebbles, but it was quieter and smelt of fish and shrimps which I liked because it reminded me of Lagos. We spent a whole day on a steamer, and the night life was good for the children. One night there was a dancing competition at which Christy and Jake won the first prize, simply by choosing one of the numbers their tap teacher had taught them. As most of the other children were amateurs and mine were professionals (they were already tap dancing in small local shows), and Jake was a natural born dancer, I was not surprised that they won. Chiedu won the third prize for singing the Negro spiritual, "O Gracious Lord, see what da white man does": the prize was free groceries from Pontins for all of us for our whole stay. It was nice. I didn't get out much, however, because the holiday was self-catering. We bought all our food from a little supermarket which had everything (but cost a little more) and someone had to do the cooking – and of course that person was me. Apart from sailing on the boat once, and going to the seaside once, I spent all the time in the kitchen. I have never been so happy to go home.

I watched dumb as my family chattered and told their friends and neighbours what a happy holiday they had had. The following morning I was so full of anger, but did not know who to vent it on. I had the type of feeling I had had the day I marched down to the *New Statesman* to ask Mr Crossman for my articles. I marched back into the flat, took a £10 note, and sat on the top of a Number 3 bus which stopped in front of our house. When the bus got to Trafalgar Square, I got out and started to mingle with some Americans and Japanese. They asked me when I came to London, and I told them that I had only come from Lagos the day before. One commented that my English was not bad for someone who had just come from Nigeria for the first time. I told them that I had attended a school called the Methodist Girls' High School. One of the American ladies told me that she knew of a half-Nigerian Methodist preacher who came from Georgia, and asked me if I knew him. I said no. She was disappointed, but we didn't let that ruin our day.

I followed them to the Mall, watched the Changing of the Guard, and saw the famous Number 10 for the first time in my life, even though I had by then lived in London for twelve years. I went with them into one of the eating places in Piccadilly, ordered and ate a lovely salad made by someone else, topped it with a huge cheesecake and drank three portions of my favourite drink, bitter lemon. I went out and bought a bobby's hat, perched it on top of my head and bought a small Union Jack which I waved at anything that passed, just like my friends the tourists were doing. I even had my photograph taken in front of Big Ben for fifty pence. It was lovely.

I got home at seven. My family had already called the police. I don't think those policemen understood that I love my family very, very much, but that I needed time to escape. If not I would have drowned. Doing things like that, rather impulsive to them, kept me afloat, kept my head above water. Now, in the 1980s, I sometimes stay two long nights at the best hotels in California all by myself, just paddling in the pools and watching other people, while my publishers and my host universities think I am already back in England with my family. Another haven I've only just discovered is the Holiday Inn in Lagos. I have now learnt to break my journey to Ibusa in Lagos, lazing for a couple of days, giving myself time to recover from my London family before facing the onslaught of my Ibusa one.

I don't think I would have thus indulged myself if I did not need it. I had an inkling that if I did not do it, nobody was going to think or dream that I needed such breaks. For how could my children ever imagine that their mother would love to wear a bobby's hat and wave a Union Jack in front of Big Ben? How could they know that I would indulge in cheesecake, when I knew that I put on weight with the very air I breathed?

Those policemen, God bless them, they thought I went to a boyfriend's house. They questioned me so much that my daughter Chiedu, whose idea it was to call them in in the first place, broke down and started to cry. I promised to be a good parent and they told me how clever my children were and how sensible. I agreed with them. Chiedu kept crying all the time. She told me she was sorry she called them: she thought I was lost and she was frightened.

I told her not to worry, that I knew what I was doing, but how could I tell her the truth? It sounded too stupid even to repeat. Years later, they knew about it, and I think they felt guilty. I was glad then that I did not tell them, because their feeling guilty would have ruined the whole day for me.

As for me, I always look back on that sunny day as one of the greatest days I have ever had in London. It was glorious!

29

A Glimpse of Success

I thought that as soon as I had enough for a deposit, I would simply scan the newspapers, pick from hundreds of houses being advertised every week and then move. Moving house in London is not that simple. I have seen huge men get really disappointed, I have seen women break into desperate tears when their dream house goes to another buyer.

Every weekend I went with the Olufunwas, peering into agents' windows, getting brochures and visiting houses. Apart from peering into catalogues, seeing other people's houses is another nosy way of knowing how the other half lives.

In 1975 I was already thirty-one, but it did not occur to me that I was fussy. It was when I started looking for a place to live that I realized that I had acquired certain tastes and so had my family. We all wanted a large redbrick house, fairly old with high ceilings. I needed a large house just in case I could not pay the mortgage and would have to sublet some rooms. So the house, which had to have at least seven or eight rooms, must not cost a penny more than £15,000.

We eventually found a narrow redbrick house in Coniston Road, Muswell Hill. It was just ideal. I liked its huge morning room that opened into an equally large although wild garden. I liked that house very much but the lady said she was not going below £16,500. I tried to see whether I could raise enough money to make up the deposit. I had to be careful as I did not wish to drag myself down with a really big mortgage. Knowing myself, I would not be able to do anything creative if I had to worry about money. Being born into poverty and having spent a greater part of my early child-hood wondering where I was going to get the next meal, I did not want that to happen to me again or my family.

The Olufunwas loved the house too, and as soon as I left to go to a book launch at the Africa Centre, they whisked my whole family off there and told the woman who owned the house to show them round. This she did and my family fell for the house. Much as I did not like making painful deci-sions, I simply had to say no. My friends meant well, but I have learnt that when things become financially difficult few friends can help. They would move into their own home, I thought, with two of them working to pay their mortgage. But to pay for this one would just be me and my Chi, biting my nails in the dark. No, we could not have it. I remember Ik saying tearfully, "Oh Mum, it's such a posh area, the son of the lady has a boat and a sports car."

I think my friends got cold feet after that, but I prayed hard that God would reserve a house for my family and myself in this area of North London and within a price range I could afford.

We went to see a huge house in Cecil Park, Crouch End. It was a really big one with large rooms, about ten of them, arranged on three floors. I particularly remember this house because it was the only one owned by a black man. He came from Trinidad. We being black, he was very frank. He laughed nervously when he recounted the unsavoury experiences he had before he could get the house. It was a very beautiful house and well looked after. I commented on that, and he laughed mischievously, winking one eye. The council gave him a grant when his neighbours kept complaining that the look of his house was bringing down the prices of the others in the street. He had been asking them for a grant for years. He used the money in improving the house, putting in two extra bathrooms and two extra kit-chens. Five years after the grant he was legally free to sell the house, as he was going home to Trinidad. I wondered why he was going home, because he was a tall, dark, nicely spoken Trinidadian. He was not old at all, and I thought he could still work here for at least fifteen years. But then I did not know him that well.

He was allowed to have tenants, which was why the house was conver-ted into three flats. One English tenant turned out to be a thief, another Arabic one a drug smuggler, a third an Irish crook who tried to take the house from him. And then there was this young black woman who had a room but was not seen for three months and then turned up suddenly accusing him of having stolen her personal effects. She took him to court saying she had left things worth thousands of pounds in the room. She was so busy claiming all this that nobody talked of the rent owed to him. He had kept the room locked for her for two months. He won the case, but it did cost him a lot and he had to stay away from work visiting this lawyer and going to that court. After that he locked up half the house and only allowed relatives to stay. Now he was selling.

The man had a passion for birds. I was struck with one parrot he had called Enoch Powell, and taught to say, "I am Enoch Powell and will die slowly and then slowly roast in hell." "That man Enoch Powell is going to roast in hell, you know. The voice of the people is the voice of the gods," the man quoted, "and it is not only the voice of the people but the voice of the birds." He gave us tea, rum and biscuits. We all laughed, but somehow I became nervous. I did not want a house with so many birds. I knew he would take them all with him, but I was suddenly uneasy. I wanted to leave. Besides, I could not afford to buy and maintain such a mansion – it was too big and who was going to give me the emotional energy to cope with so many difficult tenants?

The estate agents then showed us a house in Nelson Road. It was just the right size and fully decorated so I would not need to do much to it in the first few years. At last, I said, as I breathed a sigh of relief. We rushed to the estate agent and paid the first deposit of £500, for them to remove the house from the notice board. I would then get the building society and Mr O'Hagan to work to get the remaining £3000 I had so far managed to save. So we were going to move into our new house before Christmas. We were jubilant! Chiedu went from school to see the house but couldn't find it and I was glad, as I did not want to see again the kind of disappointment I saw on their faces when Coniston Road fell through. But they told everybody nonetheless!

People started to respect me, somehow. Generations of working-class people lived around Mornington Crescent and Cumberland Market. All the next generation wanted was to be given another new council flat, to be allowed to furnish it themselves and have a big new shiny car outside. Buying a house on mortgage and having the courage to move away from the area was something not many of my neighbours were too keen to undertake, yet many were rich taxi drivers who would have found such a move easier than people like me. That was one of the reasons why schools like St Mary Magdalene educated three to four generations of people in that area. Mr Harper, the Head, was there when many of the present children's mums and dads were kids themselves.

Some of the local women started talking to me for the first time – considering that we had lived there for six years, I thought that was not too bad. They wanted to know how much I'd had to save before getting a mortgage. When I told them that one needed at least £3000 one or two exclaimed that they had more than that in the post office. I could believe this because some of my neighbours had Jaguar and Rover cars and expensively furnished flats which their wives worked really hard to keep clean. And they went on holidays every year.

What surprised me most was when a neighbour of ours won £40,000 on the pools. I thought, gosh, give me that and all my problems would be over. I could buy my dream house in Coniston Road. The whole family went on holiday to Disneyland in California and their son had a new chopper bicycle. When they returned from California, however, we thought they were then going to move to Hampstead. But ten years later the family was still there.

Many of our neighbours, like my people in Ibusa, felt safer living next to their families and friends. They had their roots there, and would not dream of leaving their grannies or locals for new addresses, however independent such moves might make them. Many people feared the costs of house maintenance, the expense of which could sometimes shake one very badly.

I had no roots in Rothay and did not make friends there, as I had done at Pussy Cat Mansions. St Mary Magdalene, a school which I once regarded as our extended family, was about to close because it was too small. Luck was with us for by then Christy was already at Camden School for Girls, and that meant that Alice would be admitted automatically – the school likes to have sisters in the same institution. So there was nothing holding me back in Rothay.

My heart kept missing beats each time the bill for the solicitor came in and then the bill for the surveyor. It was a happy coincidence when George Braziller, my American publisher, came to tell us that all his staff in New York liked *The Bride Price* and that they were going to publish it too. I needed every penny I could lay my hands on to make my moving easier, so it was welcome news.

On 22 August 1975 I received the American edition of *Second-Class Citizen*. It was much better-looking than the first English edition and this was to me a shot in the arm. I know many publishers think that the cover of a book does not matter. Some writers don't mind either, but to me my books are akin to my children. Before any of my children were born, I planned what colour of sheet, what type of dress the baby was going to come home in. Even when I had Jake in 1962 and was a very poor, dependent housewife, I made sure that the romper suit he came home from the hospital in was new. I was sorry he had to be covered in Ik's shawl, a shawl given to me by the American Ambassador in Nigeria. Can anyone imagine what a shock it would be to a mother if her new baby was covered in out-landish clothes? The Americans seemed to have made up for it to me. Thank goodness the first English edition of *Second-Class Citizen* was soon sold out, and Margaret redesigned the cover. It was still based on the lines of the early one, but she managed to remove the huge red lips which the original artist thought I should have to emphasize my Africanness.

The next day, George Braziller invited us all to dinner. During the course of the meal, he asked me what I was going to write about next. He hinted that the age of Africa in literature had gone and that people were talking more of Australia. I remember becoming moody all of a sudden. I tried to lift my spirits and be cheerful, at least for the benefit of Margaret and Clive who were also there, but I could not. Margaret became fidgety, trying desperately to keep the conversation going. Whenever people say anything bad about places I love, I always come out with a shocking statement. My way of telling people to shut up is to shock them. So to answer Braziller's question and to stop him from repeating the fact that Africa was no longer fashionable in terms of literature, I said that I was going to write a saga. That my books about Africa would take the form of a saga. That I would go back in time and write a novel based around the Africa that my mother knew, then join this with another novel, the title of which I had not then worked out. This would be followed by *The Bride Price*, then *Second-Class Citizen*, then an autobiography that would string together and bring them all up to date. Every five years or so, I would bring the saga up to date. I made this statement ten years ago in anger, and yet when I am not angry I find that I am doing exactly that. Maybe Freud was right: "There is nothing like a slip of the tongue." Out in Ibusa people put it better: "We all speak the truth when we are drunk!"

Africa will always be a topical subject. Now, in 1985, with Botha of South Africa confused, blowing hot and cold, and the famine in Ethiopia for which Geldof organized the greatest pop festival the world has ever seen to raise millions for our starving children, and Nigeria, the richest black country, staging another coup, Africa is still very hot.

In any case, when I got home I found that I had talked myself into another novel. I was not going to let Braziller face me the following year asking, "Are you still writing your saga", and have to reply, "I am still thinking about it." I was going to start straightaway. Thus, on 16 August, I worked out all the subtitles of the book that is now *The Slave Girl*. For the first time I was going to write a book that would need research. It was going to cover the period 1920-1944 and was going to be based in southern Nigeria, to cover the history of womanhood and link it with the happenings of the rest of the world. The book starts with the nerve gas shot into Africa by Britain's enemy, because at that time Nigeria belonged to Britain, and it ends with Britain winning the Second World War, just around the time at which people like myself were born.

I normally start writing straightaway, as soon as I have a vague subject, but I could not do so with *The Slave Girl*. By then I had never been to Onitsha, where my mother spent her early childhood, nor to many of the places described in the book. I recalled most of the bits and pieces she had told me, right from the time I could first remember, and I pieced all these things together, and again went back to my Sociology and relearned my concept of slavery. There are different kinds of enslavement. The body can be enslaved, but the greatest type of slavery is the one most black African countries are going through at the moment: the enslavement of ideas. At the end of the book Ojebeta Ogbanje was happy to be married in church, happy that her bride price had been paid, but we readers know it was her embracing Christianity, and the way Christianity had been preached to her, that was her greatest enslavement.

It came out as a small book, yet I put a great deal of thought into it, and it was difficult to write because I did not have a story already made up in my mind. After jotting down the subtitles and realizing the extent of work *The Slave Girl* would need, I put it aside in 1975 as I had so many things on my mind. First the proofs of *The Bride Price* arrived, and Margaret and Elizabeth always wanted me to read the proofs, which I still do not like doing. As soon as the words have been squeezed out of my head, I really

don't like being forced to read them again. But I had to. I made sure I put
The Slave Girl right out of my mind, otherwise the ideas would start
mixing with each other.

Some flattering incidents were happening at this time as well. All of a
sudden, Innes Lloyd of the BBC phoned to ask me to write a play for television. I said yes, I could. I had read, studied and acted Gwendoline in *The
Importance of Being Earnest* and I had read many works of Shakespeare.
Those were the only ideas I had about writing plays. I had also by then read
the early life of Jackie Kennedy, and learnt from it never to say "no" to an
assignment you want and you know you could do well if given the opportunity. Had she told them at her photographic interview that she could not
take photographs, she would not have got the job and would not have met
the senator who later became her husband. I was not looking for a senator,
but I needed the money for my move and wanted to try other forms of
writing so that my whole future should not depend on my royalties.

Just a few weeks after I signed the contract with the BBC for the play *A
Kind of Marriage*, Lyn and Margaret came to say that Granada wanted me to
write an episode for their *Crown Court* series. I could not believe my ears.
Margaret's eyes were like saucers. She was really pleased and I think proud,
too. She kept telling me, "Buchi, you've made it. Many people want to get
into television because that's where the money is, not in books." I understood what she was saying years later, but I'm always condemned to earn
my living through the most difficult channel. I don't like working for
television as a career, although I would not mind turning one or two of my
books into dialogue or doing a couple of documentaries once in a while. I
know that I love people very much, but I could not work for a long time
close to people on a project that demanded a high input of emotional
energy. One writes in isolation, and the longer the isolation, the deeper the
work. I cannot cope with the pressure and artificiality of television work.
Film and television people are another set, who can raise one's hopes today
that something big is going to be done, and dash them tomorrow with
little or no explanation. As I very much hope and pray to live long, I steer
clear of these people as much as possible. But 1975 was my lucky year and
neither Granada nor the BBC broke their promises.

Elizabeth, who had worked with many writers, told me straightaway
that it might never happen again. So far she is right. I have not had so many
contracts together in one year since. Likewise Margaret had said not

unkindly that there was more money in television and she was right too. The payment Granada promised me for writing the *Crown Court* episode alone was more than I had received altogether from my two books. Yet I did not want that to be my life. It was too unsure, almost like gambling.

Working out the terms of the contract took quite a while. It was in the midst of this uncertainty that Lucy Kaye, the secretary of the Women's International League, phoned to ask if I wanted a job. The Camden Council for Community Relations was expanding. They needed three new employees, two to go into administration and one to be the leader of a new Mothers and Toddlers Group they were setting up. I said yes, I wanted a job because although I knew that I would have to stop working away from home sooner or later, I would have to do so gradually. I had not bothered to re-apply for teaching, and was still determined to finish my postgraduate work.

At the interview I met Jocelyn Barrow. When I came into the room she was busy writing, and seeing that she was black like myself, I sat down very still with my hands folded on my lap and waited. It was a short interview during which we talked and she even promised to help me look into the possibility of my getting funds to finish my research, which she found interesting. It was clear then that university fees were going to be raised to the level at which they are now, and that I would no longer be able to fund myself as I had been doing.

A few weeks later, I started the job. I was given the post of leader for the Mothers and Toddlers Group. I needed something like that: I could take my work there to read, and Christy and Alice could come with me during school holidays.

For the Camden Council, it was another thing. They wrote about us in the *Camden Journal*. They wrote about us in the *Ham and High*. I think the reason for this was that all three of us employed, two women and a man, came from minority groups. The man was from Bangladesh, the girl from Sri Lanka and I from Nigeria. I did not mind being written about in this way, although I suspected then it was simply a game of tokenism. But at least we were taken on. The pay was slightly more than that earned from teaching and the work would not be as demanding. As soon as I was introduced to Patricia Lacey, we set out looking for premises on which to start the project.

Suddenly, in October, the owner of the Nelson Road house said he was no longer selling, after I had measured for the curtains and the carpets. Mr Olufunwa and I pleaded with him but he became nasty and threatened to throw us out. This incident made me deeply unhappy, not so much because I worried about the money, but because I now knew that it could take a while to find the right house. To cap it all, if all went well with the television people I was going to be too busy to look for another one.

But things have a way of happening unexpectedly. On our way back Mr Olufunwa said he too was disappointed, because he knew I had more than enough money for the deposit, and he was hoping that my family and his would buy this house in Crouch End as an investment. The estate agents had kept the house for him for the past three months. "But how are you going to pay for it?" I asked, not very interested.

From the answer he gave I knew that he was hoping to ask me to invest in it whatever money I had left after settling in my own house. It was not a bad idea. "Please show it to me," I said.

He did. The house was not only suitable, but because it needed slight redecoration it was £2500 cheaper than Coniston Road and had all the features of that house plus a bit more. The only difference was that one was in Crouch End and the other in Muswell Hill.

"You mean you knew of this when I was going all over London looking for something exactly like it?"

"I thought we would buy it together and make a business with it, or that I would be in a position to buy it myself."

There was no way his plans were going to come true unless he won the pools. Nor was I going to buy a house with another family, and from what I heard and saw, I could not cope with tenants. So he agreed that it would be better to tell Dennel, the estate agent, that he would not be able to buy the house. His £50 deposit was refunded. He offered to take me home but I refused.

As soon as his car had turned the corner, I went back to Dennel. The old man was surprised to see me again. "I want that house," I cried.

He reluctantly took £500 from me. He refused to take £50 from a single parent and I accepted that. I was used to the fact that single female parents paid more for everything they wanted, because society thinks that we are a greater risk than our male counterparts. On the following Monday I phoned Mr Olufunwa and told him what I had done.

Having given my solicitor a free hand, I then stopped thinking about it, and stuffed my ears to all the kind neighbours who wanted to know why we did not move before Christmas as my children had told them we would. Many were beginning to think that it was a bluff. "How can she do it with all those children?"

Just two weeks before Christmas, the letter and first deposit for the Granada *Crown Court* play, "Juju Landlord", came. I felt so rich but they wanted the first draft by the first week of the New Year.

Christmas that year was wonderful, financially speaking. I made up to the children what they had lost, or I felt they had lost, during all those years we had little money. I think I spent about £600 buying presents for them. It was a good thing I was going to invest my income on a house, otherwise I would have spent it all on my family.

I was forced to do all my Christmas shopping in one day. We did not have the joy of making several trips as we used to. I bought all the food in Marks and Spencer in Oxford Street, and most of the gifts at John Lewis. I rushed back in a taxi and went on to type my "Juju Landlord". I even worked on that "Juju Landlord" on Christmas Day. In a typical three episodes of *Crown Court* there are enough words to fill two books, yet by 1 January 1976 I was able to stagger with the completed script to the Granada office in Golden Square. I skipped my agents. Even they were not fast enough for Granada!

We welcomed the New Year in with so much hope. Somehow, I could see that my very, very poor days were coming to an end. I was going to miss them. The more successful I became, the more I knew I was losing Chidi, but I could not help it. I wanted to get on, and prayed to God to help me more with the children. But one thing was certain: even when I was very poor they never worried where their next meal was going to come from. They had always had more than enough to eat and they knew it.

The children went to sleep, I toasted the New Year with Chidi, and we got drunk on a bottle of champagne. I wondered about my past and about him. For how many more years would we go on toasting the New Year together?

30

TV Plays

So much happened to me in 1975 that if 1976 had been like that, I would have collapsed. The 1975 pace did not stop with the arrival of the New Year. It went on for a while before it slowed down. I don't know about other writers, but I now notice that this pattern tends to repeat itself. One would go on for months and not be very busy, and then all of a sudden there would be three organizations wanting you to write a piece or give a talk for them. Now, in 1985, I sometimes find this a nuisance: one minute I wonder if I should go back to the book I was writing and the next minute I find myself packing it up because I have to do a talk at UCLA in California.

As a child in Nigeria we all saved up for New Year's Day. We call Christmas *Odun Kerkere* meaning "little celebration", and the New Year, *Odun Nla*, the "big celebration". This, I later learnt, was the same in most of the British colonies, not excepting the Indian subcontinent. By 1976, when I had spent almost fourteen years in London, I still resented the fact that one had to work on New Year's Day. It has changed now in the 1980s because people simply could not recover from the New Year's Eve hangover in such a short space of time.

Instead of celebrating the New Year, I fed my children on all the Christmas leftovers. We were always too full of food during Christmas week, and the big cake I had bought was partly eaten on New Year's Day. The turkey was still left, and all I had to do was use it in making Nigerian *jollof* rice and serve it with onions and mushrooms. By the time we graduated to the

Christmas pudding, it would have been the second week in January. But on that New Year's Day I did all my cooking early in the morning, brought out packets of mince pies, and left them on the kitchen table. I knew then that I would not be bothered very much.

I went back to my typewriter, and worked for six hours nonstop on "Juju Landlord". By late afternoon I was ready to carry these bulky typed scripts to Golden Square in Piccadilly. I was lucky that day because I met Alex Marshall, the then script editor of the *Crown Court* series.

I said earlier that I did not greatly respect people of my own sex, because most of them thought it was right to defer decisions to their male colleagues. I am still not sure who it was that put my name forward to write "Juju Landlord" when I was not as well known as I am now, but I wouldn't be surprised to hear that it was Alex Marshall.

As soon as I met her, I related my tale of woe about how I had missed celebrating Christmas in peace because of the Granada contract, and how my family were at home eating up the mince pies alone in celebration of the New Year, and how tired I was. I must have been very unsure about the quality of the work I had done to allow myself to wallow in this diatribe.

She looked at me and said she was so sorry Granada had ruined my Christmas, but "You have written too many words!" She asked if I had done anything like that before, and I said no. She laughed, then we both laughed, and in that laughter she was saying to me, "They are not to know, I won't tell them if you keep your mouth shut." I kept my mouth shut, and in the next few days, we worked on my script and reduced it by a third, before it was pronounced "watertight".

I went home very dizzy the following Thursday from Golden Square hoping to lie down a little before coping with our supper. The phone rang, it was the BBC, their deadline for *A Kind of Marriage* was 25 January. Not only that, I had to recommend most of my artists because I told them earlier I would rather have black actors and actresses with a Nigerian accent. And when asked if I knew of any, I had said yes – many.

I knew only Taiwo Ajayi! I met Taiwo in 1972 when I went to the BBC World Service to talk about Nigerian women in London. Sopiato Likimani, then studying to be a dentist at Guy's Hospital, was the presenter. She did some broadcasting to top up her little allowances. Taiwo was then the president of the Nigerian Organization of Women. I remember how Sopiato and I gaped at Taiwo: she had very, very large and talking eyes, her hair was plaited the African way long before it became fashionable, and she expressed herself with her long thin hands. She did not talk much to me, because I was staring at her so much. She had a silk scarf under a felt hat, and her long plaited hair was showing under it all. I have seen early movie stars cover their heads that way, but this was the first time I saw a black woman do so. And how it suited her! The only giveaway point about her was that her English was more terrible than mine. She spoke ungrammatically. Her accent was the Lagos one, like mine, but she had learnt one thing which in 1986 I still have to learn and which still annoys my foreign publishers – to speak slowly. When I warm to my subject, I never finish one sentence before jumping to the next one. But I think I make up for it by having a loud voice, the result of years of shouting at stubborn kids.

Taiwo and I left Bush House together. I was trotting behind her, because she walked like a star. I had trousers on while she was in a black flowing skirt and silk blouse. She asked me condescendingly whether I wrote *In the Ditch* and wanted to know who it was that helped me! Then I recoiled. I suspected that all those manners were just airs, part of her trade. She laughed in a funny way. And all the fear I had about her melted. Nobody helped me but God, I replied. And she told me that she was writing a novel and that she too read Sociology at Keele University. I had never heard of that university before, but I believed her. She told me how busy she was in the theatre and on television. I looked out for her, and I think I saw her once a South African play on BBC2. But I had been happy to make her acquaintance.

By 1976, when the BBC asked me to bring or introduce my own artists she was the only one I could think of. But I would have preferred her to act in Granada's *Crown Court* as Adah Obi. I was not just worrying about the two scripts, I was worrying where to get my actors. I did not want a white person blackening his or her face. I knew then of Nina Baden Semper, but her posh West Indian accent would not do for my plays. So the first person I enlisted was my son Jake! I thought they would not take him, but he was auditioned and pronounced quite suitable to act the part of Osita, the grandson of Arinze.

Mary Ridge and Anne Head were experienced hands at the BBC. I asked them if they could shift the days of shooting a little so that they would not clash with Granada's, but they could not, and most of the people I knew in the field of acting would opt for Granada, because that meant more money.

Then Mary Ridge asked if I knew of a woman called Jumoke Debayo. I told her I knew the name. The family was one of the earliest Nigerian millionaire families I knew. Bisi Debayo and myself were at school together, and so was another member of the family called Lanre. How could people from such "noble" families condescend to act in a play written by the daughter of a railway moulder? I said nothing to Mary Ridge. She said she would get all the artists, and I could choose the ones I wanted but she thought Jumoke Debayo and a Sierra Leone-born actor, Willie Jonah, would be quite good. The only problem was that Willie was busy doing some Shakespeare somewhere outside London. We could borrow him.

What I did not then know was that Jumoke Debayo and Taiwo Ajayi were sworn enemies. They were in the same profession, they were both Lagos Yorubas and they both came from wealthy families. And I, an Ibo (though a Lagos Yoruba speaker) and the daughter of a worker, was caught in the middle! It demanded extreme diplomacy. But I managed to keep the two apart. One thing they did not know was that they were alike, in their attitude, in their expectations. They were always telling me about the land and servants their parents had. Taiwo said her parents owned Tinubu Square, a very central place in Lagos, and her family had many many houses scattered all over the island. Jumoke said her parents owned part of Kakawa Street, which I knew was true, and that she went to nursery school as a child in a chauffeur-driven Rolls. That could be true too. Her address was in St John's Wood, in a flat she had inherited from her father. So Taiwo too got a flat in St John's Wood. Oh! they amused me no end, those two women. Jumoke said her son was at Eton but when she was bringing me home one day, after the rehearsals at White City, we passed in front of St Marylebone and I exclaimed and said, "Look, Jumoke, my son Ik goes there." And she said without thinking, "My son is there too."

It was then it clicked. I had seen her before at Christmas. My son Ik was in the choir and at Christmastime St Marylebone gave beautiful concerts for parents and guests. I saw that apart from my son there was another black boy in his class. One Christmas the school asked each boy present to say "Merry Christmas" in their mother tongue. I was impressed when this boy said *Eku Oduno* because my son could not speak any Nigerian (although he could manage a bit of German and French). I so envied the parents of this boy and wanted to see them. I did not need to look too far, because a

Nigerian lady answered her son's greeting with a loud laugh. It was Jumoke. But I did not speak to her then. Now it all clicked!

I still do not know why I suddenly got angry. So her son and my son were in the same school, the same class all the time. I remember telling Mary Ridge about it and she said that it was an occupational hazard, that most actors and actresses behave like that. Then she said that some would come for an audition and leave hints and letters which they had "forgotten", to show the producers that they were wanted somewhere else. Do actors and actresses have such an inferiority complex? We all suffer from it to an extent, but theirs is heavier than that of ordinary people. Maybe understanding them that much made it possible for us all to get very friendly at the time.

I felt very proud, especially that day when I took the Manchester train from Euston and accidentally walked into the cast of "Juju Landlord". I was hailed like a big somebody. Taiwo immediately insisted on buying me breakfast. I was not quite sure whether I should accept it or not, because I did not want her to spend her hard-earned money on me. I was too scared to buy one for myself, because not having ever eaten on an English train before I thought it would cost a fortune. And I needed money for moving house. So we shared the toast she had already bought and she gave me a cup of black coffee. The plastic cup had a cover and I felt the more grateful, because I thought she must have paid extra for that too. One thing really made me happy: that I was in a position to bring happiness to so many black artists. One could understand how I must have felt, after my failure to help the youth at The Seventies, Quintin Kynaston and Dashiki. The only dour-looking face I saw that morning was that of Mr Baptiste, a West Indian actor, now a leading figure in the West Indian Carnival Committee. He said that my case for the prosecution in the play was not strong enough, that a clever lawyer would have freed Mr Dawodu. I did not understand why this should bother him so much, for in real life my landlord lost the case. A few days later, with a Granada TV jury, men and women chosen at random, Mr Dawodu still lost the case. Despite his dourness and unhappiness, Mr Baptiste was glad to act in the play as a barrister.

As it was not possible to get an all-Nigerian cast, we had artists from the Caribbean, America, South and East Africa. Taiwo Ajayi was Adah Obi, and Loui Mahoney was Mr Dawodu. It was fun in the train.

The brisk business atmosphere took over when we arrived at Piccadilly, Manchester. I noticed straightaway the competitiveness of the Granada studios. As a result, few people had time to be nice to the next person. I could feel the rush, and the nail-biting tension among the producers and artists. The mood seemed to grip everybody as we waded through the rehearsal, first in a very cold room, then in the "court room". The producer did not want me there and I think he sighed with relief when I hinted that I would not be staying the night in Manchester. I had left my family on their own, and I was looking forward to working with the set at the BBC, which was to be the very following day at the White City studios.

A journalist was to do a write-up for the play in *TV Times*. He shocked me not a little by asking what part of the play was written by my friend Taiwo Ajayi. I could not be nice about such a question. I was beginning to learn to allow these actors their bit of artificiality, but not this. So I made sure that I stressed to him that I had written the play from my own book *In the Ditch*, and that Alex Marshall had edited the script.

I became sick of the whole thing and wanted to leave as soon as possible. I no longer looked forward to seeing the play take shape. I was never keen on court scenes anyway. It was always palava, palava. I wanted to get to the BBC and see how Mary Ridge would transform my village description into visual scenes, with goats, hens, kolanuts and Ibusa community noises. I wanted to go. They gave us forms to fill in for our expenses, and it was then that I found that I could have had a full breakfast at Granada's expense.

I knew then that I was very ignorant about people. I knew then that my world had been very narrow and rather too sheltered. Apart from babies, and a little Sociology, I did not know about much at all. One has to go out and meet different people in different walks of life to be able to function confidently. If I had done a thing like that I would never have forgiven myself, to say nothing of having no confidence to smile. I would forever be talking about it out of guilt. Now I knew that one of my troubles was that I never had been taught how to forgive myself, whenever I made a social slip. I thought people would hold it against me forever. Coming to know now that some people deliberately act this way and regard it as clever, I was forced to learn to understand them.

The good thing about the Manchester studios was that I saw in the flesh most of the cast of *Coronation Street*. I was a little disappointed to see that they looked so short in real life. The man who acts Ken Barlow always looks so tall that I thought he must be a giant. But he is small. And the big lady that acts Betty Turpin looked more beautiful than she does on television; I think they make her wear those dowdy clothes on purpose. And Jean Alexander (Hilda Ogden) had a different voice. The Hilda's voice is put on. I heard her saying goodbye to the men at the reception desk and I stared. Her hair was well done, with no curlers and no scarf. She had on an expensive-looking coat, well cut and neat, while Betty was in a big brown fur one. They were all laughing and joking. And that afternoon, when I was feeling so terrible, I thanked Granada for allowing me to see the stars of my favourite English series. *Dallas* and *Dynasty* may come and go, but as long as *Coronation Street* is still going strong I will always come back to Britain, wherever I have been. I was at first tempted to go up to Hilda to say "Hello, you're my best actress", but knew I would sound stupid.

I rushed to the station for my train back to London. This time I had a snack on the train, because I had collected the sum of £2 for a meal from Granada. I had coffee, a bar of chocolate and bought another bigger bar for everybody in my family. When I got to Euston, I found I still had some money left so I bought a loaf of bread and six eggs. How prices have risen since then!

We started work on *A Kind of Marriage*, my BBC play, the same week. Jake, who had the part of Osita, was spoilt by everybody. He was over the moon, walked with a swagger and told all his friends that he was going to be an actor! The rehearsals soon got started. Going to the BBC studios was joy. The producers and editors were slightly older, but the pace of life was saner.

We all enjoyed doing *A Kind of Marriage*. Even my drama agent, Sheila Lemon, came. And one could feel that life was less competitive. Mary Ridge kept asking me what I had thought of this and that. At Granada, the producer appeared to dislike me, and frowned every time I came near. But at the BBC, most of the workers like Anne Head, Mary Ridge, Alan Seymour and Innes Lloyd had travelled and met so many African people and did not think it presumptuous for an African woman to write a play they were to work on.

There was to be one slight hitch. It was in choosing the music. Mary Ridge had just bought some South African music which she thought would do as the theme music for my play. After all, was it not African music? It took a long time for Jumoke and myself to explain that South African music is South African music, that Ibusa people have their own music and that they are different. Mary did not see the difference. What she did not visualize was that it was like choosing a piece of music from Berlin in Germany for a play set in Leicester, and saying that the people are all the same simply because they are all European.

She was nice, Mary Ridge. She soon saw how important it was for us Nigerians that our country's music should be used for our play. We even had slight support from Willie Jonah, who reminded everybody that Africa was a continent and not a village. We arrived at a compromise. Only the wordless beginning of the music was used. But that beginning had the sounds of our "Agogo and Isaka and Akpele" musical instruments.

Film producers have noticed that when they now come to me to turn some of my books into films, I'm not always too keen about it. I think it's because of all these little hiccups. For example, Jumoke is a Nigerian actress, but she never got the name "Osita" right. She pronounced it in such a way that it meant "bastard", and many Ibo males who saw the play laughed. But then the typical Ibo male was never pleased about the play anyway. I wonder if that was why Nigeria never bought it. They bought "Juju Landlord" and showed it several times when I was in Calabar in 1980/81. A great many of us who write books on the so-called "Third World" pray that one day we'll have film producers, white or black, who will have a completely free hand to translate faithfully what the author has in mind. It probably won't come from Britain, it could come from the States, but it will come, some day.

I was busy. For instance, a typical day in my diary, 21 January 1976, reads, "I hurried to work at the Mothers and Toddlers Group, frightened that I would miss my seminar this afternoon, but luckily Angela cancelled her dentist appointment. I then had to go to the bank to pay in £340.50 – royalty payment. I left Mothers and Toddlers at 1.20 pm and was just in time for the seminar on Historicism. This particular theory would be quite useful for my final PhD thesis, if ever I have enough money to continue and if I have the time. Today is the first flight of the Concorde. How proud I felt that Britain and France had done this."

Reading this now in 1985, I am surprised that as far back as 1976 I was already feeling proud of Britain's achievements, and glad now that I have this silly egotistical thing about writing down the little happenings of my everyday life. I would have remembered that then I was still anti-British, but my diary entry proves me wrong. I was already then feeling slightly more British than when I came in 1962.

The BBC studio at White City was not only relaxing but the pace of work was slower than at Granada. It took us the better part of two weeks to produce a play of forty-eight minutes, whereas Granada took a week to produce a court scene of one hour forty-five minutes. Perhaps that was why they rush so much. Nonetheless, by 13 February all the rehearsals and takes were finished. I still look back on that final day with nostalgia. Everybody was laughing. The BBC lounge at White City looked particularly festive and expensive to me that evening. We ate and drank cocktails and I met the other writers in the series. I had not found writing *A Kind of Marriage* as difficult as Granada's "Juju Landlord", because, as I said, I don't like court scenes, especially long ones like those in *Crown Court*.

Before the play was shown in May, all of us who wrote the series of "Commonwealth Plays" had our photographs taken for the *Radio Times*. I don't remember the names of the others, but I'll never forget Salvon and Dilip Hiro.

31

The Move

My only regret during those hectic weeks was that I missed going to Highbury Hill Girls' open day on 12 February. Alice had to go with Chiedu, and I knew that she never forgave me for not going. That was the first time it had happened. I always attended open days and Christmas carol services at each of my children's schools. This is one of the things I now miss very much as the mother of older children. In those days, I would go to St Marylebone to listen to Bach, Handel, Beethoven and other prominent musicians played and sung by the boys. My son Ik sang soprano. At Highbury Hill, Chiedu too sang in the choir. Their music was not as highbrow as that of St Marylebone, and later we all went to St Augustine's, Jake's school in Kilburn, to see him act in *Oliver* and sing his favourite Christmas carol, "The Drummer Boy". Jake has a way of dancing and grinning from ear to ear whilst singing at the same time. By the time the other two girls left Camden school, they had become so liberated that they avoided such childish things as singing in the choir. I watched a couple of plays in Camden, but Alice and Christy never brought the school programmes home. These two were proper London girls. Camden did well for them, though, because both eventually went on to higher education, Christy to read Biological Sciences and Alice to read Economics at Manchester University. They are both fiercely independent. I have Camden High School for Girls to thank for that!

It was not possible for me to see all that in 1976. I felt really awful letting Chiedu down, and she moped for days. It would have gone on for weeks, knowing my daughter, but God intervened to rescue me from being called the most uncaring mother in the world! And His intervention took this form: it looked as if we were going to win the contractual race for the house in Crouch End!

This was confirmed on the 23rd. My family was so wild with excitement that Chiedu forgot that I was bad mother. She hugged me in sheer joy, saying that she did not believe it was ever going to be possible for us to live in our own real house: "To think, just to think, that I can now talk about decorating one's house, and one's back garden and front door." I just laughed, because she was beginning to sound like Mrs Mary Wilson who wanted her own front door rather than live at Number 10 Downing Street.

My children wanted us to move that same day. I told them that was impossible because it was a Monday, and I still had to get the deeds to be sure the house was really ours. At the mention of the deeds, they all went quiet. Chiedu asked how I knew that the vendor would not change his mind. I replied that he wouldn't because he had accepted our money, that the rest of the transaction was with my solicitor and his solicitor, and that it was just a question of a few days, during which I would have to get water, gas and electricity running in the new house. They could do without water, gas and electricity, they claimed. And Ik went on to tell us how they had lived without all those when they went camping at the country patch belonging to his school. I did not know which way to turn.

We were in this hysteria when Mr Olufunwa came to tell us that the estate agent had phoned with the good news, and that he had gone straight over and collected the keys for us. So I begged him to take us all there. Homework, Guide meetings, all were forgotten as we clambered into Mr Olufunwa's ancient car. At one time, I did not know who was the more excited, he or the children. I kept reminding him to drive safely, but Jake was sure he drove slower, "even slower than our Ma". That was something, because my family boasted that I was the slowest driver in the whole universe.

Well, we arrived in one piece, and to this day I still wonder what the neighbours thought of us, two adults and five very excited children. I remember telling the boys to comb their hair; they ignored me, and then decided that it was too cold to go bare-headed. So they sought and found my one woollen hat, Ik put that on and Jake decided to make do with the woollen tea cosy I had knitted with multiple colours when we were "in the ditch".

There was so much shouting, so much singing from Christy, but Alice stood out in her brown coat, her nose sniffing the air like a haughty dog. She did not seem very impressed. Then suddenly she said, "Ma, all you need to add to this house is a clock and a bishop and it will be a church."

Oh, Alice, the poor girl had lived all her years in council houses, with grey slabs for walls and communal open place for ill-matched families and children. She had never been inside a real brick Edwardian house with stained windows and a conical roof. The windows, the door, the red bricks and everything about the house must have reminded her of St Mary Magdalene church, which we attended in Rothay. We laughed at her remark, but I noticed that she clutched at my coat. "This house is not strong, Mum, it will collapse, I am sure of it. I like Rothay better, it's better in Regent's Park. This house is weak, the rooms are small and they are dark, Mum! Council houses are better."

I let her hang on to me as the others ran up and down stairs, hooting with joy, and Jake declared that he was not going home to Rothay, that he would like to stay and keep watch on our house just in case a thief should come in. The house had been empty since October! Jake did not want to hear that. There was a little argument over who was to take which room, and then Mr Olufunwa said we should all go and see his family. They too had just moved, to Redstron Road in Muswell Hill, not far from us.

Their house was slightly bigger than ours with a bigger garden, and was better finished. It had been owned by a do-it-yourself fanatic who had built a whole bedroom suite in the front room. He had turned the house into two separate flats, and the Olufunwas were going to live in one and sublet the other. That was a nice idea, but one look at my family and I knew I could never do that even though we had the same number of rooms. My family was too boisterous, and they had been used to having their own rooms – something I never had as a child, and which I tried all those years not to deny my kids.

I must have done fairly well, because taking Alice for a three-week holiday in California, she said that the only horrible thing the Californians do is that despite all their money they always put two children in one room. "I'll never do such a thing to my children when I have them." To think I, her mother, spent most of my childhood in rooms I had to share with husband, wife, several children and my brother, and that her father had lived in one room with his parents and nine brothers and sisters! And none of those Lagos rooms was as big as our present kitchen.

I agreed with her. But hinted as cautiously as I could that after her university career and before contemplating marriage she should do a little more travelling and see how other people live. I am sure she will learn.

It was when we visited the Olufunwas that evening in February that I learnt that Mrs Olufunwa preferred our house to the one they had bought, because ours was a whole £3000 cheaper. I sensed that she was not very pleased with my getting the house at all. She was like most of my married women friends, who felt that single women should not be able to afford such things: they should be the ''preserve'' of women who stuck to and survived in their marriages. It does not matter how dead or superficial such marriages are, many women feel that tangible buys like houses should be their reward for seeing it through. Females like me who, though not by choice, are left to raise children single-handed, should never contemplate buying a house. This was one of my reasons for shying away from married Nigerian women.

Mrs Olufunwa dampened my joy that evening. I liked their house very much, but could not afford it; I allowed my liking to stay at arms length, at admiration level, just as one admires something in a shop, knowing quite well that one could never buy it. They had a huge garden that backed onto Alexandra Palace and the all-glass breakfast room looked straight into this well-kept garden. It was lovely. She did not see all that. Ours was cheaper, with the same number of rooms, but a garden almost the size of a pocket handkerchief, and at the bottom of that garden was a primary school! They say that the grass is always greener yonder.

We got home quite late. The rest of the week was taken up with phoning the Gas Board, the Electricity Board, the telephone people and getting a removal van. A relative and an Ibusa man, Ofili, promised to lend us his car for our move. By Friday I was not only phoning and waiting for him, but also for the deeds to arrive through the post.

Then Angela, the girl who worked with me at the Mothers and Toddlers Group, had an idea. She knew of some students who had a van and who she suspected might be able to move us. She was not quite sure about it, but she would get them to phone me. I did not pin much hope on what Angela said, so I went to the Woolworths in Oxford Street to buy nails and hinges. The students chose that time to phone. My family told them to come straightaway because we were ready to move. And they came!

I stood there, like someone glued to the spot, in front of the Victory pub next to Rothay, watching this sight. I was amazed at first to see Jake and Ik and two young men carrying my bookcase into the van. Chiedu was happy with the pillows but I collapsed with hysterical laughter when I saw Alice bringing my dresses one at a time and throwing them on top of everything. I had not had time to put them in suitcases yet.

All Chiedu said to me by way of explanation was, "Look, Mum, those people are probably going to change their mind. And I have told everybody we are moving to Crouch End. We won't give them the opportunity to change their mind, not this time. Remember that horrid man at Nelson Road, he changed his mind at the very last minute, didn't he?"

I could not stop them, because maybe somehow I did not want to. If they were mad with impatience, so was I. To own my own home was a feat which my parents had never achieved in Lagos. We had in Ibusa a family compound around which we built thatched houses, some of which took only a few days to build. As my father did not live very long, he did not build one with a zinc roof. Now I was moving into one that would be mine.

The thought that it could take up to twenty years to make it really mine made my stomach rumble, and it made my legs go weak when I calculated how much I would be paying for the £10,000 mortgage I was shouldering. But then without the mortgage I could never buy a house. I was moving into Haringey, one of those London boroughs with high rates. All this went through my mind as I watched Alice struggling with our teddy bear, Stella, which they had bought me for Christmas.

Yes, they were right, the owner of the house could change his mind; I therefore had no choice but to join in the spirit of the game.

So on the evening of 27 February 1976, an evening that was very cold and damp, we moved from Rothay into Briston Grove. There was no light in the house, nor was there water or gas, but there was a happiness that was unfathomable.

We toasted with a bottle of champagne I had bought months before, the cork of which obligingly came out with a festive Yuletide pop, which made me regret our not saving our leftover Christmas crackers. Nonetheless we drank it from teacups in the dark, and Alice forgot that she was only nine and so did I. By the time I remembered it was too late; she gulped it down and announced that it was nice and fizzy.

We all went to bed without unpacking or undressing. It was mad, but nice.

32

The Bride Price is Launched

I spent the first few days after we moved mostly in bed. My whole body ached. The more I thought about all there was still to be done, the more I felt like going deeper into the sheets and never getting up. It was winter, and a very cold one at that.

Nonetheless, I had to get up. I went on Monday 1 March to thank Mr Harper, the Headmaster of St Mary Magdalene. That small school into which I had accidentally stumbled had helped me tremendously in raising my children, there was no doubt. When I went into his office, he looked rather sad and so did I. I saw and felt then that an important chapter was closing in my life. I could not shrink my family back into young children who would need primary school again. They all, with the exception of Alice, had grown beyond that. In my mind I could still hear, "Good morning Mr Yapper, good morning teachers, good morning friends."

By then most of the teachers who had taught the children in the early years had gone. Some went to other schools as the threat of school closure became imminent. Father Grant, who prepared the children for confirmations and who taught religion, got married to the black actress Nina Baden Semper and they moved to another borough. With his departure the school lost some of its glamour. He genuinely loved children, and only God knows how many barbecue parties he and wife invited my kids to. They knew them so well that on their wedding day Jake and Alice insisted on appearing in most of the photographs, and they did, even the ones that appeared in the

They were clean and well dressed, but not dressed for that type of society
ding. But Father Grant did not mind. And his wife said "it was lovely".
Now there was talk of closing the school and merging it with Christ
Church school nearby. The argument was that the resources were not
evenly distributed. There were about eighty children at St Mary Magdalene
and they had up to ten teachers. But other schools worked on the propor-
tion of one teacher to twenty-five children or even more.

I was glad I knew the school when it was at its best. I smiled as I noticed
that the witch doctor I made at a pottery class and gave to Mr Harper as a
present was still there. I remember telling him never to part with it, and
that it would always guide him like his Chi. I think he believed me because
the witch doctor shone, which showed that somebody had been polishing
and taking good care of it. It turned out to be the best witch doctor I made.
I still have some of them. Mr Harper suddenly seemed to be so alone. But
then that is the fate of all those who are involved in raising the young. The
young grow and they leave the nest. Mr Harper later went to St
Augustine's Primary in Kilburn, but he never cut the same legendary figure
he did at St Mary Magdalene in Munster Square. The new school was too
large. He had given over thirty years of his life to "St Mary Mags".

I left him and walked slowly to my old flat. Some youngsters had already
moved in and were making themselves comfortable on the bunk beds we
had left. A pair of expensive shoes Chiedu made me buy for her, and then
decided she did not like after wearing them only once, had been polished
and arranged tidily by someone. I simply had to laugh at this.

When we moved there in 1969 we were just blacks who had the audacity to
demand and take one of the best maisonette flats that Camden built at the time.
It was completely new. Our neighbours never forgave us for that audacity.
They would squash tomatoes on our doors, and our neighbours would write
all kinds of insulting graffiti over our walls. By the time we left most of these
very people smiled at me in the lift, and many even claimed to be our friends.
Now that we had left many of those youngsters, who had called my children
names and had pelted tomatoes at our door, were thankful for our cast-offs. I
could not take many of our things, because the house in Briston Grove was
overfurnished by the former Jewish owner. I had to leave the bunk beds, the
carpet cleaner and even my Hoovermatic washing machine. I was just too tired
to move them. I quickly arranged to take my gas cooker. It was better than the
one in Crouch End.

I went down the corridor to say goodbye to the old lady with the dog. We never knew her name and she did not know ours. We always called her the old lady with the dog, because she put up such a fight to keep her dog. She had a way of suddenly bursting into tears and howling her heart out. I knew why she cried, she was just lonely. So I used to pay her visits, and she would give me some sweet-smelling herbs. She said she came from a gipsy family and used to work in the circus. She was over seventy, with a heavy bosom and masses of red hair, and although she was on the plump side she carried herself erect. When she saw me on TV she said I must make sure I was fairly treated by Equity, even though she knew I was neither an actress nor a circus performer.

I also said goodbye to the old Jewish couple, Mr and Mrs Browning. They adopted me from the word go, and Mrs Browning supplied me with all my Avon cosmetics which she knew we Nigerian women love.

To me the place was already beginning to look strange and part of the past, and I began to understand Daphne du Maurier's detached description of that area in one of her autobiographies. She too had lived there by Regent's Park as a child. Somehow it looked as if places like that belonged to the very young and rootless. One gets the feeling that, yes, this is a place to live, but not to settle. The part of Crouch End where we had our new house was tree-lined and peaceful. As soon as one comes down Crouch Hill into Dickenson Road there is a kind of hush, an enveloping lull. I had lived there for less than a week and I was beginning to ask myself, "How did we manage to live in such an open and noisy place as Albany Street for so long?"

Alice started her new school that day. It was one of those large primary schools. I could tell straightaway that she was going to have difficulties. It was her first time of going to a school that did not know her brothers and sisters. And I could not see myself being too involved, because the size of it alone was bewildering. I knew that Alice was naturally clever, yet she was going to be another black child that a white teacher was being forced to teach. The teacher was distant and rather languid. I worried a little as I left her there to fend for herself, but then on my way home took consolation that she was going to be there for only a year, since I had already put her name down at Camden School for Girls where Christy was already making a good impression. She could not get too irretrievably low in one year.

When parents make a fuss about schools and their environment, some-times child-free people think they are making noises for nothing. They have reasons. My daughter Alice became wilder, and she started to enjoy telling us the trick she and her new friends played on their teachers. She became very friendly with Julie, another black child from a Caribbean family down the road. Being both black and in the same class, their teacher invariably lumped them together and sometimes she could not tell which one was doing what to her. Julie's family, a very quiet one, with a son who enjoyed playing his records for the whole street whenever the parents were out, simply accepted all the teacher said. They would rather send their children to a school round the corner because it was nearer. I could tell that Julie was an intelligent child, too, but I think their teacher saw her blackness before her intelligence. I was never close enough to Julie's mother to talk to her and soon they were given a council flat and they moved from the street and I never saw them again. But before they moved, Julie gave Alice our kitten called Titch about which Alice and I wrote a book, ''Titch the Cat'', when she was eleven and in her first year at Camden.

Whilst at her new primary school, Alice began to speak a delightful mix-ture of Cockney and Creole-patois English. It was lovely to listen to. She would prefix everything she said with ''Rass . . . man.'' I must say I did not know what she meant, and by the turn of the year when they took her on at Camden, we all breathed a big sigh of relief. I became anxious for her when she carried this boisterousness into Camden. It took the school, me, and the whole family about four years to repair the damage that school had done to Alice in one year. But the damage, thank goodness, was repaired. She got good grades and qualified herself for a university place to read her chosen subject, Economics.

If I had raised my children in Tottenham, Brixton or Toxteth, I am sure they would have been among those missile-throwing youths we saw in the riots. But if schools are smaller, say one teacher to fifteen children on average, the teachers will enjoy their pupils, and the parents and kids them-selves will nostalgically look back to that period as the best of their lives. Alice's teacher at her last school refused to pose with her pupils. She did not enjoy teaching them and I, having been a teacher in similar situations, could understand her.

I thought that all comprehensive schools were the same, and since St Augustine's, where Jake was, was a comprehensive, I thought he should change his school. Our new borough got him a place in their school in Tottenham. Jake had to go along by himself because he was then thirteen and I was working, but I had spoken to the Head on the phone. I wanted Jake to find out whether he liked the school before his final interview. He sat on a bench in the corridor waiting to see who his new teacher was. Soon after he got up and came home. I returned from work to see him looking very unhappy.

"I don't want to go there, Mum," he cried. "In that school you are allowed to bang into your teachers . . . and a big boy came to me and asked me if I was new. He said to me that the best way to survive here is never to give in to no b . . . teacher. That we f . . . blacks should stick together. Mum, I don't want to stick together with anybody, I just want to go to school and get my 'A' levels and 'O' levels. Mum, this boy really looked tough and big, and he had no school uniform."

Jake did not change school. Consequently, the borough refused to give them bus passes, claiming that they have equally good schools in Haringey. They would not listen to the argument that it was inadvisable to uproot young people who had got half way through their GCE programme and who had been used to certain teachers and a certain environment. One lady at the Education Office was so irritable at my sending the younger girls to Camden instead of Hornsey that she said she would not consider anything until I had removed Christy from Camden and promised not to send Alice there. The local schools were of the same standard, she claimed. I agreed with her but said my girls must go to Camden, and there they went.

An old acquaintance, one Mrs Ademosun, hearing that I was the leader of the Mothers and Toddlers Group in Kentish Town and that I had just moved, came to help me clean up. We threw a bit of junk outside, and settled down to watch the first episode of "Juju Landlord". We were both delighted at seeing it, and for me it was a wonderful feeling to see a simple idea take shape and become almost real on the screen. I felt so responsible. So much so that I was frightened. That my Yoruba landlord had tried to frighten me out of his house simply to exercise his power over another countrywoman with five young children, the youngest of whom was then only six days old, had moved me to include it in my first book, *In the Ditch*, and I now had that small chapter in my life dramatized, too. It came out vividly and I saw how television could help literature in the future.

Although the second and third episodes were shown over the following days and although the *TV Times* wrote a piece about it, it was hardly mentioned elsewhere. This surprised me so much that it almost hurt. All that work, all that rushing around we had done at Christmas, not to be reviewed at all. It was horrible.

Now that I have met many scriptwriters who say, "I don't feel I am a writer until I have written a book", I know what they mean. A book is always there, it is reviewed and even talked about, but plays like *Crown Court* shown in the afternoon are seldom noticed. The series was repeated later in the same year, but it failed to give me the full creative feeling I have after publishing a book.

In May "A Kind of Marriage", the BBC play, fared a little better. *The Stage* thought that I was a promising playwright or something like that. And it was listed in *The Sunday Times* as one of the best plays of the week. Many more people watched it because it was shown in the evening. But the BBC did not repeat it; they thought they would, but the management was changed and the idea got lost as a diamond might vanish in a whirlpool. This successfully crystallized my ambivalence towards writing for the television. I would put most of my literary energy into writing my type of documentary novels. My domain may be the empire of things, but there I am queen and do not have to cope with self-styled intellectual gladiators. We seldom see things with the same eye.

Partly as a result of all this, I went back to *The Slave Girl*, the outline was completed in 1975 before moving into Briston Grove, but what with writing the plays and the move, I did not have much time to put into it. With this book I started a new kind of writing, the type where one needs a detailed outline and where some is written in long hand before being typed out, unlike *In the Ditch* and *Second-Class Citizen* which just poured out of me straight onto the typewriter. After such outpouring, I always refused to edit or rewrite because I could guess that there would be mistakes on each page. I always left that to somebody else to do. But this one was different. Consequently, it took me a fairly long time, because I kept putting it down for a week or so and then getting back into it again.

It was to be the first book in chronological order of my study of the black woman from my part of the world. I could not go back to write about my grandmothers, however, because my mother hardly knew her own mother. She died when my mother was still a baby; in fact when she was discovered dead my mother was still at her breast sucking. My father never talked much about his mother, either. The little I knew about Agbogo, now my

Chi, was gleaned from my aunt, Nwakwaluzo Ogbueyin. Stories said that she waddled like a duck (the way I still walk when I'm tired) and despite all the hunger in this world, she was always plump (not much hope for me trying to be the second Twiggy!). They said she loved teasing men, and that she had to be held down on her wedding night for her husband to have sex. She was fiercely independent. I think I am like her on this last point, I don't know much about the others. And in her reincarnation she became me. I did not know enough about her to fill a whole book, however. As a result, I had to start my story with the birth of my mother, during the time of the "Felenza" (the German nerve gas). The early Europeans told our people that what was killing them was only influenza. And what the typical Ibo ear made of the word "influenza" was Felenza.

Meanwhile, by the end of March, the American edition of *The Bride Price* was out; this was before the Allison and Busby edition, even though they had the manuscript first and had sold the rights to America. It should have been the other way round. I had to put up with A. and B.'s delays, however, for by then I had not spoken to other British publishers. I left that part of my life to Elizabeth Stevens at Curtis Brown. She said that since no publisher had ever approached her, there was nothing she could do and also that they now had another writer whose work was published by Allison and Busby, so they would put a great deal of pressure on them, though they would try not to upset them. Which was all very nice, very loyal, but how was I to pay my bills?

I had by then stopped caring what Allison and Busby did anyway, I just kept writing and expressed my disenchantment to Elizabeth. Five months after George Braziller brought out *The Bride Price*, Allison and Busby were to launch the English edition at the Africa Centre. I was to do a reading and give a talk. I got all the children ready. Then my eldest, Chiedu, said she would not go – we did not know why. When I insisted, she went and shaved off all her hair and said she would paint one side red and the other white! She would look scary. In anger I said they should all stay at home. The others begged and begged, and Ik reminded me that he had had to leave school early for the launch, but I said no, they were not going.

I thought about it all on the train. I asked myself why I always wanted my daughter's (who was then only sixteen) approval. It then began to dawn on me that because I had her when I was barely her age and because she grew up so fast and because together we looked after the younger ones, she was more like a playmate and a younger sister than a daughter. I always expected her to understand what I was doing and thereby denied her the opportunity to be stupid and self-centred like most adolescents.

I was worse to my mother. I told her I would never talk to her again for marrying my uncle, as we do in our parts. My uncle who was only a grass cutter when my father was in the army, even though he was probably only an African gun carrier for an English officer. I did not stop there. Of all the men chosen for me to marry, I ran to the one she most disapproved of. I felt I was getting my own back. Tears welled up in my eyes and fell. How I wished I could take back all those horrible things I had said. Then I remembered that by then I was only fourteen!

I now wished the train would go backwards so that I could bring Ik, Jake, Christy and Alice to the Africa Centre, but it was too late. Well, I would write another book someday, and they would all be there.

It was different this time at the Africa Centre. The place was packed. All my "new friends", the actors and actresses, were there. Allison and Busby was well represented, in fact I think everybody from that office came. So did Elizabeth, my agent! I opened my mouth when I saw her. It was as if the Queen herself had come to see me launch *The Bride Price*. I think by then I was getting to be fairly well known. Allison and Busby might have cash flow problems but they were good at publicity. I don't know how they do it because Clive is a very private person and so is Margaret, but somehow they manage to get people to their authors' book launches without any problem.

That evening I noticed that Clive was rougher than usual. He looked very worried and at one time I thought it was because I read out the end of the book instead of the beginning. By reading the end, I spoilt the story for those who had just bought copies. I was not thinking; I was still worrying about my difficult daughter. I remember saying something like, "Men expect women to be mother, housewife, nurse, cook and as if all that was not enough, they expect us to be acrobats in bed . . . " It was the uneasy laughter that followed this that made me realize what I had said. I wanted to die. Why could I not write out my speech and read it like a nice lady? But then I find it difficult to be a nice lady. I am just me, Buchi Emecheta.

I made a dive for Elizabeth before the applause died down. I was so flattered that she was there, yet she was my agent and she was being paid from the money people like me made for her company. I never really understood why I should have wanted to please her: was it because she was white, and I had this inferiority complex inside me? If she had been a black woman, I would have told her where to go a long time ago. But then did not my daughter reduce me to tears a few hours before? Ah, that was me. Jelly underbelly, but hard rock on the surface.

"I have sent *The Slave Girl* to George Braziller," she said. Now this was a mild shock. Although I finished *The Slave Girl* in April, Elizabeth had said nothing about the book, and Clive had said nothing either. The only person who had bothered to make a comment was Margaret. She said the story line was not as strong as the one in *The Bride Price*. That was true, but what it lacked on that score I made up for by writing it well, or so I thought. The way Clive was saying, "Yes, next week, yes, tomorrow", I knew it would take him another year to make up his mind. In desperation, Elizabeth had sent it off to George Braziller – did he not publish *The Bride Price* first?

I made my way to the Allison and Busby group, and Clive spat, "Elizabeth had no right to send *The Slave Girl* to Braziller, at this stage."

I wanted to say, "Oh, so you read it?" but then somebody nudged me on the shoulder and gave me a bouquet of flowers and a large packet of well-wrapped chocolate. The flowers were huge and looked really lovely, and I was so delighted. Everybody around me said, "Oh!" I thought at once that they were either from my publishers, my agents, or my new friends the actors and actresses. After the initial Ohs and Ahs, I took a peep at the card that came with the gifts. It was signed "Good Luck Mum, we are proud of you, from Chiedu, Ik, Jake, Christy and me, Alice".

My initial feeling was to push everybody away and run home to my family and share with them this huge chocolate box they had bought with their paper-round money. I looked around the crowd looking for a way to escape, then saw Chidi and his friend Mr Chima talking in a desultory way by the door. Now I got it. Chidi had told me that he would not be able to come because he was going to a meeting. The children must have cried to him to bring the flowers and the chocolate because I had banned them from coming. He looked away very quickly and I was glad I did not see him before I started to talk. My words would have choked me. A sentence I repeated several times in *The Bride Price* came to me – that on the day of blood relatives, friends would go. To me all these people were friends, a few of them good ones, but my blood relatives were at home in Briston Grove.

The editor of *Africa* magazine and his wife said would I like to go to their house for a meal? I was about to hesitate when Jumoke Debayo said she would take me there. Again I wanted to escape and go home. However, the staff at the Africa Centre wanted us to have a meal downstairs at the Calabash. I was still looking around, not knowing what to do, when Lyn Allison, Clive's wife (though by then separated), came over in her casual way and said, "Buchi, you have a great fan who admired your *Bride Price* so much, she would be happy if you could see her."

I wanted to tell Lyn that she must be mad. It was getting late, and she could see that many people wanted me to eat with them. But she said quickly that the fan in question was dying of cancer. Now that was different, but who was she?

"It's Clive Allison's mother."

Now, really this was the day of blood relatives.

So without bothering to sign any more books or apologize for not wanting wine, cider or dinner at the Calabash, Lyn and I went to this flat in Covent Garden. I thought we were going to see her in hospital, but I almost fell down from shock when she said, "Oh no, she is staying with her son." And what son? Clive Allison! My respect for that man, who annoyed me every time I saw him, went up a million steps.

I wanted to hug Lyn for letting me come, but she would not understand. We entered the flat, which was painted all white with a curious-looking stove by the fireplace, and waited. Lyn went into the inner room and I could hear gentle laughter, and Lyn too came out laughing. She could not be dying, I thought, if she was laughing, and making everybody around her laugh.

I went in with my heart in my mouth and saw this beautiful lady lying there. Her face was completely unlined and she was so calm. In less than a second she calmed me down. She told me she was going to be the hostess for my next title and we all laughed. I told her in detail all that had happened that evening. (I always talk non-stop when I am worried and do not know what else to do.) I told her everything that I said and what other people had said to me. Lyn with her dry, direct, no-nonsense voice kept interrupting me and reminding me of what I had forgotten. I suddenly realized that I did not wish to go. If this was death, I would like to die like this, in my son's flat with me talking as if there was no tomorrow and no pain. Reluctantly I got up and kissed her goodbye. I walked away from that room smiling just like Lyn had done about an hour before.

It was only when I came into the living-room and saw Clive's face that I knew that she was seriously ill. He asked me if she wandered a bit, and I said no, I never noticed it. Maybe because I am a great wanderer myself. I wanted to shout at him and at Margaret who looked more solemn than her usual solemn self. I wanted to say, "You two should take your unhappy faces somewhere else, that lady there is not dying." My mind said it all, though my mouth did not give voice. I walked past them and took my train home.

I sent her a card the following day, I think it was a get well card. I just refused to accept it. A few days later, she was admitted into hospital and they said she took a copy of *The Bride Price* with her and also my get well card. She died soon afterwards, but somehow I did not feel too bitter.

That episode opened my eyes a little. I hope Clive Allison will forgive my writing about this scene, because it helped me in writing my most best-selling book to date, *The Joys of Motherhood*. That incident showed me that death can be peaceful and beautiful. That some sons can really care for their mothers. In our part of the world when a mother is that ill, people start looking for her daughter, and failing that her daughter-in-law. Whenever I saw Clive Allison after that, I always remembered how he turned his flat into a hospital room for his dying mother, even though at that time he was wifeless. I quote this incident to my sons every day! Just to let them know!

I was invited to the funeral. I had never been to one in England before, neither had I seen anyone about to die before. I came, overdressed in black. I was surprised to see Margaret and Lyn in jeans, but I did not care. My heart cried, especially when we entered the room in which only weeks before I was talking to Mrs Allison. I don't drink much – only in public to show off. I was drunk on two glasses of wine and, as nobody would talk of the lady who had died, as we do in Nigeria, I started to talk about the new film contract the BBC promised!

Funnily enough, everybody joined in. On my way home I said, "What a rotten society. They are afraid to talk of death, even that of a nice woman who passed away so peacefully. They are afraid to talk about it, because they are afraid to think it could happen to them. It will happen to all of us." I am grateful to Lyn for inviting me there on one of my greatest literary days.

33

The Joys of Motherhood

After the launch of *The Bride Price*, George Braziller told me that he did not like *The Slave Girl*. This was a surprise, because I thought it was good. He said that the language did not quite fit with my earlier books, and was not quite sure how the average American reader would take it.

Margaret surprised me. She put her foot down. She said the book hadn't a strong story line, but she liked it. Clive kept making his "Hmm" sound and not saying one thing or the other. But he did not say, "I told you so."

I kept phoning Allison and Busby, wanting to know when they would publish it, despite America's rejection. That book was symbolic and I would have liked it to be published in hardback, at least, for the people who had read my previous work. They and they only would see the connection. A new reader of my work would find it too African. Although Margaret kept assuring me that they would publish it Clive would not be committed, and for a long time no contract was signed.

When eventually the contract went through, Margaret took the first chapter, called it the "Introduction" and sent the manuscript to America without changing a single word. They said it was great. Surprised at publishers' logic, I dedicated the book to Margaret. Clive protested that dedicating it to her was "incestuous". Margaret said, "It's your book, you wrote it, you can dedicate it to anyone you like." I am glad I did because a year or so later I saw Dr Busby, Margaret's father, and he said, "Thank you for dedicating that book to our daughter. That made me feel happy."

There were now rumours that the Mothers and Toddlers Group would close, and they were suggesting that maybe I could go and start another in Kilburn. I was going nowhere. I was not going to look for another job, I was going to be a full-time writer. Money would be tight, but that was what I was going to do. I had been all my life like somebody floating on water, but come storm or high gale my head was always above, so I never sank. I then suspected that maybe Allison and Busby's delay in processing my manuscripts was because they could not afford to go on publishing one author so frequently. Margaret always hinted that I should take a break. Why should I take a break when the likes of Barbara Cartland, much older than my mother, produces twenty novels a year?

I did not know how to start looking for a different publisher. Elizabeth would not help, I knew that, she would start telling me that my books did not sell that well and that I should wait until a publisher phoned her. She had been waiting for years.

Then suddenly my phone rang. It was Margaret. Somebody from Oxford University Press wanted to speak with me; should she give him my number? I said she should. It was Mr Kahm of OUP. Could I write two books for young readers for the schools in West Africa – they would give me all the time in the world. The deposit was to be £1000 each. My heart was beating extremely fast as I agreed. All my expenses per year, including rates, were just a little below £2000, so if all went well OUP had bought me a new year, 1977. And knowing that I did not have to worry for another year about how to pay the mortgage gave me a new kind of mental independence. I was anxiously waiting for the day that Camden borough would say my work for them was finished.

To cap it all, Braziller said *The Slave Girl* was beautiful. After all the mental agony I went through for that book, it eventually won me several awards, including the prestigious Jock Campbell Award with £1000 tag money. By the time it reached that stage, though, everybody concerned had forgotten the agony of the writer.

I told Allison and Busby about my writing for OUP, and they did not object. Maybe it was my imagination, but I think they sighed with relief. That was to be my writing pattern for a long time. I would give the major books to A. and B. and the smaller ones to other publishers. I stopped using my agents. I started to arrange the royalties myself. I found that publishers were willing to pay bigger advances. It was still many years yet before I completely broke away from my agents. I think I needed them when I was starting, but as one got used to meeting publishers, one could simply arrange advances by telling them your idea for your next book.

Maybe there is something in the saying that "there is no peace for the wicked". Here I was, realizing my dream at last. Then the university announced that they were going to triple their tuition fees.

With the mortgage and the new high fares for the kids' schools, I began to feel frightened again. What would happen if suddenly one of my fingers fell off, and I could not type out the story for OUP? What would happen if Allison and Busby went bankrupt – being a small publishing house, they'd have to think of paying their printers before their authors. Well, if it came to the worst I would give up my hopes of ever becoming a Doctor of Sociology. Then the synopsis of the MPhil thesis, which was to lead me to the PhD, was approved, and I knew I would have to go on working for a few more years for the Doctorate itself.

I told Chidi about this, and he seemed happy, saying mildly that it would be nice to know that I would one day be Dr Emecheta. He said it was good news. A few weeks later he came to us and announced that he was packing in his job and leaving for America to do a PhD in Mineral Economics! He could not get a grant to do it here in England, and he would be leaving in the spring.

Pride would not allow me to argue with him. It looked as if he could stand my popularity, he could stand my writing, but the Ibo man still thinks that taking on a serious project like a PhD should be for men only. His leaving was partly my fault – how many times had he asked me to marry him and I had said no? I could not tell him that it took me a long time to forgive my own mother for remarrying when she did, and leaving us to suffer in the houses of relatives. If we had been older than seven and five, I would have not been so bitter. But I always remember my brother's running ears, due to slaps received at the hands of uncles and cousins, and his tattered khaki shirts. If our mother had stayed with us we would still have been very poor but our childhood would not have been so terrible. I did not want the kids I brought into the world to have a similar experience. And of course, with our people, marriage means more children. I did not want any more.

Christmas 1976 was not as expensive as that of 1975. Now I had to be careful because I would soon stop work, and the fact that Chidi was going away was very irritating. I kept pushing it out of my mind, but it kept coming back. He is one of those unobtrusive individuals who are always there, but never show their face. He would listen while I talked, and I would do the same whilst he went through all those heavy statistical details about oil and minerals. He is full of ideas. He is naturally stingy with money, but I encouraged him to be so. I just don't want any man to give me money when I can work for it myself. I could take from Sylvester, my husband, because I was raising our children. Although Sylvester was not prepared to support us, I would not ask another man to give me anything with which to raise my kids. What existed between Chidi and me was a very, very long friendship, spanning more than twenty years, starting when I was that tiny girl at the Methodist Girls' High School and resuming when I met him quite by accident in Camden Town, as I was returning from the Clerkenwell Court.

Chiedu had to choose this time to start making trouble. She now wanted to go to a private fee-paying school to do her ''A'' levels, because she felt she could do better there than at Highbury. The teachers and everybody concerned with her education knew that science was completely incomprehensible to her. She was, like her sisters, very intelligent but unlike them and very much like me, she found science subjects extremely difficult. I told her to do her best, and said she could start a medical career by doing BSC nursing first. I could not afford the £3000 or £4000 she would need for the two-year ''A'' level course. I could not even afford the £2000 or so I would need to complete my own PhD programme.

She kept asking me to change my mind. I told her that I would if I had the money. Then on 24 December, she got angry with my reply and threw a milk bottle at the sitting-room window. The cold wind gushed in. Hating physical violence of any kind, I simply cried, and through my tears I shouted that she should leave and go and ask for the money from her father. I did not want her to go. I wanted her to say she was sorry, that she would at least attempt her ''A'' levels at Highbury Hill. After all, the school was still a grammar school and she had got in by passing the eleven-plus.

My daughter didn't say she was sorry. She said I was not the good mother I thought I was, then marched upstairs, packed her things, and left, banging the door so hard that it shook the whole house.

My stomach lurched, and I became sick. Ik saw I was angry and cried, ''She's done it again, she's spoilt our Christmas.''

"No, she hasn't, and this time I won't let her spoil your Christmas. She spoilt our trip to the Zoo, your wanting to come to the launch of *The Bride Price*, but this Christmas she's not going to ruin things for us."

I said this almost to reassure myself. To give myself confidence, because then I saw everything I spent my whole life building collapsing like a pack of cards; because the younger children were watching and listening with open mouths, not believing what they were seeing. This type of violence had never occurred in our family before. Only Chiedu and Ik remembered the early violence with their father, but they were too young then to remember it well. We argued and shouted, but never used violence. I could see that Christy in particular was scared. She asked me what was the matter with her sister. I said that she was just growing up.

Christy was satisfied with my answer, even though I knew that she did not understand what I meant. But Ik would not buy that. Although Ik is a boy, but he is like me in everything. He is very perceptive, as well as being introspective. He saw beyond my bluff and said, "I will never forgive that girl", and ran out to get someone to repair the broken glass.

I left what I was doing and went upstairs to the room where I worked. I stared at the typewriter. This was going to be my lot. I was going to give all I had to my children, only for them to spit on my face and tell me that I was a bad mother and then leave and run to a father who had never in all his life bought them a pair of pants.

Then the phone rang; it was my husband. He was jeering. "I told you to give those children away for adoption, did I not? I told you you were too young and immature to look after them. You could not even look after yourself, now see the mess you've made of that nice baby. Where in Nigeria do you hear of a girl challenging her mother?"

I put the phone down because I was tempted to reply by saying I had challenged my mother and that here in London it happens all the time. But he had never seen anything like that before. Chiedu must have been trying to shock him by telling him about me – something unheard of in our culture.

I kept on staring at the typewriter. I wanted to think, I wanted to reassess my life, I wanted to take stock. I could do it only on the typewriter. I banged away the whole of Christmas, the whole of January 1977, and by the end of that month, almost six weeks after Chiedu left, *The Joys of Motherhood* was finished.

The following morning, I tried to pick up the phone that was by my bedside and I found I could not. One side of me was completely numb, including my lips. The more I tried to move, the more the other side seemed to be on fire. The pain was terrible. Ik screamed and called in our doctor. The poor boy was scared out of his wits. Jake simply went on howling, "Mum, do you want tea, do you want coffee?"

They stopped me from reading even newspapers. They said it was mental fatigue, I was doing too much. People talked to me. My family talked; Chidi talked himself dry. I think I started to listen when I knew that all my anger was there on paper, otherwise I would not have recovered as quickly as I did. They brought these tablets and those capsules, all of which I threw away, but I heeded what Dr Maxwell said: just a gentle massage by one of your daughters, and rest, and remember that your daughter is only growing up. I told him I had written all my anger down and he said that was good too.

In *The Joys of Motherhood* I created a woman, Nnuego, who gave all her energy, all her money and everything she had to raise her kids. She chopped wood for sale, she dealt on the black market, she did everything except whore herself to raise money. She was so busy doing all this that she had no time to cultivate any friends among her own sex.

The children grew up and left. They loved her still, but they were busy with their own lives – so much so that when she was ill they could not come to see her. When she became too tired, she died alone by the wayside with none of her living eight children to hold her hand.

In that book I said that "the joy of motherhood" was a beautiful funeral. Nnuego's sons did not give their mother a dignified death like Clive Allison did, but a horrible one. It was only after her death that they all borrowed money from the bank to give her a huge funeral celebration. It took her children years to repay the money they borrowed for that expensive funeral that went on for days. Even in my anger I could see Clive's mother's death, which to me was ideal, and imagine from what my daughter did the worst death that could ever befall me.

In a way that book, like *Second-Class Citizen*, made me accept my lot. The worst that could happen to me was to die by the wayside with everybody saying, "To think she gave all her life for her children."

I dedicated the book to my daughter Chiedu. Weeks after I finished the book, she returned. Father and daughter had quarrelled. She felt guilty to see me ill. They had all thought I was indestructible, and began to be scared every time I had a toothache after that.

"You're ill, Mum, I can't believe it! You're always there," she cried.

When she finished reading *The Joys of Motherhood*, she threatened to burn it if I kept the dedication. I removed the dedication to her, and made it to all mothers. Then she begged me please not to publish it at all. That I refused, and she laughed when she saw that I quickly made four copies and had them hidden in different places until I could give one to a publisher.

"I won't burn your book," she said in jest.

"Just in case book burning turns out to be hereditary," I said. I was not prepared to take any chances, not after the experience with her father and *The Bride Price*.

"But we love you, Mum, you must remember that. You'll never die like Nnuego, not when I'm living anyway," she bragged, not knowing that she had just a few more years to live herself.

Then she asked me a rather funny question.

"Why did you marry that man, Mum?"

"Which man?"

"The man you call our father."

"He is your father, and you must not speak of him like that. You're still partly Nigerian, you know, not all English."

"You did not answer my question, Mum, I don't want us to fight again. Why did you marry him in the first place?"

"That," I replied, sitting up in bed, "is a question between me, your father and both our Chis. It has nothing whatsoever to do with you, young lady."

We both smiled into each other's eyes, as I watched the white teeth she inherited from my mother light up her beautiful round young face.

And she went on quietly rubbing the ori oil my cousin Theresa sent me from Nigeria on my numb shoulders.

Head Above Water

By March, I was completely recovered and sent *The Joys of Motherhood* to Allison and Busby. They liked it straightaway and as usual kept it in cold storage for another eighteen months.

My American publisher found an editor who had lived in Togo for three months to evaluate my *Joys of Motherhood*. I did not like her evaluation and wrote her one of my "nasties" in which I told her where to go. Like most Americans, she took it very well. My publisher George Braziller just laughed and laughed. I think they were all simply testing me and pulling my leg because *The Joys of Motherhood* was published as it was. We had a slight argument over the title. The word "joy" is over-used in the States, and my publisher thought it would trivialize the heavy message the book contains. But his protest was not that strong, and the title in the English and American editions remained *The Joys of Motherhood.* Much later, most European countries refused the word "joy". It is known there under the ironical title *The Blessings of Motherhood*. The Germans told me that they have no irony in their language. They simply called their edition *Nnuego*, the name of the heroine in the book. The East Germans refused to accept the translation done by the West Germans, so they did their own. I am not quite sure what they call theirs as I do not read German.

All this was still very much in the future. As soon as I had sent the manuscript out, and received the first instalment from OUP, I stopped worrying about the closure of the Mothers and Toddlers Group. The clerical union wanted me to take it up as a test case, but I had other things to do. I would have won, but then I was not prepared to go to this board and that council. Many of my colleagues were surprised that I did not fight for another job. How could I? All I ever wanted was to tell my stories from my own home, just like my big mother Nwakwaluzo used to tell her stories in her very own compound with her back leaning against the *ukwa* tree. The only difference was that instead of using the moonlight and her own emotional language as her tools, I have to use electricity, a typewriter and a language that belonged to those who once colonized the country of my birth. But I am happy I mastered the language enough to enable me to work with it, for if not I would have been telling my stories only to those women and children in Umuezeokolo, Ibusa.

When Chidi eventually left for the United States in March it was not as bad as I thought. I soon got used to his not being there. I put all my thoughts into my family and my work. The friendship between Chidi and myself moved onto a new level. It became international, with constant calls, visits, cards and letters. I strictly weaned myself from emotional dependence on him or anybody else. Suddenly I found that I was becoming a new person.

As a child, I was brought up thinking that a happy home must be headed by a man, that we all had to make a home for him, not for ourselves, the women. A home without him, "Nnayin, our father", at the top is incomplete, and all those from such a home should go about with this chip on their shoulders. During my marriage, Sylvester and I did not talk much in the evenings; we rowed most of the time. Yet I still felt the nagging guilt of incompleteness just because there was no man to talk to or serve or slave for at the end of the day. Now, suddenly, with more time on my hands to do exactly what I liked, that feeling was disappearing.

A world of literary evenings – book launches, poetry readings, literary talks – opened up. Much later, another new world of the theatre opened too. I don't know how many times I've seen *Rigoletto* and the *Dance of the Dead*, or how many times I've watched *Swan Lake* or seen great artists like Nureyev dance on stage. I appreciate these operatic performances more, because I always view them from my own exotic African musical background.

I became so busy that I kept wondering how it was that only a few years back I had felt that to be a full human being, I had to be a mother, a wife, a worker and a wonder-woman. I now realized that what I was doing then was condemning myself to an earthly hell. Marriage is lovely when it works, but if it does not, should one condemn oneself? I stopped feeling guilty for being me.

I think my new appraisal of Christianity helped me to come to this conclusion. I found that it was not a sin to be happy; it was a new awareness. I love making a home of some kind and my new home in Crouch End needed years of hard work; I love telling stories and now I could tell my stories from my new home – and unlike my big mother Nwakwaluzo, I was even being paid for them. Maybe I did not have the ideal family but I sometimes wonder whether a man could have done better.

Living entirely off writing is a precarious existence and money is always short, but with careful management and planning I found I could keep my head and those of my family, through God's grace, above water.

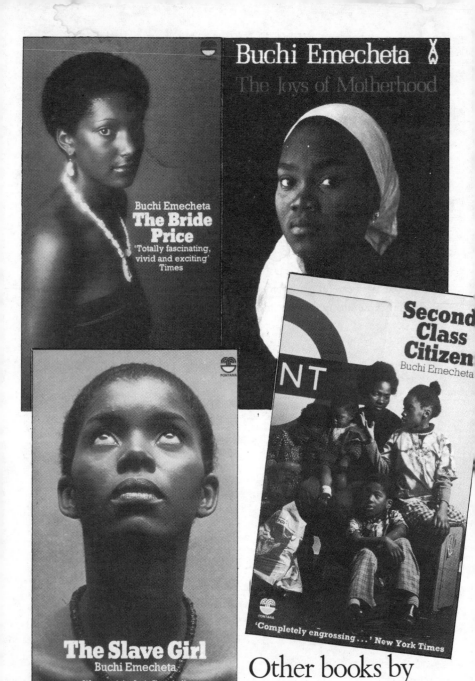

Buchi Emecheta
The Joys of Motherhood

Buchi Emecheta
The Bride Price
'Totally fascinating,
vivid and exciting'
Times

Second Class Citizen
Buchi Emecheta

The Slave Girl
Buchi Emecheta
Winner of the Jock Campbell
New Statesman Award
'A fascinating novel' Lagos Daily Times

'Completely engrossing...' New York Times

Other books by
Buchi Emecheta

Masquerade Books

The
Moonlight
Bride

Buchi Emecheta

ALLISON & BUSBY

IN THE DITCH
BUCHI EMECHETA
author of *Second-Class Citizen*
'Searing, tragic, comic and important'
— *Sunday Times*

Our Own Freedom

Photographs by Maggie Murray
Introduction and comments by
Buchi Emecheta

DOUBLE
YOKE
A NOVEL
BY
Buchi Emecheta

The
Rape
of
Shavi
Buchi Emecheta